LEVERAGE POINT

LEVERAGE POINT

GERALD N. LUND

AUTHOR OF THE BESTSELLING *THE WORK AND THE GLORY* SERIES
AND ROGER HENDRIX

BOOKCRAFT

SALT LAKE CITY, UTAH

First printing, November 1985

First printing redesigned paperbound edition, January 2000

Visit us at deseretbook.com

Library of Congress Catalog Card Number 84-72843

ISBN-10 0-87579-525-0
ISBN-13 978-0-87579-525-6

Printed in the United States of America
R. R. Donnelley and Sons, Harrisonburg, VA

10   9   8

To those few in the Middle East
on either side
who see the only lasting and acceptable solution
as resting in faith in God
and in love for one's fellow man.

Preface

Though the characters in this novel are fictional, they are based on the lives of people who do exist. For example, many of the feelings and thoughts of, and even some of the words spoken by, Alex Barclay reflect the feelings, thoughts, and words of a man who makes a lucrative living as a legitimate arms dealer. The personalities, traits, and experiences of many others in the novel, including Israelis, Saudis, and Americans, are drawn from the lives or are composites of real people. Thus, while the characters are fictional, they are true to the character and culture of their respective nationalities and social settings.

Many of the events, though changed sufficiently to protect the privacy of those involved, are based on actual happenings. There have been penetrations of Saudi air space, including the defection of an Iranian pilot who reached the massive oil complex at Ras Tanura. Covert support by the U.S. government of illegal arms sales has happened and will happen again. The introduction of Marc Jeppson, a relatively obscure educator from a small town in Utah, into the heady world of business, finance, and high technology in the culture of Southern California represents actual happenings in the lives of real people.

To insure the accuracy and realism of *Leverage Point*, the authors conducted numerous interviews and pursued considerable research in such areas as Islamic culture, Saudi Arabia and her peoples, the Mossad, Israel's intelligence agency, arms and arms sales, high-performance jet aircraft, and high-tech radar systems.

The artistic relationship between the authors has been a collaborative one. Roger Hendrix developed the original story idea, created most of the characters, and wrote the preliminary outline. Gerald Lund was responsible for plot development, more extended character definition, and the writing of the novel. Both were involved in researching, interviewing, and reviewing and editing the work.

Gerald's wife, Lynn, made numerous suggestions about characterization and plot development that improved the novel immeasureably. Jack Adamson, currently serving as senior vice president of Bonneville International Corporation, provided encouragement and valuable advice throughout the project.

Characters in *Leverage Point*

Marc Jeppson, professor of Near Eastern Studies, Claremont Colleges
Brett, his eight-year-old son
Matt, his six-year-old son
Alex Barclay, president of Barclay Enterprises; arms dealer and
    entrepreneur
Ardith, his wife
Mary Robertson, widow; Marc Jeppson's housekeeper
Valerie, her twenty-six-year-old daughter; computer programmer
Jacqueline Ashby, executive secretary to Alex Barclay
Quinn Gerritt, president of Gerritt Industries, a high-tech conglomerate
Jessica, his wife
Derek Parkin, lawyer; associate in Barclay Enterprises
Lyman Perotti, financier; reputed crime boss in Southern California
Arthur Hadlow, representative for Lyman Perotti
Russell Whitaker, Undersecretary of State, United States State
    Department
Taylor Canning, General, United States Air Force
Jonathan Taggart, engineer, Gerritt Industries; VSM-430 radar system
    designer
Mildred, his wife
Charlene, his seventeen-year-old daughter
Michael Shurtliff, Senior Vice President, Gerritt Industries
Theodore Wuthrich, Controller, Gerritt Industries
Harvey Edwards, owner, Edwards Automotive
John Talbot, Colonel, United States Air Force; senior test pilot

Israelis

Yaacov Shoshani, philosophy professor, Hebrew University; civilian
advisor to the Mossad, Israel's equivalent to the CIA
Esther, his wife
Nathan, his son; Mossad operative; team leader for Los Angeles
operations
Moshe Gondor, control officer, Mossad
Eli Weissman, Deputy Director in Charge of Special Operations,
Mossad
Yehuda Gor, nicknamed Udi; Mossad operative
Yossi Kettleman, Mossad operative
Yitzhak ben Tsur, Mossad operative

Saudis

King Abdul Aziz, also called *Ibn-Saud;* founder of modern Saudi Arabia;
died 1953
The King, current head of the royal family and ruler of Saudi Arabia
The Crown Prince, next in line for the throne; close advisor to the king
Prince Feisal, brother to the king; Minister of Defense, Saudi Arabia
Prince Khalid, brother to the king; Commanding General, Royal Saudi
Air Force
Prince Abdullah, half brother to the king; Minister of Finance, Saudi
Arabia
Sayeed Amani, General, Royal Saudi Air Force
Sheik Ahmed al-Hazzan, vice-Minister of Defense, Saudi Arabia

Prologue

It was barely past noon. The air temperature stood at an even fifty degrees Celsius—one-hundred-twenty-two degrees Farenheit—making the air shimmer so violently that only the first hundred yards or so of the twelve-thousand-foot runway was visible. The control tower, off in the distance, seemed like some sinuous serpent weaving to the sound of an unheard reed flute.

With a howling shriek, two McDonnel Douglas F-15s touched down, leaving bursts of blue-white smoke as the tires hit the hot concrete. Almost instantly the needle-nosed, twin-tailed craft disappeared into the superheated air, only to reappear a few moments later off to the left, one behind the other, taxiing toward the row of hardened shelters. On the ground, they looked awkward, almost grotesque, belying the incredible destructive power each craft carried within its bowels. Just below the cockpits, in sharp contrast to the gleaming aluminum skin, was a circular emblem—a palm tree with crossed swords beneath it. Next to the emblem, the inscription "Royal Saudi Air Force" was neatly stenciled in English and flowing Arabic.

To a thousand generations of Bedouins and village dwellers in the Arabian peninsula, the date palm had meant life and survival. The crossed swords, always unsheathed, represented strength through faith in Allah. It was that faith and the naked sword that had brought some of the world's most formidible landscape—covering an area roughly the size of the United States east of the Mississippi—under the control of the Royal House of Saud.

The whims of some geologic genie had long ago placed beneath that blistering sand a black ocean of staggering magnitude. Allah had indeed smiled kindly on the Saudis. Twenty-six percent of all the world's known oil reserves lay pooled below the desert kingdom. The Ghawar field, the largest onshore oil field in the world, contains more petroleum reserves than *all* the oil fields of the United States put together. Thirty-two of the nearly fifty other fields are capped, awaiting future need. Even with less than half their fields in current use, the Saudis still pump about ten million barrels of oil a day. The crude sells for somewhere around thirty dollars a barrel. It costs the Saudis fifty cents a barrel to extract, refine, ship, and market their oil. The arithmetic is simple but staggering. A profit of just under three hundred million dollars *per day* pours into the Saudi treasury.

It was that simple but staggering arithmetic that made the Thirteenth Fighter Interceptor Squadron of the Royal Saudi Air Force possible. It was that simple but staggering flow of oil that made the King Abdul Aziz Air Base outside of Dhahran not only possible but necessary. For while the blessings of Allah had left the kingdom of Saudi Arabia very, very rich, they had also left it very, very vulnerable.

At that moment, just past noon of August twenty-third, ten billion dollars of detection, command, and control systems failed. The Boeing E-3A Airborne Warning and Controls Systems (AWACS), one of the most expensive pieces of hardware in the world, was on the far end of its patrol duty station. An Air India 737, on its way to Riyadh, strayed a hundred miles off course. A squadron of Northrup F5-E Tigers, flying routine patrol, were vectored south to check it out. In the brief flurry of activity associated with all that, a tiny blip on one of the screens was missed.

In the pilot's lounge there was only one American, a colonel from North Carolina who served as the Commander of the Technical Assistance Team sent over by the United States Air Force to work with the Saudi squadron. He was tanned almost as deeply as his Saudi counterparts. He sat in a chair, feet up, sipping a Coke, eyes half shut, listening to the low chatter of the pilots around him.

The sudden blast of the Klaxon from the overhead speakers shattered the lazy somnolence that lay on the airbase. Airmen in the cafeteria leaped up, overturning drinks and food. Pilots in the ready room grabbed helmets and raced for their planes. Mechanics hit the buttons and started shelter doorways rolling upward. Radar and computer operators darted to consoles and terminals, hands poised and ready.

The control center, deep underground in the heart of the headquarters complex, had gone into a state of hushed but frantic urgency by the time two men burst through the doors. The first was a Saudi with stars on both shoulders. He was the base commander and director of the Eastern Coast Defense Sector. He was followed closely by the American.

The director of operations, a major with a thick moustache, saluted smartly, and broke into a stream of rapid Arabic.

"Speak English!" the general snapped. English was mandatory in the Royal Saudi Air Force.

The major stopped, took a quick breath, and started again. "A bogey just crossed the Fahad line coming in low and fast, sir."

The base commander spun around and stared at the radar screen. The Fahad line was an imaginary line running through the center of the Persian Gulf from the Iran-Iraq border on the north to the Strait of Hormuz in the south. It was the action line for the Royal Saudi Air Force. Any unidentified aircraft crossing that line was considered hostile and intercepted by fully armed Saudi fighters prepared for combat engagement.

"Aircraft identification?" the general barked at one of the airmen hunched over a console.

"F-4 Phantom, sir!"

"Iranian!" the American exclaimed. It was the most logical guess. Iran had over three hundred Phantoms in their Air Force.

The overhead speaker blared: "This is Cobra Leader to Tower. We are ready to roll."

Another voice, heavier, touched with excitement: "Cobra Leader, you are cleared for takeoff."

"We're scrambling the F-15s," the major said tersely.

"If he's across the Fahad line, they'll never make it." The general whirled to stare at the situation board and the lines appearing. "Can Blue Leader intercept?"

The major's eyes dropped. "They were vectored off to the south five minutes ago. They are three hundred miles south of the intercept point."

"What!"

The major swallowed hard, but his eyes came up and met the other's fury.

An airman behind them cried out, "Computers predict ninety-two percent probability intended target is Ras Tanura!"

Ras Tanura. The general felt his heart lurch. One of the largest oil refinery complexes in the world, a storage facility with nearly a hundred tanks—some holding a million-and-a-quarter barrels of crude apiece—an offshore loading facility that would have six to eight supertankers docked there, guzzling millions of barrels of oil into their holds. If they took out Ras Tanura, it would virtually destroy the Saudi economy and cripple the energy needs of the Western world for years to come.

"Range eighty-three miles, closing at Mach one point one."

"The F-15s will never make it." The general's voice was a whisper as he stared at the line the target tracker was making on the situation board. The F-15 Eagle can climb at a rate of seventeen thousand feet a minute at Mach 0.9, around seven hundred miles an hour. But even with that and their head-on attack capability, they would still not close on the bogey in time. At Mach 1.1, the Iranian fighter was approaching Ras Tanura at better than one mile every second. They had less than a minute.

"Cobra Leader to Charlie One," the speaker blared again. "We are leveling at zero five thousand feet. We have radar contact and are tracking. Missiles are armed. Missile range in zero eight seven seconds."

From somewhere behind them a man cried, "Ground batteries have radar contact. Will commence firing in twenty seconds."

"They'll never touch him." the American muttered. "Not at that speed and altitude."

"Time to target?"

"Thirty-three seconds!"

"Ground batteries standing by."

"General, listen to this!" The airman at a radio console had leaped to his feet and was flipping switches. The speaker instantly blared with static, then a heavily accented voice, almost incoherent with hysteria.

"Saudi Air Base! Saudi Air Base! This is Captain Mohammed Pahlavi. I am defecting to your country. Do not shoot! Do not shoot!"

Every eye had swung up to stare at the overhead speaker.

"I have approaching aircraft on my radar screen! I am unarmed! Please do not shoot!"

Another airman's voice sang out. "Bogey is zero one eight miles from the coast. Maintaining speed and altitude. Computers reject Ras Tanura as probable target."

The general leaped to the radio and snatched a headset. "Captain Pahlavi? Do you read me? This is the base commander."

"Yes! Yes! I read you!" It was almost a sob. "Don't launch your missiles. I want to surrender."

"Turn back out to sea. Turn instantly or we will fire!"

"Target turning!" came a cry from the radar man.

A burst of relief swept the room, and the general's shoulders sagged. Finally he straightened and lifted the mike again. "Cobra Leader, this is General Hammad. Did you copy that last transmission?"

"Roger, General," came back the laconic voice. "We'll bring him in."

General Hammad handed the headset back to the airman, then turned slowly to his American advisor, who was shaking his head.

"Holy Hannah, General!" was all the man from North Carolina could think of to say.

Chapter One

As Marc Jeppson turned the yellow Volkswagen Beetle onto Bridgeport Avenue in Claremont, California, he was muttering to himself. In his mind he could hear the voice of his dean—thin and reedy, almost bordering on a whine: "Professor Jeppson, you have missed the last two meetings of the faculty grievance committee. Is there some compelling reason why?"

"Two that I can think of," Marc answered aloud, wishing he had had the nerve then to say them. "First, I hate that assignment. I mean, come on! The current crisis is that no one is changing the filters in the coffee percolator in the faculty lounge."

He slowed and pulled into his driveway. "Second, I am enrolled in UCLA's MBA program because I am bored absolutely out of my gourd with my life right now, and tonight happens to be my first test in my marketing class, and I also have a ten-page paper due, and the last thing I need is to spend time worrying about coffee percolators."

He turned off the engine, grabbed his briefcase, and got out of the car. The sixteen-year-old who lived next door was bouncing a basketball in front of his garage. He grinned. "Talking to yourself again, Mr. Jeppson?"

"Yeah, I don't know if it comes from being a parent or a teacher."

"Probably from being a parent. My dad does it all the time."

Marc laughed, waved, and walked quickly into the house. He

dropped his briefcase on the couch, took off his sports jacket, and let it follow. "Mary," he called. "I'm home."

There was no answer. He turned to the lamp table where his housekeeper always put the mail. There was none. "Mary?" he shouted again, more loudly now.

Puzzled, he stuck his head in the family room. The television was on with no sound, but the room was empty. He walked over, flipped off the TV, turned back, and stopped dead. The carpet on the far side of the room was crisscrossed with dozens of white tracks that came from the kitchen, looped around the couch, and then headed for the hall. He crossed the room, still staring, bent down, and put his finger to one of the tracks. It looked and felt like flour. He raised it and touched his tongue. It was flour, with a taste of sugar to it. And the marks looked suspiciously like tricycle tracks.

With a sinking feeling he straightened and followed the tracks into the kitchen. He stopped in midstride, his jaw dropping. Five of the eight cupboard doors were open. The sugar cannister was tipped over near the blender, its contents over the edge and on the floor. A can of honey was also on its side, spreading an amber coat over a three-foot area of the counter. He watched a long drip break loose and hit the puddle of honey on the floor. Tracks marred this smaller pool and led off to the grand masterpiece. In the very center of the linoleum, someone or something had taken the flour cannister—still visible near the dinette—and carefully covered a five-by-five square of the floor. This had been the primary palette for the mobile artist. Two dozen tracks led through the flour, to the sugar and honey and then out onto the carpet canvas of the halls and family room. The avant-garde artists at the college would have been inspired by the results.

"Mary!" This time he bellowed it with desperation.

A slight noise from the garage caught his ear. Stepping gingerly so as to stay in the clearer spots, he crossed the kitchen and opened the door that led to the garage. The four-year-old heard the sound, jerked up, and stopped his tricycle dead. No question about it. This was the artist, and this was his brush. The tricycle's back tires were a gummy white, and a floury paste was caked around the fender of the front wheel. Nor had the young artist escaped fully unscathed—only by the closest of examination could one tell the tee shirt and jeans were blue.

"Matthew David Jeppson! What are you doing?"

The large green eyes lowered, half hidden by long dark lashes. "Hullo, Daddy."

The doorbell rang, and Marc looked up from spooning the honey off the counter. "Wonderful!" he muttered. He looked around to where his eight-year-old son was working on the floor. "Brett, get the door."

Brett was up and off like a shot, grateful for any reprieve. A moment or two later he was back. "Dad, it's some lady."

He turned with a quick frown. "Who?"

Brett shrugged. "She wants you."

Marc set the spoon down, washed his hands quickly, and with his sleeve wiped at the sheen of sweat on his forehead, leaving a smear of flour across his cheek. As he started for the living room, he looked down, saw that he was leaving white tracks of his own, and quickly removed his shoes.

He stopped short as he came around the hallway and into the living room. "Lady" in Marc's mind suggested a grandmotherly forty or fiftyish. But the woman standing at the door was no more than twenty-five, possibly less, and very definitely not a grandmother. She was maybe five five or six, with short dark hair that framed her face. White cotton pants and a knit top with bold red and white horizontal stripes emphasized the slenderness of her figure. He was suddenly conscious of his stocking feet and flour-smeared sweatshirt.

"Mr. Jeppson?" She smiled tentatively, dark brown eyes crinkling slightly at the corners, the lips softening.

"Yes." He brushed quickly at his pants.

"My name is Valerie Robertson. I'm Mary Robertson's daughter."

9

His face darkened almost instantly. "Where in the world is your mother?"

The smile faded. "I—She asked if I would come and take care of the boys while you go to your class."

"Well, that's nice!" Marc snapped. "I wish she had thought of that about two hours ago."

Valerie flinched, taken back by the caustic tone.

"Come with me!" He turned on his heel and started away. He stopped and looked back. "Come on! You need to see this."

Valerie followed him into the kitchen, then stopped and stared. "Oh my word!" she breathed.

"I think that would qualify as a slight understatement."

She stepped in far enough so she could see where the tracks led into the hall and the family room. "What happened?"

Brett snorted in disgust. "Matthew! That's what happened."

"Whatever your mother's doing, I hope it was worth it." Marc didn't try to contain his irritation.

Valerie turned back slowly, her dark eyes snapping, but before she could reply, a voice from behind them cut in, turning them all around. "Daddy, I'm cold."

Matthew was standing in the far doorway, a towel draped around his shoulders, water dripping from the rest of him and making dark spots on the carpet.

"Matt, I told you to stay in the tub until you're clean. You haven't even touched your face."

"But I'm cold, Daddy."

Marc went over to his son, squatted down, wrapped the towel around him, and started to rub him vigorously. Valerie watched, her anger softening. Brett was darker in both hair and complexion, and must have taken after his mother, but Matthew was a miniature of his father. Large, gentle eyes, angular features, short-cropped blond hair, firm mouth and chin. The flour smears on both faces completed the impression.

"Get back in the tub and wash your face and your hair." Marc reached up and pulled a sticky glob from behind one ear.

"But Daddy, the water's dirty and cold."

"That's no surprise. We're lucky the water hasn't turned to dough."

Valerie laughed softly, and Matthew looked up, his voice dropping. "Who's that, Daddy?"

Marc had forgotten they had company. He straightened slowly. "This is Mary's daughter, uh . . ."

"Valerie." She smiled at Matthew. "So this is the architect of the disaster?"

"Yes. This is Matt. He's four and in big trouble." He half turned. "And this is Brett."

Valerie nodded. Both eyed her with open curiosity.

Marc gave Matt a swat on the bottom. "Brett, run him more water and see that he gets all this junk out of his hair."

As the two disappeared he turned back to Valerie. "It's amazing what a four-year-old can accomplish when he is left totally on his own for two hours."

Valerie took a breath. "Mr. Jeppson, I took my mother to the hospital this morning. She underwent an operation for kidney stones."

"Oh, no!"

Valerie nodded, mollified somewhat by the instant contrition. "She's been having pain for several days. This morning it became acute."

"I am really sorry." He stepped forward. "I should have known she wouldn't leave Matthew without good reason."

"But she said you would be here when Matt came home from preschool. Otherwise I would have come sooner."

Marc hit his head, suddenly understanding. "I was supposed to be. Then I got roped into a committee meeting." His lips pulled down in a quick expression of disgust. "But we did get filters for the percolator."

Her eyebrows raised, but he went on quickly. "So how is she?"

"Much better now. The doctor said the operation went fine. She's resting now, but she wouldn't go to sleep until I promised to come over. She said you have a big test tonight in your class."

Marc nodded, feeling stupid. "Look, Valerie, I really apologize for being so rude. When I came home and saw all this . . ." His hand swept outward toward the kitchen, then dropped lamely to his side. "I feel like a creep."

"I understand. It's all right." She smiled fully now, and he saw the resemblance between mother and daughter.

It had been that warm smile that had first drawn Marc's attention to Mary Robertson at church. When Marc's wife had been killed in an auto-pedestrian accident two years earlier, Marc had been in immediate need of someone to come in and help a totally nondomesticated widower cope with caring for two small boys and a house. He had heard that Mary, herself a widow of several years, was looking for work. He approached her. She accepted. He had offered his thanks countless times since, for not only had she proven to be a cook and housekeeper of competence, she had won over his boys and became a mother to them, filling with warmth and gentleness much of the gap Lynette's death had left.

Marc smiled back at Valerie, grateful for her quick forgiveness.

"Look, Mr. Jeppson—"

"Marc, please."

She smiled again. "Okay, Marc. Let me take over now. You go to your class. Brett can help me find whatever I need. I'll take it from here."

He hesitated.

"Really. Mom sent me over to do just that."

"Well . . ."

"Go on! We'll be fine."

"Well," Marc said again, "maybe I will."

"You may want to remove some of your makeup before you go," Valerie said soberly, tapping her cheek.

Marc swiped at his cheek with the back of his hand and saw the flour on it. He grinned sheepishly. "Thanks."

Chapter Two

About twenty-five miles south of UCLA, where Marc sat taking his test, a stiff breeze pulled at the leaves of the eucalyptus trees on the Palos Verdes Peninsula. But Alex Barclay didn't mind. The winds had scoured the Los Angeles Basin clean of smog, and the city spread out below them, a vast prairie of lights, cut through with the rivers of fire that marked the freeways.

"I can't believe this!"

The woman's voice brought Barclay's head around. She was next to a man near the low wall at the back of the patio area. Just beyond it, the hillside dropped away precipitously. They were gazing out at the stunning panorama, and she waved her martini in the general direction of Los Angeles.

"He must have paid a bundle for this land!" Her voice was already thickened by the liquor.

The man glanced around quickly. "Megan, for heaven's sakes, be a little bit discreet."

Barclay set his own glass on a nearby table and moved to join the couple. "How about that?" he said amiably, nodding toward the city below.

The man turned, startled, then recognized their host. "I've got to admit, it doesn't look like this from my apartment in West Covina."

Barclay laughed softly, and then for several seconds they stood in silence, shoulder to shoulder. When Barclay spoke, it was absently, without turning his head. "Four hundred seventy-nine thousand."

"What?" They both spoke as one.

"Four hundred seventy-nine thousand dollars. That's what I paid for the lot. Then you throw in a house with sixty-eight hundred square feet on the main floor, a separate four-car garage. You're talking just about a million four for the whole layout."

The man just stared, but the woman swore, her jaw slack.

Then Barclay remembered. Peter Shapiro, senior partner in the firm that handled Barclay's legal needs, had brought them. "He's one of the comers," Shapiro had said yesterday over the phone. "He might interest you."

Barclay chuckled. "But I figure the view is worth that alone." He stuck out his hand. "I'm Alex Barclay."

"Derek Parkin, Mr. Barclay. I'm delighted to meet you." It was almost too eager, but controlled, held in check.

"My pleasure."

"This is Megan McArthur."

She transferred the martini quickly, and held out her hand.

Brunette, built well, good eyes, nice legs. Probably five years younger than Parkin's thirty or so. Hardly world class, but very nice. Except for the cool, limp handshake. Barclay let go of it quickly. "Welcome to our little ranch house, Megan."

"Little ranch house!" she blurted. A quick frown of annoyance flashed briefly across Parkin's face. "It's incredible!"

The naked covetousness made Barclay smile even more broadly. "Well, we kind of like it. You're with Shapiro and Myers?" Barclay asked, turning to Parkin before Megan's effusiveness spilled over the patio area and washed away the hillside.

"Yes, sir."

"Peter mentioned you were one of his bright stars."

"Well, thank you. I certainly enjoy working with him."

With him, not *for* him, Barclay noted with interest. Again there was the quick appraisal. Dark-brown hair combed straight back. Blue eyes, quick and alert. Rounded features that somehow still conveyed an impression of sharpness. Three-piece business suit—gray, pin-striped, tailored—with an impeccably perfect maroon tie and silk handkerchief tucked in the pocket. His was the only coat and tie at the party, and yet he did not seem out of place. In fact the appearance secretly pleased Barclay, for he sensed Parkin had wanted it this way for their first meeting. This guy was definitely *magna cum laude*, Harvard Law School.

"Peter said it was you who pulled the Clayson contract out of the fire."

Megan opened a small clutch purse she had tucked under one arm and took out a pack of Virginia Slims. She put one to her lips and turned to Parkin expectantly.

Again there was that brief flicker of irritation, and Barclay guessed that Megan McArthur had just dropped off Derek Parkin's active list. Parkin reached for a lighter, lit her cigarette perfunctorily, as though for a passing stranger, then turned back to Barclay.

"That was an interesting case. For a while I thought they had us nailed."

"*Me* nailed, you mean."

Parkin's laugh was easy and amiable. "Yes, I suppose so. But, I don't think we—you—will see any more trouble on it now."

"That's great. I—" His head lifted slightly. Ardith had just come out of the house and was trying to catch his eye. She gave the slightest jerk of her head when she saw she had succeeded.

"I'm glad to have that one over," he finished. Then quickly, before Parkin could respond, he continued, "Well, it looks like my wife is giving me the nod. Just make yourselves to home."

As he moved toward the house, he nodded here, called a quick greeting there, and moved through the crowd, leaving people smiling or laughing as he passed. Alex Barclay was well liked. He knew that. He had cultivated that natural ability until it had become one of his most important assets. He was tall, broad through the shoulders, with no more than a hint of middle-age paunch. Thick, wavy, silver-gray hair, trimmed weekly by a very high-class barber, gave him the look of a distinguished and prosperous banker. That too had not hurt him, though for a kid raised in a tenement in Chicago, it made him smile inwardly.

He speared a couple of slices of Verona salami from the hors d'oeuvre tray, popped them into his mouth, and entered the house. Ardith was just inside the family room arranging another tray of food. He stopped for a moment. Casual elegance. That was how Barclay always thought of his wife. Never overdone. She was one of the few people, outside himself, that Barclay was willing to credit for his success. He had been twenty-four, she seventeen when they had first met. It had taken him nearly a year to convince both her and her parents that he was totally serious about marrying her. Neither she nor they had ever regretted it. Nor had Alex.

She glanced up, saw him, and frowned slightly. "Russell Whitaker is here."

"Already? Why didn't you invite him to come out?"

"He wouldn't." Again there was the quick frown. "He has someone with him."

He nodded and started down the hall.

"Alex?"

He turned. Her eyes were pleading. "Don't be too long. Not tonight."

The smile was brief and cool. "When an Undersecretary of the State Department comes all the way out here to see me, I'll give him what time he wants. You can cover for me for a while."

He walked quickly down the hall and opened the door. Barclay's study was very much a reflection of his own tastes. Along the entire length of one wall ran oak cabinets polished to a rich warm luster. The top of the cabinets held four bronze pieces, one of them a Frederic Remington original. Above the cabinets, book shelves were stocked with leather-bound books, including several first editions. Two leather side chairs flanked a huge, antique mahogany desk. The mounted head of an African kudu with its gracefully spiraling horns was on the wall opposite the desk.

Two men were standing beneath it, talking quietly. Both turned as Barclay entered. The shorter of the two smiled and extended his hand.

16

"Hello, Alex."

"Russ."

They shook hands firmly, and Whitaker turned. "Alex, meet Lieutenant General Taylor Canning, United States Air Force."

If Whitaker's grip was powerful, Canning's was like getting a fist caught in the treads of an M-60 tank. He was tall, with gray eyes that seemed kindly and grandfatherly, not those of a professional man of war. His hair was also gray and short-cropped, his features heavy but pleasant. And yet there was something rock hard about the man that was felt more than seen.

"Welcome to my home, General Canning." Then to Whitaker, "We've got a healthy party going on out on the patio. Are you sure you won't join us?"

"Thanks, but we've got to meet some other people."

"Then how about a drink? I've got some stock right here." He moved to one of the cabinets and opened the door on a small refrigerator and a collection of bottles and glasses.

Whitaker started to decline the invitation, then changed his mind. "Scotch and soda for me."

"That's fine," Canning nodded.

Barclay mixed three of the same, passed them around, then gestured to the chairs. As they sat, Barclay moved behind his desk, set his drink on the gleaming surface, then sat back and waited.

Whitaker sipped his drink for a moment, glanced once at the general, then looked at Barclay steadily. "We need your help on a project."

"Okay."

"This one is a little sticky. Like the Jakarta deal."

Barclay kept his face impassive. "Go on."

"This is an official request from your government, but . . . ." He stopped and sipped again at his drink, staring into the dark liquid.

"But," Alex finished for him, "officially, it's unofficial."

"Exactly."

"Come on, Russ. The last deal like that, my man spent six weeks in a hellhole of a prison. He was lucky at that."

17

"I know." The Undersecretary's dark eyes bored into Alex steadily.

Finally Alex sighed. "What this time?"

"A certain African nation—which for the present shall remain unnamed—wishes to purchase arms to fight against Communist insurgents."

"Heavy or light stuff?"

"Light. Sixteen thousand M-16 rifles, four million rounds of ammunition."

"That shouldn't be so tough. Why come to me?"

"Same scenario as before. Officially the U.S. is neutral. The Saudis and Quwaitis are willing to bankroll the deal—they're absolutely paranoid on the growing Soviet influence in Africa—but they want their role hush hush too. It will all be strictly under the table."

Barclay was silent, then took a long drink from his glass. "All right. I think that can be arranged."

Again Whitaker shot a quick glance at the general, then turned back. "You won't be able to buy the rifles from the Colt Arms Company."

Alex snapped forward. "What?"

Whitaker spoke calmly. "Sale of arms to this particular country is strictly illegal. The State Department will not give you the permit. Don't even apply."

"Hey, come on, Russ. How do I get that kind of hardware without a permit?"

Whitaker just continued to look at him steadily. Canning watched the interchange with interest, staying out of it for now.

Suddenly Barclay understood. "The North Vietnamese!"

The Undersecretary of State sipped his drink, his eyes never leaving Barclay's face.

"Tell me you're joking."

"You're the one who told us they contacted you in Paris."

"Yes, I did," Barclay retorted, his voice rising. "That was just to let you guys know I'm completely on the up and up with you."

"We know that. That's why we've come to you now."

Barclay waved that off angrily. "If buying from Colt Arms on this deal is illegal, what does that make purchasing captured U.S. weapons from the number one country on the State Department's hit list?"

"I told you this one would be sticky."

"Sticky! Who's going to keep the CIA off my back while I work out all of these little arrangements?"

"We'll do what we can to smooth things for you, but if you're caught, we'll deny any knowledge."

Canning leaned forward. "Will the North Viets sell you the weapons if they suspect they are to be resold to anti-Communist guerrillas?"

"North Viet Nam is so desperate for hard currency, they'd sell the Ho Chi Minh Trail to the Boy Scouts of America if they'd pay in cash. No, that's not the problem."

Agitated now, Barclay got up, started to pace, thinking quickly. "You're talking a four or five million dollar deal at best. Small stuff like this, I'm lucky to clear one or two percent. I could lose everything, not to mention facing Joliet or Leavenworth. The profit doesn't justify the risks."

The Undersecretary flashed General Canning the briefest of looks. Canning leaned forward, the kind gray eyes unreadable. "What if we were to sweeten the deal a little?"

That brought Barclay around.

"Three weeks ago," Canning went on, "an Iranian fighter pilot defected to Saudi Arabia. By the time they'd picked him up on radar and scrambled their fighters, he was right over the most important oil installation in the Middle East."

Barclay whistled a low soundless whistle.

"Had he been hostile . . ." He shrugged.

Whitaker picked it up. "About four months ago, another plane—this time a cargo jet with a full crew—defected from Iran to Egypt. They not only crossed the Persian Gulf, they crossed several hundred miles of the northern edge of Saudi air space. The Saudis didn't even know until Egypt announced the plane had landed and the crew was asking for asylum."

"There have been other similar incidents," Canning added.

"Needless to say," Whitaker went on, "the Saudis are not the only ones who are worried. Take out the oil, you topple the royal family. Take out the Saudis, and the stability of the whole Middle East—not to mention the world's energy supplies—is in jeopardy."

They were working him like a pack of wolves bringing down a caribou. The general paused briefly. "Another deal is in the wind. A little larger deal."

"How much larger?"

Canning spread his hands. "About two billion."

Alex's jaw dropped, and Whitaker nodded slowly—the stag was down. Whitaker continued, "The president is about to authorize the sale of sixty of the most sophisticated jet aircraft in the world—the F-22 Barracuda—to the kingdom of Saudi Arabia."

"They go for around twenty-five million apiece," Canning added. "Add in parts, support systems, additional radar . . ." He sat back, rolling his drink back and forth in his hands. "Because of the nature of this deal, the Saudis are willing to set aside the law that no commissions be paid on arms purchases. It could run as high as fifty or sixty million."

Barclay could scarcely restrain himself from shouting the figures. He finally managed a shrug. "How soon?"

"Don't misunderstand," Whitaker said, his voice flat. "We can't promise you the deal. We can only promise you a good shot at it."

"What's that supposed to mean?"

"There will be others trying to put together a package. The Saudis are pretty shrewd negotiators—they'll take the best one. But we'll put you on the inside track. That should give you about ten jumps on anyone else."

"*If* I pull off the African deal," Barclay said slowly.

Whitaker smiled. "But of course."

For several long seconds, Barclay looked back and forth between the two men. Then, "I'll need some help on this. If this is as big as you say . . ." He turned to Whitaker. "I have my eye on

20

one man—in fact, he's here tonight. But I'll need another. Can I tap your computer banks again?"

"Certainly. I'll have Bates out here Monday."

"Does that mean you're willing to accept the risks on this other deal?" Canning asked.

Barclay looked surprised. "Risks? What risks?"

Valerie heard the garage door opening and quickly took off her apron. She stuffed it in a drawer, made one last swipe at the counter as the car door slammed, then turned as the door opened and Marc entered. He stopped, staring around the room, then he started to back out the door again.

"Sorry. I must have the wrong house."

She laughed, pleased at his reaction. He came back in, spun around slowly. "My kitchen has a two-year supply of flour and sugar and honey on the floor. Surely this could not be the same room."

"The boys and I had nearly as much fun cleaning it as Matt did creating it."

He set his briefcase down. "Hey, I didn't mean for you to do all this." His hands came up quickly. "Not that I'm complaining, mind you." He moved to the doorway and looked into the family room. "And you had a new carpet installed as well."

Again she laughed with pleased merriment. "It was mostly on the surface. The honey gave us a few challenges, but the rest came up pretty easily."

"Really, I never expected this. Thank you very much."

"You're welcome."

"How's your mother?"

"Doing very well, really. I talked to her earlier."

"You said she's been having pain for several days? Why didn't she say something? Here she worked all day yesterday, came this morning and cooked breakfast for the boys while I was at my early class, and I didn't even know she was having problems."

"Mom didn't want you to worry about it. She says you have enough on your mind already."

"Thanks," he said ruefully. "That makes me feel wonderful."

She shook her head quickly. "You know I didn't mean it that way. To hear Mom talk, you're more like a son to her."

The lines around Marc's eyes softened. "And she is much more than housekeeper to us," he said softly. "I don't know what we would do without her. She's like a grandmother to the boys. They both absolutely adore her."

"And she them." Valerie turned to look down the hall toward the bedrooms. "And no wonder. Matt is such a delight."

Marc hooted. "You can say that after tonight?"

She nodded. "We had a wonderful time together. And Brett. So sober and yet so sweet."

"Well, I really appreciate you coming. I don't know what I would have done."

"How did you do on the test?"

He shrugged. "Who knows?"

Valerie watched his face as the smile faded and he was lost in thoughts of the class. Finally she straightened. "Well, I'd better be going."

That pulled him back. "Look, we have some lemonade in the refrigerator—" He pulled a face. "At least we did before Matt started his hatchet job on the kitchen. Would you like a glass? You've earned that, at least."

For a moment she hesitated, then smiled. "Yes, thank you."

When they were seated at the table, Marc watched her sip from the glass. "So you're Valerie."

She looked up in surprise.

"Youngest in the family, graduated from Cal Poly, Pomona, majored in math and computer science. After graduation spent eighteen months in Hong Kong knocking on doors."

While he was reciting soberly, as though to a class, she saw the amusement dancing in his eyes.

"Plays the piano," he went on, "dabbles in watercolors, currently works as a systems analyst for a large oil firm in Denver."

"You forgot my shoe size," she laughed, shaking her head. "I can't believe my mother."

"She's very proud of you." He took a drink of lemonade, watching her. Mary kept a snapshot of her family in her wallet—a family shot at a cabin, the men holding fish, the women in jeans and woolen shirts. She had pointed out her youngest daughter to him, but Marc hadn't paid much attention. He had expected her to be . . . what? He wasn't sure, but certainly not this. "So when did you come out? Your mom didn't say anything about that."

"She didn't know. She started having pain a week or two ago. We had a family council." Her shoulders lifted and fell. "I'm the only one not married, and I've been threatening to come out anyway. All my brothers and sisters live out of state, and Mom's getting older."

Now it was Marc that was surprised. "So you're moving here?"

"Moved," she corrected. "My stuff is a few days behind me, but I got here yesterday."

"Well, welcome to California. If you give us a little advanced warning next time, I'll have Matt do the living room and bedrooms as well."

She groaned. "This was sufficient, thank you!" She finished her lemonade and pushed back from the table. "Well, I'd better go. I want to stop off and see how Mom is."

"How long will she be in the hospital?"

"Three days."

"Then rest for some time, I would imagine."

"The doctor said it would be two to three weeks until she's really back up and at it again."

The lines around his eyes deepened. "Well, tell her not to worry about us. I'll see if I can get a girl from the college."

Valerie had started toward the living room. She stopped. "Oh, no. That's one of the reasons I came down."

"It is?"

"Yes. Mom didn't want to lose her job with you."

"Well, she doesn't have to worry about that. But I don't expect you to have to fill in for her. I can find someone."

Valerie smiled, faintly teasing him. "Does that mean my work is not satisfactory?"

23

"Are you kidding? I had planned on renting a back-hoe to clean up the kitchen. This is terrific!"

"Then it's settled."

"Are you sure?"

"Yes. If that's all right."

"All right? It's great! Thank you."

They moved from the kitchen to the living room. Valerie opened the door. "Well, good night. I'll be here tomorrow in time to fix breakfast and get Matt off to his preschool."

"Thanks."

She opened the door, started to exit, then hesitated. "Do you mind if I ask you a question?"

"No."

"Mom said you're working on a Master's of Business Administration at UCLA."

"Yes."

"But you teach in Near Eastern Studies at the Claremont Colleges?"

He nodded, amused. "Is that your question?"

She shrugged, suddenly embarrassed. "I was just wondering if I had gotten it straight."

"Why is a man who has a doctorate in Near Eastern Studies working on a master's degree in business?"

Now he had really flustered her. "Well, yes. It is a little curious. But I didn't mean to pry."

The amusement in his eyes slowly died. "That's what the dean of the college wants to know," he said slowly. "I wish I could think of a clever answer."

Chapter Three

The man at the computer keyboard let his fingers drop and started to type rapidly. Alex Barclay watched him idly. He hardly fit the typical image of the computer expert. With his blond wavy hair and tanned features, he looked more like a naval cadet or the captain of the Yale University rowing team.

Lines of data began to flow across the terminal screen, and Alex started to watch what was coming up on the screen.

```
PROFILE SEARCH COMPLETED
TOTAL PROFILES SEARCHED: 82
PROFILES MARKED AND SAVED: 9
DO YOU WISH COMPLETE FILES ON THOSE PROFILED? Y/N
```

Without looking up for affirmation, the man hit the Y key, then leaned back. "This will take a few minutes. It has to go back to the original database and add complete files on each man."

Benjamin Bates stood, drew heavily on his cigarette, then stubbed it out in an overflowing ash tray. He was an oak of a man—short, thick, facial features like weathered bark. He stretched, limbering up his body. They had been at it for over three hours, Barclay leaning over the man at the keyboard, reading each profile quickly as the computer spewed out the data feed, Bates alternately smoking and dozing in the corner.

Barclay ran his fingers through his hair and turned to Bates. "Just exactly how big is that data base you tap?"

Bates smiled. This was part of the ritual. Four times Barclay had asked Russell Whitaker of the State Department for help. Four times Whitaker had sent Benjamin Bates. Every time Barclay had asked that same question, Bates had given the same response, "We left out Idaho. That helped."

Alex laughed softly and let it drop. In fact, he didn't even know if Bates was from the State Department or some other agency. He just always came with some bright-eyed assistant whom he never bothered to introduce, a terminal, a phone modem, and access to a data base that always left Alex feeling slightly uneasy. He leaned over and picked up the phone.

"Jackie, is lunch ready?" He listened for a moment, then, "Good. I'll be out and help you." He hung up and exited the room.

The man at the keyboard rubbed his eyes, then moved his fingers up to massage his temples. Bates watched for a moment, then grinned. "If Jackie brings lunch in, that'll rest your eyes."

The even white teeth flashed. "Hey, isn't she something?"

"And every bit as sharp as she looks. Barclay calls her his executive secretary. But I've watched them operate. I think she's more like a partner."

"On or off the job?"

Bates pulled out another cigarette, retrieved a lighter from a crumpled coat pocket and lit it thoughtfully. "I've wondered that myself," he said finally, "but according to Whitaker, it's strictly on the job. He says Barclay takes great pride in playing it straight with his wife."

"Who is this Barclay, anyway?" the man demanded of his boss. "I can't believe the way he races through the data. He's got each individual marked or rejected while I'm still reading the stuff."

Bates just shook his head. "The uncanny thing is yet to come. Just watch him. Sight unseen, he seems to have a sixth sense about who will work out for him."

"Work out for what?"

There was the slightest shrug. "Depends which project he's putting together. Whenever he's starting on a major project, he goes on a hunt for help. Sometimes he gets him through his own means. Other times, if it has to do with a government project, he searches our data base."

"Why does he need help? I thought you said that he and Jackie ran this whole operation."

"They do. Oh, there's the hired help—warehousemen, drivers, custodial staff, that kind of thing. But no other executives. Just Alex and Jackie—and temporary help as needed."

"Like this Derek Parkin who picked us up at the airport last night?"

"Yeah. He's brand-new from what Alex said. Hired him away from some law firm." Bates drew out a crumpled pack of cigarettes, extracted one, and lit it. He drew deeply, then blew the smoke at the ceiling. "This must be some project. To my knowledge Alex has never brought on more than one new man before."

"Why doesn't he use the same men over again?"

Bates looked surprised. "Oh, they never survive."

The other visibly started, which brought a laugh from Bates.

"No, I don't mean that. Though one did end up in an Indonesian prison with his knuckles broken."

The blue eyes widened, which only added to Bates's amusement. He took another heavy draw on his cigarette. "No," he went on, "it's not like that. Barclay just burns them out. By the time he finishes with them, they're either too frustrated or too disillusioned or too exhausted—" He paused. "Or too scared. Alexander Barclay goes at hired help like sixteen linebackers at a rookie quarterback."

"Scared? Scared of what?"

Again there was an enigmatic shrug. "The world of the arms dealer—even the legitimate arms dealer—has its ups and downs."

"Like what?"

But before Bates could answer, the door pushed open, and Jacqueline Ashby pushed in a cart carrying white sacks emblazoned with a bright yellow sun and the words CASA DEL SOL RESTAURANT. Both men watched her appreciatively. Barclay paid her well, and she obviously spent a goodly portion of it on clothes. The white skirt and navy blue blazer were accented with a soft, red and blue plaid blouse with a white bow at the neck. It was elegantly understated and complimented the slenderness of her figure. Cool green eyes, looking out from under eyebrows as black as her hair, held a faint touch of amusement, as though accepting the unspoken praise being directed at her as part of her due.

Barclay followed close behind her, carrying a tray of Coke and Seven-Up and glasses filled with ice. With swift efficiency, Jackie had napkins and the food spread out across the desk.

For a few moments they were all occupied with getting their food and drinks sorted out, then Alex turned to Bate's assistant. "Okay, let's get started. I've asked Jackie to stay."

It was not a request, and Bates nodded almost imperceptibly as the other man shot him a startled look. Barclay and Jackie noted both reactions without expression. "Bring up number six," Barclay went on.

"Number six?"

"Yeah. His name was Jeppson."

The computer operator took a huge bite of a chimichanga and a quick swig of drink, then banged out the commands quickly. All three of the others inched their chairs closer so they could watch as the data started to fill the screen.

```
PROFILE: MARC ALLEN JEPPSON
AGE: THIRTY-TWO
ADDRESS: 717 E. BRIDGEPORT AVE., CLAREMONT, CALIFORNIA
OCCUPATIONAL PROFILE: MISSIONARY SERVICE IN URUGUAY/
     PARAGUAY, THE CHURCH OF JESUS CHRIST OF LATTER-DAY
     SAINTS (72-73); TEACHING ASSISTANT, U OF U (74-75);
     PEACE CORPS, EGYPT AND SUDAN (75-76); ASSISTANT PRO-
     FESSOR, GEORGETOWN UNIVERSITY (80-82); ASSOCIATE PRO-
     FESSOR, CLAREMONT COLLEGES (82-PRESENT)
EDUCATION: BA, POLITICAL SCIENCE, UNIVERSITY OF UTAH (75)
     MA, MIDDLE EASTERN STUDIES, UNIVERSITY OF UTAH (77)
     PHD, NEAR EASTERN STUDIES, UC BERKELEY (80)
     CURRENTLY ENROLLED, MBA, UCLA GRADUATE SCHOOL
     OVERALL GPA: 3.92
```

LANGUAGES: ARABIC (FLUENT), SPANISH (FLUENT), HEBREW (CONVERSANT), PARSI (CONVERSANT)
PERSONAL: MARRIED LYNETTE THOMPSON ('78); WIFE KILLED IN AUTO ACCIDENT ('83); TWO SONS, BRETT MARC, 8, AND MATTHEW DAVID, 4. INTERESTS/HOBBIES: WRITING, SKIING, WATER SKIING. NO RECORD OF ARRESTS, NO KNOWN DETRIMENTAL HABITS. CREDIT RATING 1A. KNOWN DEBTS, ABOUT $12,000. ACTIVE CHURCH ATTENDER. MEMBER CLAREMONT KIWANIS CLUB

"Well, well," Barclay said as the lines finally stopped coming up.

"Not bad," Jackie agreed. "Ph.D. in Near Eastern Studies. Fluent in Arabic. Not bad at all."

"And working on an M.B.A. at UCLA," Barclay said. "That's an unexpected dash of frosting on the cake."

"And he lives in Claremont," Jackie added.

"Is that nearby?" Bates asked.

Barclay turned. "Out near Pomona. About thirty miles east of L.A."

"What about the others?" Bates's assistant asked, sensing a decision had already been made.

Barclay stared at the screen, lost in thought for several moments. Finally the words registered. "No, I don't think so. Mark the others so we can retrieve them if we need to."

The man was shaking his head in disbelief as he tapped out the instructions.

"Attach to our printer and get Jackie a printout of Jeppson's profile, will you?" He turned to Jackie as the man nodded. "Get a copy of it to Jarvis this afternoon. I want a full report on this Jeppson by the time I get back from Paris next week."

He took Bates by the arm. "I need to have you take some things back to Washington. Let's go in the other office."

It was nearly half an hour later when the man brought from Washington to run the computer set down his magazine in the outer foyer of Barclay Enterprises and looked at Jackie. She was at the reception desk, her head bent to her work.

"Can I ask you a question?"

She looked up. "What?"

"What happens now?"

"What do you mean?"

"With this Jeppson guy. How does Mr. Barclay go about getting him to join his staff? I mean the guy *is* happily employed as a college professor."

"Maybe," she agreed with a half smile. "Maybe not. Why the M.B.A.?"

He shrugged. "Who knows? But suppose he is unhappy. I mean, how does Barclay even approach the guy?"

"It varies. About a week ago, Alex was invited to be one of the guest lecturers at a seminar sponsored by the UCLA Graduate School of Business. He declined." Her smile broadened, showing flawless white teeth. "Among other things, I suspect that sometime this afternoon, I'll be calling UCLA to tell them Mr. Barclay's plans have changed and that he can lecture there after all."

"And if Jeppson doesn't come to the lecture?" He shook his head. "Even if he does. Then what?"

She laughed right out loud. "You don't understand, Mr. Davies. That is the part Alex enjoys the very most. Marc Allen Jeppson will never know what hit him."

Chapter Four

Marc Jeppson stopped abruptly as he came out of the front entrance of the social sciences building. The rain was coming down in sheets, sometimes almost horizontally as the wind caught it. It was only the first week in October, which made this first real rain of the season early, but it was coming in with a vengeance.

For a moment he hesitated, glaring up at the heavy grey sky. He started back, then glanced at his watch. He lowered his head, hunched his shoulders, and darted across the quad toward the faculty parking lot.

With the rain, the traffic was moving even more slowly than usual down Euclid Avenue, and he caught three red lights in a row. It was already nine twenty-eight, and he had promised Mary Robertson he would be on time, if not early. His past record was not totally impeccable, so she had made him swear solemnly that he wouldn't add another black mark to the list.

As he approached the next intersection, the light turned yellow. He hit the gas pedal. The 1977 Volkswagen Beetle had a hundred and twenty thousand miles on it, and it lurched forward like an old plow horse. It was too little too late. Marc jammed his foot on the brake and slid to a stop squarely in the middle of the crosswalk.

Two middle-aged women joggers, their sweatsuits dark with rain, detoured around the front of his car, and shot him a dirty look. The one yelled something, and while he wasn't up on lip-reading, he was pretty sure it was a comment you wouldn't hear from the pulpit.

"May your shin splints multiply and your gym socks turn to mold!" he shouted after them through the closed window.

It was a quarter to ten when he swung the beat-up VW into a parking place outside the mall and darted through the rain to the main door. As he entered, the smell of the rain on his sportcoat made him wrinkle his nose. He took out a handkerchief and wiped the moisture from his glasses and made a quick pass at his damp hair with one hand.

Before he reached the center plaza of the mall, he could see Mary and Valerie standing at the top of the escalators looking around impatiently. "Oh, brother!" he muttered, then ran up the moving stairs lightly, bracing himself for the attack. Valerie spied him first and touched her mother's arm.

"Marc!" There was more exasperation than anger in Mary's voice. "You promised!"

"I know," he started lamely, "but some students caught me after class—"

She grabbed his arm. "We'll have to hurry. They open the main doors about six minutes to. They always do."

Suddenly she turned and surveyed the rain spots on his clothes. "Marc, where's your raincoat? I sent it with you this morning."

Valerie was smiling as Marc rolled his eyes. "I didn't know it was raining until I came outside, and then I decided I was already late and—"

She dragged him into a quicker pace. "We've got to walk faster!"

"Mother," Valerie cried. "You've only been out of the hospital a week. You shouldn't be hurrying."

The older woman waved that aside as if she were waving away a fly only half noticed.

"Now listen, the toy department is closest to the main door so you'll go in there. Valerie and I will go to the south door, but that little man up there never opens the door until two minutes to. It's maddening!"

He nodded. "Probably has to take a belt of something or other to build his courage."

She shot him a quick look. "What are you mumbling about?" But she didn't wait for an answer. "Remember, the Super Cycle is not just on sale. It's what they call 'the door crasher.' The quantities will be limited, and they'll go fast. You can't be timid or polite, or they'll be gone."

"Yes, sir!" he barked crisply. "Chin down, bayonet up, and watch my back, sir!"

That finally broke through to her. She stared at him for a moment and then laughed. Valerie was trying hard to maintain a straight face. "Will you stop it!" Mary said firmly. "I'm just saying that you'll have to get in there and hold your own."

"Mary, if this is going to involve hand-to-hand combat with other women, why don't you or Valerie do it?"

"Because the winter coats for the boys are also on as a door crasher, and it will take two of us to get one for both Brett and Matt, so by the time we could get down to the toys, all the Super Cycles will be gone, and you know the Super Cycle is the one thing Matt wants for Christmas more than anything else."

Marc was awed. She had got it all in one sentence without missing a step or taking a breath. "Tell me again how much we're saving."

"Normally they're forty-nine ninety-five. On the door crasher they're only nineteen ninety-five."

"Thirty bucks!" he yelped, causing a lady headed in the opposite direction to turn and stare at them. "I'll give you that thirty, and throw in another twenty if I don't have to do this."

Instantly, Marc knew he had pushed her too far. Her back stiffened, and her heels popped sharply on the marble floor. "You think *I* like it? I try to help you get a little Christmas shopping done, and this is what I get."

"Mary, I was just kidding."

"I try to save you some money, stretch things so your kids can have a nicer Christmas, and the one time I ask you for help—"

"Mary, for crying out loud! I was just trying to bring some humor into the morning. Heaven knows I could use some." He heard Valerie snicker and shot her a dirty look. "I'll be happy to buy the Super Cycle." He glanced quickly upward, wondering what it would take to get forgiveness for that one. "Okay?"

They rounded the corner, and Marc could see the clot of women already milling in a tight circle around the main entrance to Mervyn's.

"Okay," Mary said, only partially mollified. "We'll meet you back at the escalators." She gave him a little push toward the crowd of women. "Remember, you've got to get in there and go for it. Okay?"

He nodded glumly as the two of them turned and hurried away. With a quick eye, Marc surveyed the crowd, estimating there were close to a hundred women milling in a tight circle around the door. He moved around the periphery, looking for an opening of any kind, drawing several curious looks as he circled. He was the only male in the group.

"Ain't no use," a voice behind him said in a slow drawl. "They're packed in tighter than a quart of pickles in a pint jar."

Marc turned in surprise. An older man, near seventy, sat on a bench, a look of infinite patience carved into his features. Marc grinned. "Couldn't have said it better myself," he admitted. "But I have no choice. I either throw myself into the breach, or face a fate too horrible to contemplate."

The older man just shook his head slowly. "May as well sit down No one's going through that herd until they disperse across more of the prairie."

Marc laughed, turning and eyeing the women again. "You may be right, but it occurs to me that this may be more a time for strategy than for strength."

He went up on his tiptoes, peering over the sea of heads. Through the glass doors, at the far end of the store, he saw a man in a dark suit coming toward them, dangling a ring of keys in his hand. Marc checked his watch. It was nine fifty-four. Six minutes to ten. Uncanny, he thought. His housekeeper couldn't fill the car with gasoline, but she knew the door opening routine at Mervyn's down to the second.

"Watch this," he called softly to the old man. "Strategy doth prevail."

Walking swiftly back around to the center of the crowd, he took out his car keys, held them high in the air and began to jingle them vigorously. "Excuse me, ladies," he called in a loud voice. Again he rattled the keys. "Ladies, if I can get through here, we'll see if we can get the doors opened for you."

Several of the heads in the rear swiveled around to stare at the keys suspended in the air, and then as if by some invisible hand, a path started to open directly in front of him.

"That's it," he sang sweetly. "None of us can get in until the doors are unlocked."

In less than twenty seconds Marc was standing at the door, the Red Sea of women closing in tightly behind him.

Through the glass, the man in the dark suit was coming, but was still about twenty yards away. A rather frowsy-looking woman in a brown ski parka standing next to Marc was eyeing him with open suspicion. Fumbling with the keys, he gave her one of his best smiles, turning his body enough to block her view of the lock.

"Double locking system," he said, lowering his voice to a half whisper. "Can't be too careful." He raised his other hand to cover the fact that his key did not even come close to fitting into the lock.

The clerk from Mervyn's, obviously deep into boredom already, reached the door. The keys came up, and in a moment the bolt clicked. Marc helped him slide the door open about two feet, then slipped in quickly and pulled it shut again, cutting off the surprised cries from the women and catching the clerk off guard as well.

Marc patted him warmly on the shoulder. "The supervisor said to hold them here for another couple of minutes."

The man stared at Marc, his pencil thin-mustache twitching. "What?"

"She said two more minutes, but I'd trust your own instincts."

"What?" It was obvious the man was still opening doors because of limited mental speed.

"I'd give them thirty seconds, then get out of the way."

Marc moved off with a friendly wave, leaving the man staring.

Six minutes later Marc was standing in the line waiting to pay for his purchase, a Super Cycle tucked under one arm and a smug look on his face. He felt a little sheepish for hassling Mary over this. These sales weren't so bad after all—even door crashers. One merely needed to know exactly what door crasher meant.

"*You!*"

For almost a full second Marc could not place the woman standing there, pointing her finger at him like a policeman's nightstick. He knew he had seen her before . . . Then it came. This was the woman in the brown parka. At the time he had thought her frowsy. Now all he could think of was a mother grizzly coming down on him like a heat-seeking missile.

Marc managed a grin. "Well, hello again. I hope you're having a wonderful day here at Mervyn's." The line moved forward one place.

"I *knew* you weren't a store employee. How dare you use deceit to get in ahead of the rest of us?"

"Deceit? I never said I was a store employee."

"You got a Super Cycle and I didn't because you wouldn't wait your turn like everyone else."

Marc shook his head, not about to be intimidated. "As the saying goes, the race is not to the swift, but to the sneaky."

With a "Hmmph!" she turned abruptly and left.

He had only moved three places forward when she reappeared. Several other women moved closer to hear. "I want that Super Cycle," she demanded. "I was here half an hour early."

"Lady," Marc said wearily, "in the Guiness Book of Records, you just took the lead for poor losers."

There were some angry murmurs around him, and Marc felt his face going red. This was getting to be ridiculous.

"So you admit that you got a Super Cycle by impersonating a store employee."

"I held up keys and rattled them. Some impersonation."

"That's what I wanted to hear!" she cried triumphantly, beckoning vigorously behind her. A man in a dark suit stepped out from behind a display. "Allow me to introduce you to Mr. Abbott, head of store security."

Valerie and her mother were standing in almost the exact same place at the top of the escalators, only this time when Mary spotted him, carrying a large polyester sack, she almost ran to meet him.

"Marc, for heaven's sake! Where have you been? We've been here almost half an hour."

Swinging the sack around behind him, he merely grunted. "Where's your car?"

"Marc! Where were you? We've looked all over. Val even went back down to the toy department."

"Look," Marc said wearily. "Do you want me to carry this to the car for you or not?"

Valerie eyed the sack, and Marc turned slightly, keeping it behind him. This time Mary moved, and he turned again, but it was a feint. She had the sack, turned it, then gave a cry of dismay. "Marc! This is a J. C. Penney's sack!"

"Mary, a group of Serbo-Croatian terrorists are about to bomb the Orange Julius stand. I suggest we get out of here immediately." He heard Valerie cough. She was trying hard to maintain a sober demeanor.

Mary stared at him in disbelief, then she rummaged inside the sack. "And you paid *full price?*" she cried when she finally came up with the sales slip. "Marc, I could have gotten it anywhere for forty-nine ninety-five. I told you Mervyn's!"

Marc sighed, a deep, weary sound of resignation. "Remember the deal I offered you earlier?"

"Deal? What deal?"

"I offered to give you the thirty dollars we were saving in the sale plus an additional twenty if I didn't have to go in there."

"Yes, I remember. So?"

"I'll double that on one condition."

"What?" she asked, thoroughly exasperated now.

"From now on, I'll give you whatever money you need. Just don't make me help you spend it."

Chapter Five

Allahu akbar!
The words of the *muezzin*, the crier who calls the faithful to prayers, blared from the loudspeakers atop the graceful minaret of the mosque. "God is great!" the voice cried with great solemnity, repeating the cry four times.
Ashhadu an la illallah.
"I bear witness that there is no God but Allah."
Each *muezzin* throughout the Muslim world calls more than half a billion Islamic worshippers to morning prayers in his own distinct tone and style. Some make it a low, mournful dirge; others make it a cheerful, lighthearted chant. The voice calling the faithful to prayer from the stunningly modern and beautiful mosque at the King Khalid International Airport at Riyadh, Saudi Arabia, made it into a fierce, almost threatening, command.
Ashadu anna Muhammad rasulu Allah.
"I bear witness that Mohammad is the Messenger of God."
It was that time of day when, as the law stated, one could first distinguish the difference between white and black threads without artificial light. The sky in the east was showing the faintest of pale yellows and golds, but full dawn was still some time away.
Hayya ala-as-salah. Hayya ala-as-salah.
As-salutu khayrun mina-an-nawn.
"Come quickly to prayer. Come quickly to success. Prayer is better than sleep."

39

A dozen men in flowing robes and headdresses were gathered in the courtyard of the mosque around the place of washing, performing the *wudu*, the partial ablution. Each man went through the cleansing process quickly but thoroughly. The hands, the feet, the arms and the face—each were washed before coming before the face of Allah. Almost as one the men were finished. The king nodded, almost imperceptibly, then stood and led them inside the mosque.

Alahu akbar, Allahu akbar.
La illaha ilallah.

"God is great! God is great! There is no God but Allah!"

The Muslim prays with more than his mouth. The entire body is involved as first he stands, then kneels, then prostrates himself so he touches his forehead to the ground. It is a solemn ritual, and the king felt a familiar thrill as he thought of this same act being repeated at that very moment all over the kingdom. In palaces, mud huts, mosques, fields, or even kneeling on a small prayer rug in front of a Bedouin tent—across the breadth of his land, his people were beginning another day by renewing their allegiance to Allah.

Finished, the king stood up, glancing at his diamond studded Cartier wristwatch. "It is time," he announced to the crown prince, and they walked swiftly out of the mosque and headed for the main terminal and the departure lounge reserved for the royal family.

Twenty-five minutes later, a line of black limousines left the terminal building and the mosque behind, moving in the direction of Riyadh. As the sleek and lushly furnished automobiles reached the outskirts of the airport, they pulled off to the side of the road. The king stepped out of the lead vehicle and moved around to the front of the car. No one else followed suit, just rolled down mirrored glass windows to watch. It was still a few minutes before sunrise, and the sky was a brilliant burst of pink and turquoise. The air was pleasantly cool but held the first promise of the coming heat.

The king turned his head, thinking of those he had just embraced and sent onto the plane. The king was a handsome man, round of face, quick to smile and with dark, jet black eyes that could flash with fierce anger or soften with quick humor. Now the corners of his mouth pulled down as he thought of the crown prince and those who accompanied him. What kind of reception would their proposal find in America? The king had great respect and admiration for America, and yet he knew his allies too well. There would be a great outcry from the Zionists and their supporters when they learned the president was considering the sale of F-22 Barracudas to an Arab nation. Could the president hold to his promise?

The king sighed. While he did not have a Congress and voting constituents to worry about, he knew that a ruler is never truly his own man. In his own country there were the royal family, the council of ministers, the *ulema* or council of religious scholars who interpreted Islamic law, the tribal sheiks, and a host of others to satisfy.

The rumble of massive engines brought his head around. He watched impassively as the jumbo jet lifted off the ground, letting the sound batter at him like a cleansing wind. Slowly the huge craft banked around to the north. It caught the first rays of the sun, flashing them back at him as though they were a signal.

"The light of Allah is upon you," he murmured. "Go with God, my brothers."

Aboard the plane, the crown prince; the king's half brother; Prince Feisal, Minister of Defense; and half a dozen others chatted quietly as the 747 climbed steeply, then banked to the west.

A few minutes later the seat belt sign winked out. The crown prince stood, and the others followed. They moved across the sumptuously furnished cabin to private compartments. Long, ankle length robes and cotton *thobes* came off and went into closets. Out of those same closets came three-piece business suits, gleaming Gucci shoes, and hundred-dollar ties.

When they gathered back in the lounge of the Royal family's private airliner, the transformation was nearly complete. Except for the dark olive skin and the white headdresses held on with braided black cords, they had crossed that invisible line that separates the Orient from the Occident.

The same sun that caught the burnished skin of the 747 over Riyadh had risen above the Mount of Olives enough to bathe Jerusalem in the first golden-pink glow of morning. Nathan Shoshani put his head back and drew in a deep breath of the cool, fragrant air, listening to the sounds of an awakening city. In an hour or so the roads would be swarming with tourists and Arab street hawkers selling olivewood camels and Holy City bookmarks. But now there was only the braying of a donkey, out of sight somewhere below him in the village of Silwan. Behind him he heard the soft cooing of a dove.

He glanced at his watch grudgingly, knowing that this would be his last look for some time to come at the city he loved so deeply. He was tall and broad across the shoulders. His hair was black, thick and curly, as was the hair on his arms, chest, and back. Dark-brown eyes looked out from heavy brows that almost touched when he frowned. At thirty-six he still had the lean look of an athlete, with trim waist and rock-hard stomach. But then, a field agent for the Mossad—Israel's intelligence agency—was expected to stay in top-notch physical condition.

Like most Israelis, he was casually dressed—leather sandals with no stockings, faded jeans, and a plain cotton shirt, open at the neck. He too would change into a business suit before his arrival in New York. But for the long Atlantic crossing he much preferred the comfort of something less confining. With a sigh he turned and climbed the few steps to his car, thinking of the coming confrontation with his father.

A few minutes later, he pulled into a parking place outside a small apartment building in West Jerusalem. Like most other buildings in the city, it was made of the beige-white Jerusalem stone that gave all of Jerusalem—even the most modern of buildings such as this one—a sense of antiquity in keeping with the history of the ancient city. As he stepped out of the car he could see the gleaming white dome of the Shrine of the Book, home of the Dead Sea Scrolls. But his mind was not on Jerusalem stone or the Shrine of the Book. He ran up the three flights of stairs and rapped on the door sharply.

For someone in her midsixties, Esther Shoshani was a strikingly handsome woman, slender of build, fine of feature, with only the first streaks of grey touching her hair. When she opened the door and saw her son, her face softened instantly into a radiant smile. "Ah, Nathan, we were afraid you wouldn't have time to stop by before you had to leave." She spoke in nearly flawless English.

He gave his mother a perfunctory kiss on the cheek and a quick squeeze, then pulled away and moved into the apartment. "Where is he?"

Esther Shoshani was not only still attractive at sixty, she was also very perceptive, especially when it came to the two men in her life. She caught her son's hand. "He's in the alcove," she said, holding him back. "He'll be out in a minute."

But Nathan pulled free and strode across the small living room. He stopped as he caught sight of his father near the window of the small room off the kitchen. The morning sunlight streamed through the window, backlighting his father and leaving him in dark silhouette. Nathan stepped back. It was forbidden to interrupt in any way a person engaged in morning prayers.

Yaacov Shoshani was shorter than his son and beginning to stoop slightly at the shoulders, but any sense of age was dispelled by the graceful dignity of his movements as he rocked slowly back and forth. The prayer shawl or *tallit* was over his head, the square shape of the *tefillin* on his forehead silhouetted in the light. More commonly known as phylacteries by Christians, the *tefillin* were small, hollow boxes made of one single piece of black leather. Sealed inside were intricately inscribed scrolls containing selected passages from the Torah. One was worn on the forehead, a second on the bicep of the left arm.

Though it had been almost a decade since Nathan had donned the *tefillin* and prayer shawl on other than special occasions, he knew every move, every word of the blessings, every phrase of the recitations. He felt a curious mixture of the old childish awe and a growing irritation. This particular set of *tefillin* had been in his family for five generations. To know that his great-great-grandfather had donned those same phylacteries in the same exact ritual over a hundred years ago touched him with a sense of continuity that was unlike anything else he had experienced.

He turned and saw his mother watching him, her eyes pleading. "Do you have time for breakfast?" she asked.

"No, Mama, thank you. My plane leaves at nine. And I have to stop by the office in Tel Aviv before I go."

"Some coffee, maybe?"

"No, thank you."

Her eyes looked past him, and he turned to see his father coming to join them, holding the folded *tallit* and the velvet bag that held the *tefillin*.

"*Boker tov, Nahtan.*"

"In English," Esther chided. "He is going to America. He needs to practice his English."

"I know he is going to America," Yaacov mocked her gently.

Nathan's mouth tightened. "Eli told me about your assignment." It was spoken harshly, more than he had intended.

Yaacov's eyebrows came up slightly, quizzically. "Eli?"

"Eli Weissman, the deputy director."

"Oh yes, of course."

"Why, Papa? Your field is not intelligence work."

"Nathan!" Esther said sharply.

Yaacov laid his hand on her arm and smiled sadly. When he spoke, it was to her rather than to his son. "The president of the United States is informed that Saudi Arabia has had two or three very sobering incidents with enemy aircraft penetrating their airspace. He panics and authorizes the sale of the most advanced fighter aircraft in the world to our sworn enemies. When our own prime minister hears of this, he personally asks me to serve as an advisor to the intelligence team set up to prevent the sale from occurring. Personally mind you. The prime minister himself.

And my son asks why I did not decline. I should have said perhaps, 'But Prime Minister, my son will not like it. Surely you must reconsider your request.'" He turned to Nathan, and hurt finally crept into his voice. "Tell me, Nathan? If this upsets you so much, why didn't *you* refuse the assignment?"

Their eyes locked for a long moment. It was Nathan who looked away first. "All right, Papa, I'm sorry."

"When the Prime Minister called last night, he did not tell me that you would be the team leader. I learned that later, when the director called to brief me."

"Okay, okay. I'm sorry."

"Is it so terrible," Esther Shoshani asked softly, "to have to work with your father?"

"You know it is not that, Mama. It's just that—"

"It's just that he's afraid that I'll bring my *tefillin* and *tallit* to the meetings and embarrass him."

"No! No, I'm not!" Nathan retorted hotly. "But I do fully expect that we will hear a lecture or two about this being a time for faith, that what Israel needs is not good intelligence or a strong military, but more prayers, more dedication to Torah."

Now it was his father who was nettled. "I have never said that a strong military or good intelligence work is not necessary. But I do say that those who trust in man's arm alone, including my own son, are sowing the seeds of destruction for the very Israel they think they are defending."

"Please," Esther pleaded, looking first at one, and then the other. "Not now. Not again."

"Do you really think," Nathan shouted, "that standing in the alcove every morning, putting on a piece of cloth and two leather boxes is going to make one bit of difference in this world?"

"It could make as much difference as sending a team of faithless men to America!"

"Enough!" Esther cried. "That is enough!"

Both men stopped, breathing hard, shocked by the fierceness of the woman who had stepped between them.

"Nathan is leaving today,'" she went on in a hoarse whisper.

"Must it always be like this? Can you never speak of things without attacking one another like two blind scorpions? Now sit down, both of you. I will get some coffee, and then we will visit like normal human beings."

She glared up at them, daring either to challenge her command. They looked at her, then at each other. Finally Yaacov smiled ruefully. "She is well named, this woman of ours. Even the king of Persia would not have dared to cross such an Esther."

Nathan laughed, nodding and putting his arms around his mother.

"Well, I mean it," she said, much of the storm blown out of her by the sudden switch of moods. "Now, sit down, and I'll get some coffee." She pushed her husband and son toward the couch and then disappeared into the kitchen.

"I'm sorry," Nathan said. "I shouldn't have said those things."

"You say what is in your heart," his father answered sadly. "That is what causes me the greatest sorrow."

Chapter Six

Marc broke off what he was saying as a Western Airlines DC-10 thundered past, rattling the windows, and both he and Valerie turned to watch. The Proud Bird Restaurant sits just a few dozen yards south of the main runways of Los Angeles International Airport, where a plane lands on the average of about every sixty seconds. The whole north side of the restaurant is glass, providing a perfect view of the planes as they approach final touchdown. Marc and Valerie sat next to the window, the remains of two excellent prime rib dinners still on the table.

The DC-10 lumbered over Aviation Boulevard and disappeared; and they turned back to face each other. "I'm sorry," Valerie said. "What were you saying?"

Marc turned his glass idly, watching her. "Your mother tells me you're a runner."

She shook her head. "Not really. I just jog four or five times a week for the exercise."

"Oh."

"Why? Do you run?"

Marc looked up in mock horror. "Not me. I collect articles on the dangers of running." That startled her for a minute, but then she laughed merrily, and a tiny smile broke through his sober expression.

Valerie sat back, liking the way the smile danced in his eyes and softened the line of his jaw. All through dinner he had been

47

tense and on edge. This was more like the Marc she saw fathering his two sons around the house, or joking with her mother.

He was watching her as well, and finally spoke. "Tell me what you were thinking just then."

She blushed a little and dropped her eyes.

"Come on."

Finally she looked up. "I was thinking now that you've survived dinner, you're feeling a little more comfortable."

There was a flicker of surprise, then the smile was in his eyes again. "That obvious, huh?"

She shook her head slowly. "Not really."

He looked out the window and watched an American Airlines 737 gliding downward. "It's been a while," he mused. "I'm out of touch."

"Well, now that I know it's my running that makes you nervous, I don't feel quite so bad."

He chuckled softly, then the green eyes seemed to deepen as he became more serious. "I just wanted to say thanks for these last four weeks. We wouldn't have survived without you."

"Thank you. It's been a delightful time for me. I'm going to miss being with your boys now that Mother's back up to full steam."

"What do you mean you're going to miss them?"

"I've been unemployed long enough. I've got to start looking for a job."

"Well, that's fine, but you'd better not stop coming over or you're going to have two very disappointed young men on your hands." He gave her a searching look. "Maybe three."

That caught her completely off guard, and she felt a sudden rush of pleasure. "Well, Mother's not completely better," she said softly.

He smiled. "Definitely not up to heavy work yet."

"Definitely."

Marc pushed his chair back and looked at his watch. "We've got a lecture to catch. Are you ready?"

She nodded, and they both stood.

As they left the restaurant and headed for the car, Marc suddenly slowed his pace. "Will you answer me something?"

"If I can."

"Did you think it was odd when I invited you to attend the lecture at UCLA with me?"

"Odd? No, why do you ask that?"

"I happened to mention it to one of my colleagues today, and he about fell off the chair laughing. Like I said, I'm out of touch with this dating scene."

Valerie slipped her arm through his. "It's been a delightful evening so far, and I look forward to the rest of it. Thank you for asking me."

As the applause filled the lecture hall, Marc looked around, joining in. With less than two hundred graduate students present, it couldn't be described as a thunderous ovation, but it was warm, sincere, and enthusiastic. He turned to Valerie, who smiled and nodded. "That was very interesting."

Before he could answer, the dean of the graduate school stood to join the lecturer at the podium. The applause continued for another few moments, then died out quickly.

"On behalf of UCLA and the Graduate School of Business, thank you, Mr. Alex Barclay, for a stimulating and thought-provoking lecture." The dean glanced at his watch. "We still have about ten minutes. Mr. Barclay has agreed to answer questions from the floor."

There was a brief smattering of hands as the dean sat down and Barclay stepped forward again. "Thank you, Dean Sandberg. And thank you, for being a warm and gracious audience. Okay, any questions?"

A hand shot up directly in front of Marc and Valerie.

"Yes, please."

It was a girl, midtwenties, thin boned, with short, cropped hair and huge round glasses. "Mr. Barclay." Her voice was stronger than Marc had expected. "You titled your address, 'The Creation and Use of Leverage in Effective Business Transactions.'"

Alex nodded.

"You said that one way to create leverage with clients or potential clients is by doing special things for them, things that are not directly related to your business. Sometimes, you said, those acts of service may actually be disadvantageous to you or cost you considerably."

"Yes, I feel that is very important."

"I understand that and agree totally. My question is, how do you get clients in the first place so you can create leverage with them?"

"Ah!" Barclay leaned forward, his face thoughtful. "That is a very good question." Let me answer it in two ways. First, I have one rule in business I never violate. I call it performance integrity. No matter how small or insignificant the deal or the client, you deliver"—he punched the air with his finger as he hit each word emphatically—"always. On time. As ordered."

He smiled easily. "Do that without fail, and word starts to get around. Your reputation creates leverage for you—it becomes an important basis for client attraction. Do you see that?"

Marc was nodding along with the girl and several others.

"But there is a second way. This is more subtle, and in some ways not as easy to see. But I consider it almost as important as the first. Besides clients and potential clients, there is a third group of people—those who will never be clients. Now," he said, warming to his subject, "we've already talked about creating leverage with the first two groups. But most businessmen ignore the last group. If they aren't potential clients, they write them off. That's a mistake. I do things for this group as well—even when there is not the slightest chance they will buy my services or my products—and it often pays off with rich dividends. The more markers you have out on the table, the greater the likelihood you can call them in when you need them."

Marc's hand shot up, surprising himself almost as much as Valerie. Barclay stopped. He adjusted his glasses and looked more closely. "Yes?"

Marc stood up tentatively, aware that he had acted before thinking. He took a deep breath. "On the surface, that philosophy sounds a little manipulative and self-serving, doesn't it?"

There was an instant murmur of disapproval, and Barclay noted several dirty looks directed at the questioner. He opened the folder he had brought with him to the podium, studied the black-and-white photo attached to the first page and then looked up. Bingo! No doubt about it. The young man standing before him was Marc Allen Jeppson. He looked up and smiled.

"No, that's all right," he said to the audience. "That's a fair question." He turned to Marc. "I suppose it does sound a little manipulative and self-serving the way I stated it. But I assure you, I do not view people as mere chips in a poker game."

He removed his glasses, took out a handkerchief, and began to polish them. "Let me use an example to make my point a little more clear. Suppose I'm in the business of making widgets. I have a neighbor who has no use for widgets—never has had and, as far as I can determine, never will. Okay?"

Marc nodded.

"One day I find out my neighbor has a problem. Or, better, let's say he has always wanted something that I happen to be in a position to get for him. So I do it. It even costs me. Why do I do it? Because I like to do nice things for others. Okay? My motives are sincere. I'm just a nice guy." He grinned. "Will you grant me that?"

"Yes," Marc agreed with a smile.

"How is my neighbor going to feel toward me?"

"Grateful," Marc responded.

"Does the fact that my neighbor feels gratitude toward me make me manipulative?"

"No."

"Opportunistic?"

Marc sensed that he was being boxed in, very neatly and with great finesse. Yet he couldn't resent it, for Barclay was doing it with such charm. He shook his head. "No, of course not."

"Okay, good. Let's continue the example. Several months later, my neighbor is at his men's club. He's having lunch with some of the guys, and, lo and behold, the conversation happens to turn to widgets. Mr. X mentions that he needs a whole trainload of widgets and is trying to decide where to get them."

He paused, savoring the moment, for the trap had just shut tight. "Now, tell me, what is my neighbor very likely to do at that moment?"

Marc grinned good naturedly, conceding defeat. "He's going to say, 'Well, Mr. X, I just happen to know a man . . .'"

Barclay chuckled, a deep, rich, pleasant sound. "Exactly! I have created leverage. Not through manipulation. Not through caculating narrowness. But through being a good guy. Agreed?"

"Agreed. Thank you." Marc sat down, feeling a bit foolish. Valerie touched his arm in encouragement.

And so the questions went for the next few minutes. Barclay was candid, witty, and direct. Even when he occasionally attacked the logic of the questioner, he did it with the greatest of charm. And when the Dean finally stood up to cut off the questions, the applause swept the hall again—warm, appreciative, and enthusiastic.

"Well, what did you think of Alex Barclay?" Marc asked as they exited the building and started for the car about ten minutes later.

"Fascinating. I guess I've always known there were people who make a living selling weapons, but I've just never thought about it I guess. I would have pictured them as having swarthy skin, hair that was glossy black and slicked straight back with a comb, pencil thin mustache, trench coat."

He laughed. "With the collar turned up."

"And mirrored sunglasses."

"Right. Barclay certainly doesn't fit that."

"He's very charming, almost delightful."

"What did you think of his idea of leverage?"

Valerie pursed her lips slightly. "Well, I can see what he's saying, but like you, I find it still seems pretty calculated and self-serving."

"And yet," Marc chose his words carefully, "if you could keep your motives right, it would be exciting. I mean, to know that what you were doing—your own creativity, your own ingenuity, the ability to bind people to you with positive relationships—was what made the difference."

She looked up at him and made a shrewd guess. "And that's why a man with a doctorate in Near Eastern Studies is pursuing an MBA."

He glanced up, then looked out across the campus. "Yeah," he finally said. "I guess it is. I've always enjoyed teaching, but I've felt so stifled lately, so boxed in. This kind of stuff just rejuvenates me."

They had reached the Volkswagen. Marc unlocked the door and threw his briefcase in the back. Valerie looked up at him and smiled. "Well, tomorrow when you see your colleague, you can tell him that the last laugh is on him. I really enjoyed the lecture."

"Good." He shut the door and came around to the driver's side. As he slid in and inserted the key in the ignition, he paused. "Would you like some ice cream or something?"

She leaned her head back against the headrest. "Not really, unless you do."

"Would you like to do four laps around the parking lot before we drive home? I'd be happy to drive along with you."

"You're never going to forgive my sins, are you?" she laughed.

He turned the key, liking the way she laughed—deep, with softness and rich with enjoyment. But instantly his face fell. The engine of the VW did not turn over. Not even a whimper. Surprised, he released the key, pumped the gas pedal twice, then tried again—with exactly the same results. Valerie sat back up again and turned to watch. He waited a full ten seconds and tried again. Nothing.

"Wouldn't you know it," he said in disgust. He opened the door and got out.

Valerie was fighting back a smile. "My mother warned me about California boys. Are you sure this isn't a put-on?"

He pulled a face at her and walked around to the rear of the car, mumbling to himself. He opened the hood, wiggled a couple of wires, tentatively poked at something that resembled a greasy tin can, put his foot on the bumper, and bounced the car up and down a couple of times, then came back around and slid in alongside Valerie.

Now Valerie was appropriately serious. "Can you see what's the matter?"

He shook his head. "I was only joking about the four laps around the parking lot. How about a quick fifty-mile run out to Claremont?" He turned the key once more, without much hope. His expectations were correct. The car was dead.

"Wonderful!"

"What if we push it?"

Thoroughly disgusted now, Marc surveyed the situation. There was a slight incline to the parking lot, but he had parked facing uphill. "It's worth a try. Can you steer if I push us around? There's a bit of a hill going the other way."

"Sure."

As Marc got out, Valerie slid across into the driver's seat, careful not to snag her nylons on the gear shift. He rolled down the window, then shut the door and leaned down. "Have you ever done this before?"

"I used to drive a Beetle. How do you think I got started into running?"

Getting the car turned around was easy enough, and Marc stepped to the window again. "Is the ignition on?"

"Right."

"Are you in second gear?"

"Yes."

"Then here we go." He leaned into the door, and the little car began to roll.

"Now!"

Valerie popped the clutch. The car bucked heavily, lurching to a stop. They tried it three more times with exactly the same result.

"It's no use. She's not going to start."

Valerie shook her head, feeling bad now that she had teased him about it. She could tell he was terribly embarrassed by it all.

"Problems?"

That brought both Marc and Valerie around with a snap. Two cars had pulled up alongside the VW. The first one was a white Mercedes 450 SL convertible. The second he didn't recognize. It was low to the ground—not much higher than Marc's belt buckle—and a gleaming metallic blue. It looked like a cross between a Formula I racer and air-to-air missile. The engine purred deeply, like some jungle cat after a successful kill.

The window of the sports car was down, but in the glare of the overhead arc lights Marc couldn't make out the driver. Then the doors of both cars opened. A stunning black-haired woman got out of the Mercedes, then Alex Barclay stepped out of the blue sports car. Surprised, Marc opened the door for Valerie, and she got out of the VW as the two joined them.

"Won't she start?" Barclay asked.

"No way. She's gone."

"I can help push it."

Marc shook his head. "We tried that. It's no use. It's completely dead. Thanks anyway, Mr. Barclay."

The older man's eyes widened. "You know me?"

"I was in the lecture."

"Oh, of course. In fact—" He peered at him. "You asked a question, didn't you?"

Marc flushed slightly, pleased to be remembered. "Yes. My name is Marc Jeppson. This is Valerie Robertson."

Barclay stuck out his hand, gripping Marc's firmly, and nodded to Valerie. "This is my executive secretary, Jacqueline Ashby. Jackie, actually."

"How do you do?" Jackie smiled and stuck out her hand to

both of them. First class all the way, Valerie noted, feeling suddenly very plain. Hairdo, makeup, clothes, figure. This was a very lovely woman.

"The faithful secretary sacrifices evening at home to listen to the boss's lecture." Alex made it a compliment even though it was said lightly. Alex turned to survey the VW. "That's too bad about your car."

"Yeah," Marc answered glumly. "I don't understand. I just had it tuned up two weeks ago. And it ran fine all the way in."

"So what are you going to do with it?"

"Why? Do you want to trade?"

For one split second Barclay looked startled, then he laughed deeply, Jackie and Valerie joining in.

"Well," Marc added, straight-faced, "You'd have to throw in the all-leather steering wheel cover."

"Whoo-ee," Barclay chuckled, "that isn't exactly what I had in mind."

Marc shrugged. "What kind is it, anyway?"

"A Lamborghini Contach Five Thousand."

"How about my car and a couple of thousand?"

"How about your car and *ninety-five* thousand?" Jackie laughed. It could have been barbed, but her look made it clear she had joined in the game.

Marc whistled softly. "Ninety-five thousand! My eight-year-old son would go bananas just to see it."

"Then we'll have to make sure he sees it," Alex went on. "But actually what I was going to ask was, where do you live?"

"Claremont."

"Let's see . . . ."

"That's out near Pomona, isn't it?" Jackie broke in.

"Yes."

"Do you have a mechanic in this part of town?" Barclay asked.

"No."

"Well, I do, over in Culver City. He's terrific. If you have it towed to Claremont, it's going to cost you a bundle. I'll call him and have him pick it up." It was obvious that in Barclay's mind, the whole thing was settled. "Just leave the key in the ignition."

Marc shook his head. "Look, Mr. Barclay—"

"Alex, please."

"Okay, Alex. I—"

"You're worried about how you're going to get home, right?"

"Well, yeah. The thought had crossed my mind."

"I'd be delighted to run you and Valerie home."

Marc's mouth dropped open, then snapped shut again. "That's fifty miles from here! If you could just get us to a bus stop, that would be great."

"At this hour of the night? In this part of town, even the bus drivers mug the passengers."

Jackie stepped forward and touched her boss's arm. "Alex, I have an idea. There's not room in either of our cars for three people. Why don't we let them take one of the cars? We can switch back once Harvey checks out the VW."

Alex quickly cut in on Marc's protest before it was fully formed. "Great idea, Jackie!" He reached into the Lamborghini and pulled out the keys. "Here, Marc, you take this, and I'll call you tomorrow—"

"Mr. Bar—Alex! I can't take your car!"

"Why not?" he asked as if the answer were not really obvious.

"Well, for one thing, I live in a very high-class neighborhood. You just don't drive up in any old car. What would the neighbors say."

Again that won him a hearty laugh from Alex.

"How about mine?" Jackie asked. "Even I'm intimidated by Alex's Lamborghini."

Marc was completely nonplussed now. "Really, this is very kind of you, but I can't."

"It's the company car," Jackie smiled. "If you wreck it, I'd have to get a new one. That wouldn't be all bad."

"Then it's settled," Alex said firmly. "Jackie only lives a few miles from my home. I'll drop her off."

"Alex," Marc tried again. "I just can't."

"Nonsense." His eyes suddenly narrowed suspiciously. "Do you belong to a men's club?"

"What?"

"A men's club. Do you belong to any men's clubs?"

Valerie nodded, understanding, but Marc was still lost. "No, why?"

"Do you know anyone in the market for widgets?"

Marc smiled, finally catching up. "No, I don't think I do."

Alex clapped him on the shoulder. "Then what's to worry? Grab your things—you just got yourself a ride home."

Marc swung the Mercedes into the driveway of the Robertson home, which was only one street over from his own, and turned off the lights and the engine. Valerie's head was back against the seat, and he looked to see if her eyes were open.

She turned her head slightly. "I appreciate you bringing me home in the style to which I've grown accustomed."

"Isn't this something? I can't believe it. I can't believe the whole night, as a matter of fact."

She pulled a face. "Thanks a lot."

"I didn't mean you—that part has been delightful. It's just everything else."

"I know. When you think about it, it really was something for him to lend his car to a total stranger."

He wrinkled his nose. "I still can't believe the VW. That is really strange. I just had it tuned up."

Valerie opened the door a crack. "Well, in spite of it all, I had a delightful time. Thank you very much."

"Thank you. I really enjoyed it too."

She swung her legs out.

"Valerie?"

She turned back.

"Running *is* really hard on your body. Have you ever tried racquetball?"

"Once or twice." She shook her head. "I'm terrible at it."

He grinned wickedly. "That's wonderful. How would you like to try a game tomorrow night?"

Chapter Seven

Nearly eight thousand miles east of Claremont, California, the sun was just coming up over the peaks of the Jungfrau Massif in central Switzerland. Quinn Gerritt stood at the bedroom window of his luxurious chalet, watching the light tip the peaks with gold. He reached for a set of binoculars on the dressing table, adjusted the focus slightly, then began sweeping slowly down the narrow valley, past the tiny village of red-roofed houses. The sound of the helicopter was growing louder. Then he had it. The helicopter was coming in from the direction of Interlaken, and though it was still too far away to see the circular GI logo, the red-and-white markings were unmistakeably those of the Gerritt Industries.

Behind him, Jessica Gerritt stirred lazily. "Is that them?" she murmured.

"Yes." He turned. She was sprawled across the bed like a contented cat, one hand tucked under the spray of honey-blond hair that covered the pillow.

Gerritt walked to the bed, leaned over, and kissed her. Her eyes opened, and she smiled, then reached up and touched his cheek. Jessica Hawthorne had been on her way to a highly successful modeling career, with screen opportunities likely to follow, when Quinn Gerritt had met her, dazzled her with a jet-set courtship, and proposed three weeks later. Seven years later, it was one of the few things that virtually everyone agreed he had done right.

"Are you sure you don't need help down there?" she asked.

"I'm sure. Freda set everything out before she went in to the village. And Karl is out back if I need him."

The clear blue eyes closed slowly again, long lashes lying softly on her cheeks. "Good," she purred. "This is a ridiculous hour to hold a meeting anyway."

"Anything before noon is ridiculous to you," he agreed amiably. Then, conscious that the noise from the helicopter had ceased, he straightened. "We may have to go back to the States tomorrow."

Jessica turned over on her side. "Whatever," she mumbled, already sinking back into sleep. Gerritt patted her arm softly, then rose and exited the room.

The east end of the living room of the chalet was a two-story wall of glass framing a panorama that stunned the eyes and made one involuntarily draw in a breath. To the south, the village of Lauterbrunnen lay below them, looking much like a miniature cluster of Monopoly houses flung across a board of unbelievable green. Behind it, a sheer granite cliff provided the leaping-off point for a thundering waterfall that dropped nine hundred eighty-four feet to the valley floor. Above and beyond the falls were the knife-edged peaks of the Jungfrau—the Wetterhorn, the Schreckhorn, the Eiger, the Monch, the Jungfrau itself—jagged masses of granite towering to the thirteen-thousand-foot level and beyond.

Gerritt sat with his back to the window, facing the two men who had come on the helicopter to the village, then motored up to the chalet. As they sipped their coffee, he studied them. Rarely were these men totally at ease in his presence, though he had worked with them for a combined total of over twenty years. But it was more than that now. He had seen it in the nervous flutter of their fingers, the quick aversion of the eyes when he looked at them, the shifting of their weight now as he watched them steadily.

These were shrewd, bold men, tenacious in every respect.

One did not come into senior management positions, at least not in Gerritt Industries, by ducking confrontations or sidestepping the unpalatable. But they were on edge, more than he had ever seen them before.

Quinn Gerritt had been born to wealth, and the fates had seen fit to dress him in the physical presence that his position required. In his midfifties, his blond hair was still thick and full with only the first touches of gray. His face was sharply cut, angular, almost too narrow, but a full mouth and ready smile softened it without making him look weak. Most people found Quinn Gerritt charming, witty, and immensely likeable. Only his eyes hinted at the combination of drive, power, and ruthless determination that was the real Quinn Gerritt. And now he focused those eyes on Michael Shurtliff, senior vice-president of Gerritt Industries.

"All right, Michael," Gerritt finally said, "cut the fancy dancing. What's the bottom line?"

Shurtliff, a short but stocky man with jowls that made him look a bit like a bulldog, took a deep breath. "The bottom line is, Gerritt Industries is bankrupt."

A nervous tic started pulling at the corner of his mouth. When Gerritt continued to watch him with those pale blue eyes, he licked his lower lip quickly. "The final blow came yesterday. Bank of America called. We have until the first of the month to meet that twenty million dollar note or we go into receivership."

Theodore Wuthrich, controller and senior accountant, jumped in. He was a small man, nervous and quick, and his voice was high-pitched now with the strain. "We've been late on payroll in three of the four divisions for the last two pay periods. The unions have given us the ultimatum. One more and they walk."

"Ted, you've been crying in your beer for a year and a half," Gerritt said contemptuously. He slipped into a whining, sing-song voice, "'We can't make payroll. We can't pay the suppliers. We're behind on our taxes.'" His voice suddenly took on a knife edge. "We haven't gone belly up yet."

"Yes we have!" Shurtliff cut in sharply. "What is it going to take to convince you? Come the first, we *are* belly up! Belly up, gutted, stuck on the spit, and roasted over the open coals."

"It isn't the first yet!" Gerritt snapped.

"Come on, Quinn!" Shurtliff shot back. "We've been on a collision course with disaster for five years. We haven't put a dime into research and development. Our plants are ten years out of date. The last four products we've introduced have bombed. Our stock has fallen to three dollars a share! Three dollars. I mean, come on! We've begged and pleaded and warned, but all we ever get from you is there's always tomorrow. Well, tomorrow is here. It's over! We're finished!"

Shurtliff sat back, breathing hard. Wuthrich was staring at him, half in awe, half in astonishment. For almost a full ten seconds, Gerritt stared at his senior vice-president, his mouth hard, but Shurtliff was through dodging. He met Gerritt's gaze with a fury of his own.

"Did you tell the bank about Taggart and the radar system?"

"Sure. Bring a signed contract with Taggart's name on it, *and* a ten percent payment on the note, then they'll talk."

Gerritt loosed a string of bitter expletives describing the mental capacities of all bankers in general, and the Bank of America specifically. "And what about Taggart?" he finally asked.

Wuthrich rich looked quickly at Shurtliff, who nodded. "Meet his price and he'll sign tomorrow," Wuthrich said. "Otherwise, he won't budge."

"Why should he?" Shurtliff blurted. "Jonathan Taggart has developed the most significant breakthrough in radar technology in the last ten years. If he goes to Hughes or TRW, they'll snap him up so fast he'll wonder why he ever gave us first option."

"He gave us first option because he's one of *our* engineers!" Gerritt shouted.

The senior vice-president sighed and leaned forward. "Quinn, we've plowed that ground a thousand times. We have no legal hold on him. He developed this totally on his own. It was not a Gerritt Industries project."

Off somewhere in the house a phone began to ring. Shurtliff turned to look, but Gerritt ignored it.

"I'll talk to him again," Gerritt said, for the first time badgered by the brutal finality of their logic.

"You've talked to him already!" Shurtliff exploded. "Four different times. I've talked to him. Ted's talked to him. We've wined and dined and cursed and pleaded. He's not going to change his mind. You either put four hundred fifty thousand dollars on the table or you're whistling in a wind tunnel."

The sound of a door opening and closing caused them all to look up. Jessica Gerritt came to the railing of the loft above them, tying the sash on her robe. She leaned over, ignoring the two men with her husband. "Quinn, that was Maurice on the phone. He's having a private showing of his winter designs this afternoon. He wants me to fly up."

"Fine. Tell Peter to keep the jet in Paris. I'm going home tomorrow. I'll meet you there."

She blew him a kiss, started to sweep away, then turned back. "I'll need a letter of credit. Ten thousand dollars should be plenty."

Gerritt nodded absently. "Ted, there's a typewriter in the study. Can you draft that for her?"

Theodore Wuthrich just stared, his mouth open.

"Quinn!" Shurtliff was also widemouthed in disbelief.

"What?" Gerritt was still preoccupied.

Shurtliff threw up his hands. "Hasn't anything we've said all morning gotten through to you?"

Gerritt's eyes narrowed, and he leaned forward slowly. "Yes, Michael, it has. Why do you ask?"

Shurtliff flinched, chilled by the sudden tautness in Gerritt's voice. But then he straightened. Quinn Gerritt was not the only one going down with this ship. "I ask," he retorted bitterly, "because normally—" He stopped, suddenly realizing that Jessica Gerritt had returned to the rail and was watching them with a faint smile of contempt.

He took a deep breath. "Because normally, a man staring bankruptcy in the face doesn't send his wife on a private jet to Paris with a ten thousand dollar letter of credit in her purse."

Gerritt shot out of his chair, his face livid. "You listen to me, Mr. Senior Vice-President! The day I cannot take care of my wife's needs will be the day you and this toadie you brought with you will be out on the streets peddling toilet paper! I am Gerritt Industries! Do you understand that?" His voice had gone shrill and piercing. "*I am Gerritt Industries!* We are bankrupt if and only if I tell you that we are bankrupt. Is that clear?"

The color completely drained from Shurtliff's face as the withering onslaught smashed at him. Wuthrich's hand fluttered to his tie, which bulged out momentarily as he swallowed hard.

"I asked you a question, Mr. Shurtliff! I said, is that clear?"

"Yes, Mr. Gerritt."

"Are we bankrupt, Mr. Shurtliff?"

"No sir, not until you say we are."

"Then why is Mr. Wuthrich standing here with his thumb in his ear like some retarded tree sloth? Why isn't he in the study typing a letter for my wife?"

Wuthrich jumped as though someone had stuck him with a red-hot sliver of iron. He was up and out of his chair and scurrying across the living room like a startled chipmunk. Shurtliff looked up in time to see Jessica give him a tiny smile of triumph and disappear. Disgusted he stood up abruptly. "I need a smoke."

"Not in here, you don't!"

"I'm well aware of your habits, Mr. Gerritt," he muttered. "I'll be outside."

He moved to the door, not waiting for Gerritt's permission. As he opened it, Gerritt spoke softly. "Michael."

Shurtliff stopped, not turning around.

"When you hear the crack of the hammer and the cry of 'Sold!' then you can talk to me about bankruptcy. But not before, Mister. Not one minute before."

Shurtliff paused for only a second, then walked out, shutting the door firmly behind.

Chapter Eight

This close to the coast, the sky was gray and overcast, with just a trace of mist in the air. Marc was driving the Mercedes convertible slowly down Sepulveda Boulevard in Culver City when Brett leaned forward pointing. "There it is, Dad!"

"Where?" Matthew cried.

"See the red-and-blue sign? On the other side of the street."

Marc saw it then, pulled into the left lane, and started blinking. Even this early on a Saturday morning, the noise of the traffic on the San Diego Freeway, which ran parallel to them, was a steady roar.

"Edwards Automotive." Brett read slowly as Marc waited for a break in the oncoming traffic. "Yup. That's it, Dad."

"Yes, it is." He made the turn and drove through the chain link gate that had been pulled open. "Look, Alex is already here."

"I see the Lamborghini!" Brett shouted excitedly.

"Where?" Matt said, not knowing what he was looking for.

"The blue car, Matt. Isn't it cool?"

"I dubs it!"

A Ford pickup was parked next to the sports car, and Marc pulled in alongside it and shut off the motor. Edwards Automotive consisted of a small fenced yard with several cars parked around the perimeter, some in the process of being dismantled. The building itself had three high garage doors marking the repair bays, and a regular door on one end, with "Office" written on it. Above the larger doors, in red-and-blue letters ran the options:

"Tune-ups—Alignment—Major and Minor Repairs—Radiators—Transmissions."

As they got out, Alex Barclay came out of the office door, followed by a black man in coveralls. Alex was dressed casually—gray plaid shirt, heavy-knit white cardigan sweater with shawl collar, white trousers, and grey mesh duck shoes. The top two buttons of the shirt had been left open. A gold necklace lay against the thick tangle of black and grey hair on his chest. It was, Marc supposed, what some of his students would call laid back and mellow. And it reeked of money.

"Good morning, Marc," Alex called. "Looks like you found it."

Marc took Alex's outstretched hand, and they shook firmly. "Yes, your directions were easy to follow."

"Good. Harv, this is Marc Jeppson. Marc, meet Harvey Edwards, the best darn mechanic west of the Mississippi."

"Well, at least west of the Colorado," Edwards said with a grin. "Pleased to meet you, Mr. Jeppson." His voice was a rich tenor and pleasant. He was close to forty, built like a long-distance runner, and had quick dark eyes. They shook hands, Marc finding himself liking the man almost instantly.

"These are my sons, Brett and Matthew." He turned, but there were no boys alongside. He looked around in surprise as Alex chuckled deeply. Both boys were at the Lamborghini, Brett pointing out the features in a low voice.

"Brett, Matt! Come over here."

They came over immediately, Brett looking sheepish. "This is Brett, and this is Matthew. Boys, this is Mr. Barclay and Mr. Edwards."

They shook hands shyly, then Brett glanced quickly over his shoulder. "You sure have a neat car, Mr. Barclay."

"Why thank you, Brett," Alex said seriously. "Would you like to sit in it?"

Brett's eyes widened in disbelief. Matt's head bobbed up and down like a piston.

"Oh no," Marc said quickly. "You just look at it from outside."

"Come on, Dad," Alex chided. "A couple of good-looking boys like these two won't hurt anything. Will you?"

The deep sobriety as they both shook their heads caused Edwards to laugh in delight. "Well, you've got to admit," he said, "they know class when they see it."

"Go on," Alex said, waving his arm. "It's all right."

"Brett, watch Matt!" Marc called as they darted away. "And don't touch anything."

"They'll be fine, Marc. Those are two fine boys you have there."

Edwards clapped Marc on the shoulder. "Well, let's go in and take a look at this car of yours." He turned and went through the office door. As they followed, Marc noted the sign in the window giving the hours of business. The last line read: Closed Saturdays and Sundays. Closed Saturdays for everyone except Alex Barclay, Marc decided.

The repair area was neat and well kept, with tools and other equipment lining the walls. They were the only ones in the shop. Marc's Volkswagen was on one of the hoists, about three feet off the ground.

Edwards slapped it on the rear fender. "This look familiar?"

"Afraid so. How bad is it?"

"Well, let's just say if I were a doctor, I'd call in the family to break the news."

Marc's face fell.

"The engine is gone."

"Great!" Marc muttered, eyeing the rusting fenders.

"So it's beyond hope?" Barclay spoke up.

"No, I said *this* engine has had it. But I've found a good rebuilt engine. They'll deliver it Monday. I can have it in and running by next Friday."

"Great!" Barclay said. "That's really great, Harv." He turned to Marc. "See what I mean?"

"But I can't—" He stopped as both men looked at him. "Look, I really appreciate this, but a new engine will cost more than the car is worth."

"If you're talking resale value," Edwards agreed. "But with it you can get another fifty to seventy-five thousand miles."

"I know, but what's a new engine going to cost?"

"Is that your only concern?" Edwards said with a slow smile. "The money?"

Barclay watched, amused. Marc looked down. It grated on him to have to admit it in front of Barclay, but reality was reality. "Yeah," he said shortly, "that's a problem."

"Well, then, let's negotiate a price you can live with."

"Look," Barclay said quickly, "while you two are doing that, I need to make a call. Can I use your phone, Harvey?"

"Sure thing. You need a book?"

"No." Barclay turned on his heel and went in the office.

"Well, let's see what we can do, Mr. Jeppson," Edwards said, his smile even broader than before. Marc had the distinct impression Edwards was enjoying this.

"Really," Marc went on. "I appreciate your looking at it, but . . ."

"Are you familiar with Griswold's?" Edwards asked, still smiling.

"What?"

"Griswold's Restaurant. Do you know it?"

"Yes. In fact, there's one not far from our home."

"I know. Mr. Barclay said you were from Claremont."

"Yes, I've eaten there several times."

"Is it as good as they say?"

"I like it very much."

"Good. How about this? If you and your wife treat me and my wife to dinner at Griswold's, my crew and I will put a new engine in your Volkswagen. Does that sound fair?"

Marc just stared at him.

Edwards laughed right out loud. "I'm deadly serious." Then

he held up his hands. "Look, before you answer, let me tell you a story. A true story, in fact."

"Okay." Marc was still reeling, trying to catch up with what the man was saying.

"Three years ago, this guy comes in to my garage. He said his gas tank had a leak in it. I checked it out, found that it did, and fixed it. I billed him something like thirty-three bucks. Okay?"

Marc nodded.

"Two weeks later this guy's wife is rear-ended by a delivery truck. The car bursts into flames. She escaped but had second- and third-degree burns over a good part of her body. She was hospitalized for several months. Next thing I know, I was slapped with a three-and-a-half-million-dollar law suit for negligence and malicious dereliction of duty.

"Things started to unravel pretty quickly then. Within two weeks, my insurance company had managed to wiggle out on a technicality. I'm on my own, they politely inform me. The other guy's lawyer, dripping with sorrow for my plight, generously offers to settle out of court for half a million bucks."

The smile had disappeared, and a deep bitterness had hardened Edwards mouth. "Three different lawyers told me I didn't stand a chance of winning, that I was crazy not to settle. You with me so far?"

"Half a million!" Marc echoed.

"Right. It meant my garage, my home, my savings—a life's work and then some."

"So what happened?"

"Well, one day I was working on a car for one of my regular customers. By now I have ulcers, I've lost twenty pounds and look like an anemic zombie. So this guy asks me why I look so terrible. Before I know it, I've spilled out the whole story to him, him all the time nodding, first with sympathy, then with anger."

Suddenly Marc saw where all this was leading. "Alex Barclay!" he blurted.

"Exactly," Edwards said. "He left that day without saying

much more. But that afternoon, I got a call from one of the most prestigious law firms in Los Angeles. They send a lawyer out. He takes everything down, nods, makes notes, nods, makes notes, shakes my hand, says, 'Mr. Edwards, we think we can help you. You'll hear from us.'"

He stopped, his eyes glistening. "Three weeks to the day, the same lawyer comes out again, shows me a paper. It's from the law firm of the guy suing me. The suit has been dropped. All action on their part is suspended. The lawyer shakes my hand, says, 'If you hear anything more—anything at all—let me know.' He waves good-bye and drives away, leaving me standing there bawling like a baby."

"There were no legal fees from the firm?"

"None. At least not for me. I don't know what they did or how they did it, but it was done!"

"Just like that?"

"Just like that! Ever since then, I've been trying to find a way to say thank you to Mr. Barclay. I give him free service, but shoot, he only drives brand-new luxury cars. I change his oil and give him a tune up now and then, but that's all. Your little VW is the first real chance I've had to pay the man back. There'll be no cost to you, and no cost to him. Do you understand, Mr. Jeppson?"

"I understand," Marc said softly, looking past Edwards to where Barclay was talking on the phone. "I understand even more than you think."

"Good. The dinner at Griswold's isn't necessary. The engine is on me, either way."

Marc stuck out his hand. "Harvey, my wife died a couple of years ago, but I think I know a young lady who will join me, and we would be delighted to spend an evening with you and your wife. And the dinner is on us."

Edwards grinned, his eyes sparkling. "Then, Mr. Jeppson, it looks like you and I have a deal."

Valerie was at the sink, peeling potatoes, when she heard a car door slam and Brett's voice crying, "Mary! Mary!"

Her mother looked up from her needlepoint. "What's that?"

"It sounds like Brett."

There was a pounding on the back door, and Valerie wiped her hands on her apron and walked over to open it. Matt and Brett were there, grinning like they had just won a year's supply of jelly beans.

"Valerie! Come and see!" Matthew grabbed her hand and started tugging on it. "Come and see what Daddy's got."

"Come on, Mary," Brett joined in. "You'll never believe it."

As they came out the door, Valerie stopped. Marc was leaning with casual nonchalance against the blue Lamborghini parked in the driveway. Matt dragged her forward again. "Isn't it cool, Valerie?"

Brett, striving to be more adult, simply went and stood by his dad, beaming proudly.

"Well," Valerie said, as she walked around it slowly. "I suppose a Mercedes convertible is a little tacky."

Marc grinned, no longer able to contain himself. "I fought him, believe it or not. But saying no to Alex Barclay is like spitting into high surf. You may feel a little better for doing it, but it doesn't make a whole lot of difference."

"You mean he let you borrow this one too?" Mary said.

"Yup," Brett said matter-of-factly. "Ours won't be done until Friday."

"Which is a story in and of itself," Marc said. He quickly told Mary and Valerie about Harv Edwards.

"I can't believe it," Valerie said when he finished. "A new engine for two dinners."

"Remember what Alex said in the lecture about creating leverage? I think we just witnessed it in action. Harvey Edwards was actually delighted to find a way to repay Alex."

"He took us to his warehouse," Brett broke in, his eyes shining. "I got to shoot an Uzi!"

"A what?" Mary said.

Matt stuck out his chest proudly. "Even I know what an Uzi is."

71

"Well, I don't, so you'd better tell me."

"An Uzi is a gun," Matt said solemnly. "It shoots real fast."

Brett nodded. "It's the world's best submachine gun. It's made in Israel. It's named after the man who made it."

"He shot a submachine gun?" Valerie turned to Marc in surprise.

"Among other things," Marc answered. He nodded to Brett to continue, not wanting to lessen his moment of glory.

"Mr. Barclay sells all kinds of guns," Brett went on. "He's got a whole firing range in the basement of his warehouse. I shot pistols and rifles and submachine guns. It was so neat! You should have been there."

Matt was tugging at Valerie again. "I got to put ear muffs on while Brett and Daddy shot the guns."

"Well," Mary said, shaking her head at Marc, "I'm glad that at least you had sense enough not to let Matthew shoot them."

"Matt got to drive the boat instead."

"The boat?"

"Yeah!" Matt's eyes were round and shining with excitement. "It's a great big boat, and I got to steer it all by myself."

Marc's face still registered disbelief. "He took us down to the marina. You wouldn't believe it. This is not some motorboat. It's a small yacht. I mean, a full-blown yacht. It sleeps ten comfortably."

Valerie went down to one knee so she was looking Matt in the face. "You've had quite a day of it, haven't you?"

He nodded solemnly. "And besides that, Jackie took us to lunch, and I got my very own can of pop."

"Jackie?" Valerie looked up at Marc, who nodded.

"She's Alex's secretary," Brett supplied. "She's really nice."

"And she's pretty too," Matt said.

Valerie straightened. "I know," she said slowly. "I met her last night."

Matt tugged at her again, and when she leaned down, he put his arms around her neck and whispered in her ear, loud enough for all of them to hear, "I think you're pretty too."

"Well, thank you, Matthew. What a sweet thing to say." She hugged him back, and he ducked his head in embarrassment.

"I'm really hurt," Mary said, making a long face. "I thought you were my boyfriend."

Matt immediately pulled away and darted to her side. "You're not just pretty," he said loyally. "I love you."

"Oh, brother," Marc laughed. "Talk about the diplomat."

Brett tapped Marc's arm. "Can I go tell Jed now, Dad?"

Marc shook his head. "We'll be going home in just a minute."

"It's only a couple of blocks," Brett pleaded. "Please!"

"Oh, I don't care. Go on!"

Brett gave a whoop and was off on a dead run.

"Well," Marc said, as he turned back to Valerie, "I came over to see if we might take a rain check on that racquetball tonight."

There was one brief look of surprise and disappointment, then she recovered. "Sure. That's fine."

"Trying to wean you away from your running habit with racquetball is the easy way out. Wanna go cold turkey?"

She looked at him quizzically.

"How about spending an hour or two perfectly motionless in the bucket seat of a Lamborghini Contach Five Thousand?"

Valerie's eyes were sparkling, though she kept her expression sober. "Could I think about jogging just a little?"

"No way. Cold turkey is cold turkey."

"I'll come over and stay with the boys," Mary said, trying not to appear too pleased.

"No," Marc said. "I can get a baby-sitter."

Mary put her arm around Matt's shoulders and gave him a squeeze. "Nonsense. After the compliment Matt just gave me, I wouldn't think of sharing this boy with anyone else."

"Well, all right," Marc said.

"Yippee!" Matt yelled, throwing his arms around Mary's legs.

Valerie turned back to Marc. "What does one wear to go riding in a Lamborghini?"

He shrugged. "I'm sorry, Miss. Alex Barclay is Lamborghini people. Marc Jeppson is pure Volkswagen Beetle."

Chapter Nine

Quinn Gerritt, president and CEO of Gerritt Industries, was at the window of his office, staring down at the traffic on Wilshire Boulevard thirty-three stories below him. It was a gray, drizzly November morning, and the cars were moving slowly, though his thoughts were far from centering on the traffic flow. The intercom buzzed, and he moved to his desk and punched a button.

"Mr. Gerritt. A Mr. Andrew Hadlow is here to see you."

Gerritt frowned. Andrew Hadlow? Somewhere far back in his mind that rang a bell.

"He doesn't have an appointment, but he says he met you at a cocktail party at Mr. Perotti's house several months ago."

"Oh, yes."

His secretary lowered her voice. "He said it's about our financial problems. That's all he would say, Mr. Gerritt."

"All right. When I buzz you, send him in. And hold all calls."

He sat down and leaned back. Perotti. The enigma. When he and Jessica had gotten the invitation to the cocktail party at Perotti's house, Gerritt had been totally surprised. And totally intrigued. Perotti lived more than a mile away in a massive home on the crest of a ridge overlooking the Pacific. He had said then that he wanted to get to know some of the neighbors, but many closer "neighbors" had not been invited. Afterward, Gerritt checked to find out who Perotti was but turned up little. He was into real estate, owned an import-export business, had major interests in some financial institutions. There were recurring hints that Perotti was tied to organized crime, but Gerritt had shrugged those aside. Someone always threw in organized crime when they couldn't pin down a man's source of wealth. But whatever it was, one thing was certain. Lyman Perotti was big money.

Gerritt opened the lower drawer on his desk, checked the cassette in the built-in recorder, flipped a switch, then shut the drawer again. He leaned forward and punched the intercom. "Send Mr. Hadlow in, please."

Hadlow was short, no more than five seven. His hair was jet black and graying at the temples. He combed it straight back, which added to the severity of his angular features. His eyes were a pale blue, like Gerritt's, but alert, always moving. The suit was custom tailored; the shoes, Italian. Even the briefcase was pure elegance. Clearly, Mr. Hadlow did very well in his own right.

Gerritt came from behind his desk and extended his hand. "Mr. Hadlow, good to see you again."

"Thank you."

Gerritt motioned him to a chair, then drew another up across from it. "Can I get you a drink?"

Hadlow smiled as he shook his head. It was a smile that only touched the surface of his face. The eyes remained cool and aloof.

"How is Mr. Perotti?"

"Fine. He sends his regards."

Gerritt nodded and leaned back. Hadlow had obviously not come to see how things had gone since the party.

"I apologize for coming without a prior appointment."

Gerritt waved that away.

"But we understand the timing is critical."

"Timing?"

"Yes. Before Gerritt Industries goes into receivership."

Gerritt swore inwardly. He knew that rumors about the company's troubles were rampant, but the receivership was strictly hush hush . . .

"Look, Mr. Gerritt, I'll come right to the point. My people

know all about your situation. We know about Bank of America. We know about the union's ultimatum. We've seen the receivership papers that are being drawn up."

Gerritt was struggling to keep his face impassive. Whoever "my people" included, they were up to the minute on the death struggles of Gerritt Industries.

"We think we could arrange some financing, if certain conditions were met."

"Oh?"

Hadlow nodded in satisfaction. "Thank you. Expressions of shocked surprise and bland denials would have been a disappointment."

Gerritt smiled fleetingly. "I must admit, you have my attention."

"Please turn off the recorder and we can proceed."

Again there was the quick temptation to bluff, instantly rejected. Gerritt shrugged, stood up, and walked around behind his desk.

As he came back to his chair, Hadlow was getting a paper from his briefcase. He handed it to Gerritt as he sat down again. "Are these figures correct?"

As Gerritt studied the sheet his amazement grew. It was all there—the note to Bank of America, the missed payrolls, back taxes, research and development needs, operating capital. It wasn't to the penny, but the dollar figures were almost right on the nose. He looked up, not trying to disguise his surprise. "You've got it all."

"All right. We have a group that will fund you the total amount, one percent above prime. Seventy-five percent of all profits will go toward the payback until fifty percent of the principal is paid back. Thereafter, fifty percent of the profits will go toward the pay back until the debt is retired. Agreed?"

Gerritt looked at him for several seconds. The conditions were stiff, but not unreasonable under the circumstances. Gerritt Industries was hardly providing the top collatoral. Finally he nodded. "Are those the only conditions?"

Hadlow's eyes were expressionless. "First, two questions. Is the radar device your engineer developed—I think his name is Jonathan Taggart—as revolutionary as he claims it is?"

This time, Gerritt was openly stunned. Only he and his two top executives knew about that. In a world of rampant industrial espionage, secrecy was paramount. "Yes," he said slowly.

"How long would it take to bring it into full production?"

He took a deep breath. "Two to three months to develop the prototype. If we pushed hard, we could complete testing in another six to eight weeks. We could also start tooling up during that time. I'd say six to nine months, altogether."

"You've got six. Here are the conditions. You will meet with Jonathan Taggart at nine o'clock tomorrow morning. The appointment is already made in your name. You will offer him one hundred thousand dollars cash now, one hundred thousand more when the prototype is tested, and ten percent royalties on all sales."

Gerritt was staring. "Are you crazy? I've offered him twice that, but he won't budge. If we don't give him four hundred fifty thousand by—"

Hadlow's eyes had narrowed, and Gerritt felt a sudden chill. "Second condition. I will be appointed to the Board of Directors of Gerritt Industries as of this morning. I will not be a member of record or attend any meetings. You will continue to serve as Chairman of the Board, but I will be senior member next to you."

Gerritt swallowed hard, then nodded. "Go on."

"A Mr. Alex Barclay of Barclay Enterprises in El Segundo is beginning preliminary work on a major sale of jet aircraft to Saudi Arabia. There are a lot of competitors. Your radar package would go a long way to cementing the deal for him, not to mention creating about fifty or sixty million dollars worth of immediate business for Gerritt Industries."

"How do you know all this?"

"When you make contact with Barclay, you are not to mention Mr. Perotti or myself in any way." He paused, but Gerritt didn't speak.

77

He took a small slip of paper from an inside pocket. "You will be having some openings on the night shift at the Hawthorne plant. These two men will be hired."

He sat back, watching Gerritt closely.

Gerritt knew some kind of response was expected, but he was still a bit dazed.

"We have no desire to take Gerritt Industries away from you, Mr. Gerritt. If we did, we would have taken action after Bank of America made its move."

"I understand that. Your offer is very generous."

Hadlow stood, moved to the desk, and scribbled on a pad. He tore it off and handed it to Gerritt, who stood now also. "If the conditions are satisfactory, call me at this number once you have Mr. Taggart's decision. Funds will be transferred immediately. If you decide you do not wish to work with us, simply cancel your appointment with Mr. Taggart."

"What if I have further questions?"

"You know the conditions. You know the arrangements on the loan. There are no further questions. It's either play or pass, Mr. Gerritt."

Jonathan Taggart had come into the office of Quinn Gerritt promptly at nine o'clock the next morning. He had been in a jubilant mood then. Now he stared at the contract before him with disbelief. "A hundred thousand dollars . . ." He looked up. "Is this some kind of a joke, Mr. Gerritt?"

Gerritt was tipped back in his chair, fingertips pressed together. "No, Jonathan. In the long run, considering the royalties, you could come out of this with much more than what you are asking for."

Taggart shook his head. He was a large man, thick through the shoulders and chest. He removed his glasses. "I told you before, I told Shurtliff, I told Wuthrich. I know what my design is worth." His voice rose. "I didn't have to come to Gerritt Industries. I've been more than fair with you." He tossed the contract back across the desk with contempt. "And this is what I get."

Gerritt picked up the contract and looked at it curiously. "I think you ought to consider this very carefully, Jonathan. Take the longer view."

Taggart shot to his feet. "I don't appreciate playing games, Mr. Gerritt. Good day." He turned and stalked to the door.

"I'll keep the offer open until tomorrow morning," Gerritt called. Taggart didn't break stride, just went out, leaving the door to close softly behind him.

Charlene Taggart was a junior at Cypress High School and one of the varsity cheerleaders. She and the rest of the cheerleading squad had just finished the pep assembly for that night's game with Long Beach, and she was still flushed with excitement as she came to her locker.

"We're gonna kill 'em tonight, Char!" a student called out behind her.

"You better believe it!"

"Good job, Charlene!"

Charlene half turned and smiled at her English teacher as she opened her locker. "Thanks, Mrs. Townsend."

As she turned back to get her books, the smile on Charlene Taggart's face froze. Then she threw her hands to her face and screamed and screamed.

Staring out at her from the top shelf was the head of Charlene's pure white Persian cat, Muffy.

Mildred Taggart looked up from her counted cross-stitch, then reached over and turned down the stereo. This was her favorite of all the Mozart piano concertos, and she had immersed herself in the sound. She waited, her head cocked. Then the doorbell rang again.

The man was dressed in a suit and a tie, and as she opened the door wider, she saw he had a wallet in his hand. There was a quick flash of a badge.

"Karl Belknap, Los Angeles Police Department, Ma'am. Are you Mrs. Jonathan Taggart?"

She felt a sudden lurch of fear. "Yes."

"I'm afraid there's been an accident."

Her hand flew to her mouth. "Oh no!"

"May I come in?"

"Of course." She opened the door and stepped back. He smiled sadly as he entered, and she shut the door behind him. Mildred started for the living room when suddenly she felt him move behind her. There was not even time for a surprised gasp. One hand grabbed her arm and yanked it up viciously behind her, the other clamped over her nose and mouth. She fought wildly, flailing with her free arm, twisting her body, but she was like a child in the grip of some gargantuan creature. He pulled her body in against his, lifting her off the floor.

"Come on, Mrs. Taggart," he hissed in her ear, "this won't take but a minute."

He pushed her, then dragged her down the hall toward the master bedroom. She clawed at him over her shoulder, tried to gouge his shins with her heels, but he just laughed and jerked her arm up higher toward her shoulder blade. The scream of pain choked off in her throat as he tightened the pressure across her nose and mouth. The terror of the man gave way to the greater terror of suffocation. Now her body fought too, chest heaving, muscles contracting in agony. But the grip only tightened, crushing her nose and lips against the bones of her face.

And then suddenly they were into the bedroom. He flung her away from him, sending her crashing into a chair, then onto the bed sprawling. In an instant she was on her back, scrambling away from him, eyes wide, gulping air in huge, desperate gasps.

The man watched her for a moment without moving, then straightened his tie, pulled down his coat, and ran his hand quickly through his hair. He smiled, that same sad smile she had seen in the entryway. "I would suggest you call your husband before you talk to the police, Mrs. Taggart."

He nodded, turned, and was gone. Mildred Taggart leaped off the bed and ran to the door. She slammed it shut, fingers scrambling at the lock. When she felt it click, she collapsed to the floor and began to sob.

The car rounded the corner with screeching tires, hit the driveway with a bang, and slammed to a halt. Jonathan Taggart was out and running for the house, leaving the car door wide open. The hysterical, nearly incoherent call from his wife had completely shaken him.

He burst in the door, looking around wildly. Everything was in order. He darted down the hall to the bedroom, rattled the knob. Through the door he heard a soft cry, filled with terror.

"Mildred, it's me!"

There was a sob of relief, a quick fumbling at the door, then it jerked open. Mildred Taggart threw herself into her husband's arms. "Oh, Jonathan!"

"Daddy!" Charlene Taggart rose shakily from the bed. He opened one arm and swept her into his grasp along with her mother.

It took almost five minutes to calm them to the point where they could stammer out their stories, and even then he had to let them pause, as the horror of the morning would overwhelm them again and again. But when they were finished, a fury lay on Jonathan Taggart.

"Everything's okay, now," he soothed, moving them both over to the bed. "You just lie here. I'm going to call the police."

"Don't leave Jonathan!"

"I won't, Mildred. I'll be in the kitchen. But we need to get the police. You just stay here with Charlene." He patted her hand and then pulled loose from her grip.

The muscles along his jaw pulled into a tight line as he picked up the phone and angrily punched out the 911 number. He put the phone to his ear. There was nothing. He hit the numbers again. They beeped in his ear, but again nothing happened. Then a sudden prickling went up his spine as he realized someone was breathing into the phone.

"Who is this? Who's on the line?"

"Mr. Taggart?" It was a man's voice, deep, rich, pleasant, and yet full of chilling menace.

"Who is this?"

"The police cannot help your family, Mr. Taggart. Only you can. If you choose to be difficult, we can find them anywhere, any time."

"Who are you? What do you want?"

"Remember, only you can keep your family safe. Look on the front porch."

There was an audible click, then the dial tone cut in.

Taggart stared at the phone, then put it back in its cradle slowly. He moved back into the entry hall and opened the front door. There was nothing on the porch. He opened the screen door to step outside, but it bumped up against something soft. He pushed harder, felt it give, then recoiled in horror. A dark red stain was on the cement. Taggart gave the screen a hard shove, stepped around it, and stared.

The headless body of Muffy was blocking the door through which he had entered his house just minutes before.

"Mr. Gerritt, Jonathan Taggart is on the phone."

Gerritt was startled. It had been little more than an hour since Jonathan Taggart had left his office. "Put him on."

"Mr. Gerritt?" There was a deep bitterness, but also resignation.

"Yes, Jonathan, this is Mr. Gerritt."

"I've been talking over your offer with my wife."

"Yes?"

"We've decided to accept. I'll be in this afternoon to sign the contract."

"Well," Gerritt said, feeling a sudden chill of his own. Barely an hour! What had Hadlow done. He shrugged the thought off, not wanting to know. "Well, that's a pleasant surprise. I know you won't regret it."

"Just tell your people."

"What?"

"You know what I mean!" Taggart nearly shouted, then fought for control. "Just tell whoever you need to tell that we have accepted your offer."

Chapter Ten

It was one of those winter days for which Southern California was justly famous. The overcast had burned off, and the temperature was nearing seventy, even though it was the first of December. Golfers were out on the course of the Wilshire Country Club in great numbers, taking advantage of the day.

The clubhouse sat at the eastern extremity of what surely must have been some of the most expensive recreational acreage in California. Sprawling fairways, immaculate greens, sand traps, water hazards, palm trees—hundreds of acres rambled through the heart of high-rise condominiums, office buildings, and expensive private homes in the heart of downtown Los Angeles.

Jacqueline Ashby and Alex Barclay were on the front steps of the clubhouse, waiting for Marc. They had been chatting leisurely, but had fallen silent. Without looking at him, Jackie finally spoke. "I can take Marc to get his car, if you'd like."

That brought a sharp look from Alex.

She smiled, knowing there was no hiding from his razor-sharp intuition. "Does that surprise you?"

"Well, yes, a little."

"At first, on the night of the lecture, I just thought he was kind of cute. And nice. But then last Saturday, when he came to the office . . . " She shrugged. "I don't know. I could get interested."

"Well, I did have an appointment right after lunch and was

going to ask if you might have time to run Marc out to get his car."

She laughed lightly. "You're incorrigible."

"I know, but adorably so, don't you think?"

Again she laughed.

"Derek will be envious."

Jackie gave a derisive hoot.

"No desire to return the rather obvious interest of Mr. Parkin?" Alex chuckled. "He'll be crushed."

"Only his ego, and I'm not sure it's possible to crush that."

"True. Derek does think rather highly of himself. But he's competent. He'll do for what we need."

"How about Marc Jeppson?"

Alex bit his lip thoughtfully. "Still a little too early to tell. But so far, just as you, I kind of like what I see. Today will give us a better idea."

"Well," she said, looking up. "Here he comes, so let's both of us move in a little closer and see if we like what we see."

As Marc pulled the Lamborghini into the parking lot of the Wilshire Country Club, he was suddenly grateful Alex had insisted that they pick up the VW from Edwards Automotive after lunch and not before. The lot was like a dozen new car showrooms rolled into one. Mercedes dominated, with Lincolns and Cadillacs close behind. Sports cars were sprinkled liberally throughout. Marc could identify the Porsches and Corvettes, but several other sleek-looking ones were beyond him. Ferraris? Maseratis? Jaguars? He wasn't even sure he knew all the names.

As he pulled into a parking space he took a deep breath. When he had called Alex the previous evening to arrange for the exchange of cars, Alex had insisted on lunch and named the place. After Marc hung up and told Mary and Valerie about it, his tone was awestruck enough that Mary had chided him a little for being so intimidated.

"Come on, Mary," he had said, "this is one of the most exclusive country clubs in California. A membership costs twenty-five thousand dollars and monthly dues run just over a thousand a month. Wouldn't that make you a little nervous?"

Valerie had looked up from the puzzle she was helping Matt and Brett put together. "He does that quite a lot, doesn't he?"

"Who? Does what?"

"Alex. He likes to tell you how much things cost, doesn't he?"

Marc, a little to his surprise, had jumped to Alex's defense. "Why do you say that?"

She shrugged. "You know how much his car cost. He told you about his yacht and what he paid for it. Now the country club."

"Well, it's not like you think. It's just that he—I don't know. It's just not like that."

He shut off the engine of the Lamborghini with some regret. This would be his last time with it. After this, driving the Volkswagen would be like going from piloting high-performance jet aircraft to driving go-carts at the Kiddie Track. He gave one last look around, caressed the upholstery, then opened the door.

"Hello."

He looked up in surprise and climbed out. "Hi, Jackie. I didn't know you were coming."

She was dressed in a light grey suit, white silk blouse with a ruffle at the throat, and matching gray hose and high-heel pumps. With her dark black hair and green eyes, she was stunning. Marc noticed the guard watching them with open admiration.

"I wasn't," she responded, "but Alex wanted me with him to check some things downtown, so he invited me along." She tipped her head slightly to one side. "Do you mind?"

"Mind? Between driving up in the Lamborghini and you coming out to meet me, the security guard just violated every commandment ever made about coveting."

She glanced quickly at the man, then laughed, a warm and delightful sound. She slipped her arm through his. "Then let's make him think you're the luckiest man in the club today."

•　　　•　　　•　　　•　　　•

As he took another sip of his Perrier water with a dash of lime, Marc kept his face impassive. The stuff was awful. Flat bitterness with strong carbonation. The lime was the only redeeming quality to the whole drink. Well, maybe the ice too.

There had been no drinks listed on the menu. When the waiter—a young man in black coat and bow tie—had asked about their drinks, Jackie had said water was fine for her, but Alex had ordered the Perrier water. Feeling suddenly awkward, Marc had simply nodded. "That's fine for me too." He had barely stifled a shudder at the first sip, and now, with lunch cleared away, he was still nursing two thirds of his glass.

The other thing Marc had noticed about the menu was that there were no prices listed. Too gauche, he decided. A person shouldn't be here in the first place if cost mattered.

"The other day you mentioned you teach at the Claremont Colleges," Alex said, bringing Marc back to the present. "Is that in the college of business?"

"No. I'm in the Near Eastern Studies department."

"Oh!" Alex seemed surprised. "I guess I assumed you were in business after seeing you at the lecture at UCLA."

"No, I just started an MBA for fun."

Jackie wrinkled her nose. "Fun? I could suggest half a million better ways to find relaxation."

"Hmmmm," Alex mused. "Near Eastern Studies. What does that include?"

"Oh, a variety of things. I teach classes in Islamic culture and religion, Near Eastern geography and history, that sort of thing. I also teach beginning and advanced Arabic."

"Really?" Jackie said. She reached in her purse and brought out a long envelope. "Write me something in Arabic. I always thought their writing was so mysterious and so beautiful."

Marc felt inside the pocket of his jacket and brought out a felt-tip pen. "Well, actually, I've been playing with some Arabic calligraphy lately. I'm not very good yet, but . . ." He lapsed into silence and went to work on the envelope. Jackie pulled her chair around a little closer to watch him as he worked.

"The Islamic faith prohibits the representation of the human figure in art, and so calligraphy was developed as one of the alternatives. I think it's one of the most beautiful of art forms."

Long, flowing lines were starting to appear on the paper, curling, jutting up sharply, only to flow back in on themselves.

"That is beautiful," Jackie said, more impressed than she had intended to be. "I mean really beautiful. What does it say?"

Marc finished, capped the pen, and pushed the envelope toward her. "That's what is known as the *Shahada*—the profession of faith for a Muslim. It says, 'There is no God but Allah. Mohammed is his messenger.'"

She handed it to Alex, who studied it with interest. "That really is remarkable, Marc."

"Only because you don't know Arabic. This is crude and poorly done. I have a framed picture in my office with the *Shahada* done fifteen different ways, each one its own work of art. What they do is really incredible."

"How about Saudi Arabia?" Alex asked casually. "Have you ever been there?"

"No, unfortunately. I've studied a great deal about it, but it's nearly impossible to get in there without a sponsor."

"That's what I've heard." Alex leaned forward. "Say, if you're an expert on the Arabs, let me ask you a question."

"Okay."

"A couple of weeks ago, I met a Saudi delegation in Washington, D.C. It was led by the crown prince himself. What a charismatic man he is."

"Really?" Marc was impressed. He knew enough about the Saudi royal family to know that not just everyone met the designated successor to the throne.

Alex shrugged, somehow conveying the impression that he had not meant to drop names. "They were here working on some business deal. I happened to be in town, and a friend at the State Department invited me to sit in. I may get a little piece of the action. In fact, it may turn out that I get a chance to go over there."

"Really! I'd love to go there. Saudi Arabia is the heart of the Islamic civilization. That's where it all began."

"Well, actually, I'm a bit intimidated by it all. I understand they are very strict about their religion."

"Absolutely. There are places where they still stone a person for committing adultery."

"Well," Alex grinned, "that's not all that bad, considering the whole place is sand."

Jackie and Marc both laughed aloud. "Good line," Marc said. "I'll have to remember that one."

They fell silent as the waiter cleared the table. Finally Marc turned back to Alex. "You said you had a question."

"Yes. If this business deal with the Saudis starts to shape up, I'd like to get a gift for the crown prince. I understand that is appropriate."

"Most appropriate. Gift-giving is very much a part of their culture."

"That's what I thought."

"There is a famous story about King Abdul Aziz ibn-Saud, the first king of modern Saudi Arabia. One day a visitor presented the king with a magnificent gray Arabian stallion. The king was delighted. Such a gift called for a return gift of thanks. He called for the great leather-bound book in which he kept a record of all gifts given to his visitors. Next to the man's name, he started to write 'three hundred riyals.' This was considerably more than the horse was worth. But as he wrote, the nib of the pen snagged on the paper, then flipped loose, showering three ink blobs across the line. The Arabic zero is a dot, so . . ."

"So he added zeros?" Alex asked.

Marc nodded. "Instead of writing 'three hundred riyals,' it now read 'three hundred *thousand* riyals.' His advisor, noting what had happened, pointed out the problem. The king looked closely at the ledger. 'Pay it immediately,' he said, 'for I will not have it be said that the hand of King Abdul Aziz is more generous than his heart.'"

Jackie's jaw dropped. "So he paid it?"

"Without hesitation."

"Jackie," Alex said with a frown, "let's be sure we type everything to the Saudis. No nibbed pens."

Marc chuckled at that. "Let me give you another example." Then suddenly he shook his head. "No, I'm doing all the talking, and I'm not really answering your question."

"Yes. Yes, you are," Alex insisted. "Go on."

"Well," Marc said hesitantly, but when they both nodded, he gave in. "All right. Just one more, to show how much understanding their culture and choosing a suitable gift can help."

"Near the end of World War II, America and Great Britain had come to realize that this little desert kingdom had become a pivotal power in the politics of the world. Both Churchill and Roosevelt started to woo the Saudis. As you know, America won out, and while there are probably many reasons why this was so, a good part of it revolved around the fact that Ibn-Saud liked President Roosevelt and did not like or trust Churchill."

"Now you're talking my language," Alex said enthusiastically. "This is leverage you're talking about, right?"

"Exactly."

"So what made the difference between the two?"

"Two things. First, though the Islamic religion has no specific ban on tobacco, it does forbid liquor. The sect of Islam that dominates Saudi Arabia is strongly fundamentalist, and so they don't just forbid liquor, it is strictly outlawed. King Abdul Aziz neither smoked nor drank. As you know, President Roosevelt was a chain smoker, but he knew the king's code and didn't want to smoke around him. One night, after a long meeting, they went directly to dinner. Roosevelt was so desperate for a smoke, he sent the king on a separate elevator to the dining room. Roosevelt hit the emergency stop button on his elevator and hurriedly smoked two cigarettes before going on, blaming a stuck elevator for his delay. He also had no alcohol served at the dinner."

Alex was watching this young professor with great interest. Besides being more and more impressed with his abilities, he found himself taking a real liking to him. That didn't happen very often with the men he brought on board for projects.

"When it was over," Marc was saying, "Roosevelt presented the king with a DC-3 as a gift."

"You mean an airplane!"

"Yes. It was a huge success with Ibn-Saud. He was the first to own one in all of Saudi Arabia."

Alex grimaced. "I wasn't thinking of something quite that elaborate."

Marc smiled. "Let me finish the story. Three days later the king met with Winston Churchill. None of this self-sacrificing attitude for him. Right off he told the king that abstaining from alcohol and tobacco might be part of the Saudi religion, but he, Churchill, considered smoking cigars and drinking alcohol as a sacred rite in and of itself. He proceeded to puff on his cigars and sip whiskey throughout their meetings.

"In his memoirs, Churchill makes it all sound hilariously funny. And while the king was a man of the world, and didn't expect others to observe his standards, Churchill's cavalier attitude set the relationship off to a bad start. Churchill had also heard about Roosevelt's gift, so in a grandiose, off-the-cuff gesture, he told the king that the first Rolls Royce off the assembly line after the war would be his."

"Hmmm," Alex mused. "Airplanes, Rolls Royces? You are really starting to discourage me."

"Ah, but here's the point of the story. One would think a Rolls Royce would be a pretty impressive gift. But when it finally arrived, it had the steering wheel on the right side, like all British-made automobiles. When the king went to get in, he saw that this would leave him sitting on the left-hand side of his driver. In Saudi culture, the left hand is the inferior hand. One doesn't even eat with it. And the left-hand position is definitely the inferior position. For the king to be on the left of a servant was unthinkable. So he gave it away."

"You're kidding! He gave a Rolls Royce away?"

"That's right. And America, not Britain, became the Saudi

choice for an alliance." Marc paused, suddenly a trifle embarrassed by his long speech. "So you are absolutely right to be concerned about what you give the prince."

Alex was sober. "That's unbelievable. The whole of history changed by the choice of a gift."

"Well, as I said, there were many other factors too."

Alex ignored that, watching Marc closely. "Would you ever consider doing me a favor?" he finally asked.

"After what you have done for me on my car, are you kidding? What do you need?"

"Could you help me choose the gift? Give it some thought, then tell me what to get the prince? I'd really appreciate it."

"Of course."

"Terrific!" He lifted a hand, and the waiter moved toward them instantly. "You just made this a very profitable luncheon for me."

"Oh no," Marc said swiftly. "This one's on me."

Alex shook his head firmly. "No way. I invited you to lunch, remember." He turned to Jackie. "Do you want anything else?"

"No, thank you. The lunch was lovely."

"I think that's it, then," he said to the waiter. "We're ready for the check."

"Yes, sir." The young man disappeared.

"Alex, I mean it," Marc persisted. "I've had that incredible car for almost a week. You got my car fixed for nothing. Please, let me buy lunch." He pulled his wallet out.

Alex was both pleased and amused, but he finally shrugged. "If you insist."

In a moment the waiter was back, carrying a small tray with the bill on it. He started to hand it to Alex, but Marc quickly slid his American Express card onto the tray. The waiter turned slowly, stared first at the card in disbelief, then at Marc with such a look of contemptuous scorn that Marc visibly flinched, his face flushing almost instantly.

Alex burst out laughing. He reached across, took Marc's card, and tossed it back to him, then signed the bill with a quick flourish.

"Thank you, sir." The boy retreated, shooting Marc one last look of total disbelief.

"I'm sorry," Alex said, fighting back another round of laughter.

Marc was blushing. "What's the matter?"

"Did you see that look?" Alex said to Jackie. "You would have thought Marc was offering to pay in wampum or sea shells or something."

"Don't they take American Express?" Marc persisted.

"They don't take anything!" Jackie laughed.

Alex leaned across the table and patted Marc's arm. "I'm sorry for that, Marc. Here in the club they don't take any money. Not even if you purchase golf balls in the pro shop. You just sign. For everything. Then they put it on the monthly bill. I really do apologize. I wasn't trying to embarrass you. I've never tried paying before. I wasn't sure what the waiter would do."

"It was good of you to offer, anyway," Jackie said, sensing Marc's humiliation.

Marc managed a thin smile, but inwardly he was deriding himself. The Lamborghini and lunch at the Wilshire Country Club and Jackie's arm through his as they passed the guard had temporarily dazzled him. When the toad is the guest of the peacock, he told himself, it would be well if the toad remembered who is the toad and who is the peacock. A few minutes later, as they walked out into the sunshine, Alex stopped and peered at his watch. "It's two thirty already. Listen, Marc. I've got to stop at the law office. Would you mind if Jackie rides out to the shop with you to pick up your car. Could you do that, Jackie?"

"That's fine with me. I was just going back to the office anyway. I'll leave your car at the warehouse."

"Great." He turned to Marc. "It's been a delightful lunch. Your knowledge of the Saudis was an added bonus."

"I'll get that information on the gift to you right away."

"Super. Just put the bill in with it."

Marc shook his head firmly. "No way. This is my way of saying thanks for the car."

"Don't be ridiculous. I planned to find a consultant to help me on this. I wasn't suggesting you do it for nothing."

"Am I going to have to pull out my American Express card?" Marc asked, dead sober.

Alex chuckled. "Okay, okay. Thanks."

"Thank you for lunch."

"Let's do it again." He started away, then suddenly turned back. "Say, Marc?"

"What?"

"If I get into this Saudi deal very big, I might need a consultant with some expertise in dealing with Arabs. Would you consider that?"

Marc was completely caught off guard. "I . . . I've never done any consulting. The Saudis aren't really my area of specialty."

Alex turned to Jackie. "What do you think, Miss Ashby?"

"Based on what we saw today, I think he would be terrific."

"I agree. Are you busy between Christmas and New Years?"

"Well, no. I . . ."

"Great. We're taking the yacht on a cruise to Baja, California. The weather in Mexico is great this time of year. We'll do a little deep-sea fishing, play a lot, work a little— just enough so we can take it as a tax write-off. Anyway, will you join us? I'll be ready for some real help on the Arabs by then."

Marc was shaking his head slowly, a little dazed. "Alex, really, I'm not qualified."

"You let me be the judge of that. Plan on the twenty-seventh to the thirtieth. All you need to bring are some clothes and personal things. We'll have everything else. I'll have Jackie call you."

Jackie nodded, but before Marc could respond, Alex continued. "By the way, Jackie, did you get those tickets for Universal Studios?"

"Yes, I did. They came today."

"Good. Marc, every now and then we get what we call 'trades,' free tickets for services we render. How would your boys like to spend the day at Universal Studios?"

"They'd be delighted." He was suddenly suspicious. "Are you sure they're free?"

"Jackie, tell him."

"Completely. And they're VIP passes."

"In fact, just the other day, Jackie was saying how long it's been since she's been out there." He nudged Marc. "We've got four passes."

"Alex!" She blushed instantly, and it was clear that Alex had caught her by surprise too.

"I'd be delighted," Marc said. "But going with two boys is hardly the way to enjoy the day."

"I think your boys are darling. I'd love to go with all of you, but . . ." She shot Alex a dirty look, but he was beaming innocently.

"Then it's settled," Marc said. There was no need to feign his pleasure. To spend the day with Jackie would be tough duty indeed.

Alex was pleased with himself and didn't try hard not to show it. "That's great. Well, I've got to run. See you later. We'll keep in touch, Marc." And he was gone.

For a moment the two of them stood there, both a little embarrassed. "Look, Marc. I didn't expect that. Alex sometimes—"

"You heard the man. If you really don't mind taking the boys, I really would be delighted to have you with us."

She looked up at him closely, then smiled. "I would like that too. Very much."

"Good." He reached in his pocket and extracted the car keys. "Do you want to drive?"

She gave a quick shake of her head. "Are you kidding? And ruin your image with the security guard?"

Barclay's black Lincoln Mark VII came out of the parking lot first, followed closely by the blue Lamborghini. The Lincoln

95

turned south, the sports car north. In a parked car half a block away, Nathan Shoshani lowered his binoculars and picked up a microphone. "Shana, did you get confirmation on those plates yet?"

A woman's voice, heavily accented, responded almost immediately. "Both the Lincoln and the Lamborghini are registered to Barclay Enterprises in El Segundo."

"Thank you." Shoshani pushed the button on the mike again. "Yehuda, you take Barclay. We'll take the new man and the girl."

There was no response, but a second car a block down the street pulled out and fell in a discreet distance behind the Lincoln. Nathan let the Lamborghini pass him, waited for two more cars, then started the engine and pulled a quick U-turn. As he accelerated, he reached across to a pad and jotted down some quick notes.

Chapter Eleven

"Mom?"

Mary Robertson looked up from the book she was reading. The late afternoon sun came in from the window, framing her in soft back light.

"Mr. Williams called today."

"Mr. Williams?"

Valerie was on the couch, folding Matt's shirts and jeans. She paused, not looking up. "Yes, my boss in Denver."

The book lowered slowly to rest in Mary's lap. "Oh?"

"My job has come open again."

There was a brief deepening of the wrinkles around her eyes. Valerie looked at her more intently, trying to read the expression, but with her face in shadow, it was difficult. "He offered me a substantial raise if I come back."

"I see." Mary picked up the book again.

Valerie waited a moment, but when her mother continued reading, she sat up straighter. "You're pretty well back on your feet again now, and it's time I go back to work. The only thing I've been able to find here is in downtown L.A. I don't relish driving forty miles in that traffic twice a day."

"And Marc is on a yacht in sunny Mexico, with one Jacqueline Ashby, who is charming and very beautiful."

"Mother!"

"Well, as long as you're listing the reasons, let's get them all out on the table."

"Mom! You've been trying to match Marc and me ever since you started working for him."

"That's right, and it took having kidney stones to finally do it."

"Well, it isn't going to work."

"Not if you go back to Colorado."

"Not if I stay, either!" She dropped her head and started folding the clothes with quick, hard strokes. Mary watched her for a minute, then closed the book and set it aside.

"Valerie, don't let Jackie blind you."

"Blind me!" she blurted. "What about Marc? She's all he seems to see lately. He's taken her to dinner, to a concert. And two weeks afterward, Brett and Matt still talk about what a wonderful time they had with her at Universal Studios. And Baja!" She spit the word out with distaste.

"I guess you're right," her mother mused. "The fact that Marc invited Jackie for a cruise on his private yacht does put her one up on you."

Valerie bit back a sharp retort, then got up and moved over to sit on the floor in front of her mother. "All right, so Alex invited him. But Jackie's there!"

"Not by Marc's doing."

Valerie sighed and started drawing patterns idly on the carpet.

"And who did Marc take to that Christmas party at Mr. Barclay's house last week? Jackie was there too. If Marc was as serious about Jackie as you seem to think, would he have taken you to that, knowing she would be there?"

"And do you know how I felt around those other women, Mom? I felt like a little girl in pigtails, come to a grownup party to stand in the corner and watch. Jackie, Jessica Gerritt, Ardith Barclay. Everyone with their hair just done, and their elegant clothes, and . . ." She stopped, biting her lip, close to tears.

"I thought you liked Ardith Barclay."

"I do. She is a lovely and gracious woman. I think she and I could be good friends. But even she is so far out of my class, Mother." She shook her head forlornly.

Mary leaned forward slightly and waited until Valerie looked up at her. "I chided Marc once for thinking he was outclassed by the Wilshire Country Club. Am I going to have to start giving you lectures on what constitutes real class and what doesn't?"

Valerie sighed, smiling in spite of herself. "Tell me how classy I am. I could use a little propaganda right now."

Her mother didn't return the smile. "Valerie, you know I'm hoping and praying that something will work out for you and Marc. Nothing could make me happier. But I'm not interfering. I have not pushed Marc in any way—not hinted, not arranged things behind the scenes—which," she added with just a trace of asperity, "is not true for Alex Barclay, as near as I can tell. But be that as it may, I know my daughter, and I know Marc Jeppson."

She took a deep breath, picked up the book again, and found her place. Then and only then did she look at her daughter again. "I'll only say this. I think you're selling yourself short, and I think you're selling Marc short. And your boss in Colorado better make that raise a mighty big one, because it's going to take a lot to cover what you'll lose by leaving here."

Valerie would have been quite surprised to know that at that very moment Marc was not with Jackie, but sitting in a deck chair, eyes wide open behind his sunglasses, watching the people around him. They had been anchored off Ensenada for a full three days. The first two days had been filled with skin diving, deep sea fishing, shopping in the village, and long walks along the beach. Now, everyone seemed content to spend their last afternoon languourously and lazily on board ship.

Alex was deep in conversation with Quinn Gerritt and General Taylor Canning at a small table. The large beach umbrella kept their faces in shadow and hard to read, but the talk was earnest, and Marc suspected this was the real reason for the cruise.

John DeLorean. That's who Marc thought of when he looked

at Gerritt. His physical presence was almost electric, but there was something deep in the man that was like rock. No nerves, no blood, no pulse.

Taylor Canning was military all the way. He was genial, open and friendly, yet always precise and ordered, cutting through any superficialities. Marc liked him.

Alex? Marc smiled inwardly as he watched him. There was a lot of depth in the man yet to be probed, but Marc knew he would like what he found there. Not that there weren't weaknesses and flaws—a tendency to flamboyance, the attitude that people were markers in an intriguing game, a slight streak of underlying cynicism. But there was also his enthusiasm for life, the acceptance of every challenge as a shot of adrenalin in life's blood stream, his total devotion to Ardith.

Marc turned to where she sat talking with Jackie and the general's wife. Casual elegance. That was Alex's phrase for his wife, and Marc nodded now as he thought of the term. Here was one of Alex Barclay's most important assets.

Jackie looked up, saw him watching her, and flashed him a warm smile. He smiled back, then turned to look at the two figures sunning in the deck chairs near the main cabins. Derek Parkin lay next to the latest bauble he had added to his string, his pale skin sharply contrasting with the tawny gold of hers. Gaylene. Marc could never remember her last name. She was a stunning ash blond with flawless skin, bright green eyes, and beautiful features that covered one of the most inane minds Marc had yet encountered. But then, one didn't have to be too shrewd to guess that Gaylene's mind was not what had won her Derek's invitation to join the cruise.

Marc shifted his gaze slightly to Derek. Here was a hard one to read. The outer man was quick, competent, and very assured. The inner man? Marc had decided to set aside judgment on him for now. But one word kept cropping up when he thought of Derek. A user. Derek Parkin was a user. Of things. Of people. Of opportunities. It surprised him a little that Alex had hired him as an executive vice president of Barclay Enterprises.

On the other side of the deck, Jessica Gerritt lay tanning in her white bikini. Marc was warming to his little game of categorizing people in a single word or phrase. Iced mink, that was how he thought of Jessica Gerritt. Cool, infinitely poised, sophisticated down to the tips of her brightly painted toenails. And as aloof and superior as her husband.

And what of Jackie? He swung back to watch her talking with the two older women. He studied her, comparing her to Jessica and Gaylene. And Valerie. That brought a slight frown, and he lay back and closed his eyes. Though many might have chosen either Jessica or Gaylene over Jackie on the basis of pure physical beauty, with Marc it was just the opposite, though he knew his judgment was colored by what each was like inside as well as out. In contrast to Jessica's icy superiority and Gaylene's mental vacant lot, Jackie was bright, warm, genuine, and open. She had an ability to put him completely at ease, and yet did so without becoming doting or patronizing.

Last night, on their way back from shopping and dinner in the village, he and Jackie had left the others to walk along the beach. They had stopped and talked, and he had felt himself drawn to her powerfully. But at the last moment, as she tipped her head up to him, he backed away, turning to stare out across the water. It had been an awkward moment, and the hurt was evident on her face.

He suspected Jackie had blamed his sudden loss of nerve on the memory of his wife floating up at the last moment to jab him with guilt. But now, with more clarity than he had had then, Marc realized that what had come between him and Jackie was not the memory of Lynette. It was Valerie—Valerie with a loveliness all her own; Valerie with an inner depth like a quiet pool where one came for strength and rejuvenation.

He took a deep breath and let it out slowly. For two years he had gone on with life, lonely and missing Lynette, fiercely at first, but later content to be alone with the boys. He had firmly and successfully resisted the numerous efforts of the inevitable matchmakers and maintained his stance. Then suddenly, almost at the same time, two remarkable women had entered his life. Most men would have accepted such a fate with joy. Marc only found it more and more frustrating.

Suddenly, he felt hands on his shoulders. He opened his eyes and removed his sunglasses. Jackie was standing behind him, and began to massage his neck muscles softly. She smiled. "Did I wake you?"

"No."

Closing his eyes again, he let the relaxing pressure on his shoulders soothe him. "Ardith has sent me over with a request."

His eyes opened again.

"Alex would like to take us to dinner tonight. Just the four of us."

"Oh?" He sat up, and she came around and sat beside him. Her hand lay easily on his arm.

"I don't know for sure, but I think you are about to become the official Near Eastern consultant for Barclay Enterprises."

"Really?"

"Really." She smiled. "And I'm glad. I think you'll be a great asset."

"Thank you." That meant Alex had liked his report on the prince and his recommendation for a gift.

"Want to go for a swim?"

He looked up at her, sensing her hesitancy at leading out after last night's rejection. She submitted to his scrutiny with a faint smile. There was no question about it, he concluded. She was one lovely woman. He rubbed his arm, feeling the heat of the sun on it, then stood and pulled her up. "Why not?" he said with a grin.

It was past ten when they finally finished dessert, and Alex pushed back his chair. He fumbled in the side pocket of his jacket and came out with a package of cigarettes. Ardith's eyes widened, and then she frowned.

"Alex." The gentle reproof was evident.

"Now don't you be Alexing me," he said with mock severity.

"This is my first cigarette in almost a week." He took a matchbook from the table, lit the cigarette, and inhaled deeply.

"You know what Dr. Goodrich said about your heart."

"I know, I know. And I've almost quit." He turned to Marc. "Have you ever smoked?"

He shook his head.

"Smart. I wish I had never started." He inhaled again deeply, then set the cigarette in the ashtray and blew the smoke toward the ceiling. "Well," he said, looking steadily at Marc, "I suppose you guessed there may have been more to this invitation than just a chance to get to know you better."

How did you answer that? Yes, that's all I've thought about for the last four hours? No, Alex, I've always trusted your surface motives, and I never gave it a second thought? He just watched, keeping his face expressionless.

"You probably sensed that General Canning and Quinn Gerritt were invited on this trip for more than social reasons."

Marc nodded.

"There are some things starting to shape up. One of those opportunities that doesn't come along every day."

Marc picked up his spoon and toyed with it absently, his eyes never leaving Alex's face.

"It could be very big." Pause. Alex was choosing his words carefully. "It will heavily involve the Saudis."

Here it comes. Marc felt his excitement rising.

Alex leaned back, picked up the cigarette, looked at it, then set it back down again. "Marc, what would it take to get you away from the Claremont Colleges?"

Marc had started to twirl the spoon, but it stopped in midair.

Alex grinned. "I thought maybe I could catch you off guard with that."

Marc set the spoon down slowly.

"I happen to know what your current salary is. I'll double it."

Marc looked at Ardith, who smiled gently at his dazed expression. Then he turned to Jackie. She reached over and squeezed his hand. Finally, he looked back at Alex.

Alex laughed aloud at the expression on his face. "You didn't suspect it at all?"

Marc shook his head. "I thought maybe you wanted to talk about me being a consultant, but . . ." He shook his head again.

"Well, then, while I've got you reeling, let me close in for the kill. I took the liberty of speaking with the dean of your college. I wanted to know what the possibilities were before I approached you."

"The dean?"

"Yes. I explained the whole situation." He laughed again. "Well, at least enough of it to let him know that this would be a great opportunity for you, and that the experience you'd gain would benefit the college as well. He agreed. If you accept, they will grant you a one year's leave of absence, beginning January first."

"January first! That's the day after tomorrow!"

"Well, actually, that's when your official leave of absence begins. But since you're already on holiday, how about saying that you started working for me the day we left Los Angeles? Can you handle being paid full salary for lying around in the sun?"

Marc was speechless, much to their amusement. Jackie spoke first, to Alex. "I do think you should point out to Marc that this is not a typical work week."

"Wait until we have a yes answer from him, then we'll break the realities of life to him."

"The leave of absence is ideal in a way," Ardith said. "You can try this for a while. If you don't like it, you can go back to Claremont with no real loss. And if you do like it, well, who knows what might come of it?"

"But—what would I do?"

"Well, for starters, you said you've been dying to get into Saudi Arabia. If all goes well, we'll both end up going there in the next few months. Probably several times."

Marc held up his hands. "Whoa! Would you stop throwing right hooks at me until I get my head cleared."

Alex now became very serious. "This may seem sudden to

you, Marc, but it isn't for me. I've been thinking about this ever since that day at the Country Club. You're exactly what I need."

"But I'm not a businessman."

"No, though you are halfway through your MBA. I've hired Derek to help me on the business end of things. I need you to help me walk through the Arabian labyrinth."

He pushed his chair away from the table. "Look, we're not holding you hostage here until you give us your decision. Take all the time you need." He got that impish look that made him look ten years younger than he was. "At least until we get home tomorrow."

They all stood. Alex extracted a fifty-dollar bill from his wallet and tossed it on the table. Then he looked up at Marc. "You think it over, Marc. Think it over very carefully. This kind of opportunity doesn't come along every day."

Marc gave him a long, quizzical look, then a tiny smile pulled at the corners of his mouth. "Does this mean I have to sell my Volkswagen?"

It was almost midnight when Ardith and Alex Barclay finally came to their cabin and began preparing for bed. Alex sat on the edge of the bed and slipped off his shoes as his wife went into the bathroom to brush her teeth.

"Gerritt cornered me a few minutes ago," he called quietly, mindful that others were just on the other side of the bulkheads.

Ardith poked her head around the door. "Oh?"

"He asked me why I brought a college professor along on this trip."

"And what did you say?"

He laughed and let one shoe drop. "I told him I thought he was a promising young man and refreshing to have around."

There was a pause as she rinsed out her mouth. Then she reappeared with a towel. "It's called integrity."

"What?"

"The thing you find so refreshing about Marc Jeppson."

He looked at her sharply. Even after so many years, she could still bring him up short with her insights. "Yeah, I suppose it is. I don't deal with many who have it in great abundance anymore."

"So, did that satisfy Gerritt?"

He finished undressing and slid under the covers. "No. Gerritt is sharp enough to know I didn't bring Marc along just to provide a refreshing change."

Ardith turned off the light and slipped in beside him. "Gerritt is too sharp. I'm not sure I like him."

"If I did business only with people you like, or that I like, for that matter, we wouldn't be sitting in a yacht off the coast of Mexico nor would we be considering building a new home in Pacific Palisades."

In the dark he couldn't tell whether she agreed. They were both silent for several minutes. Finally Ardith turned her head. "Do you know what it is about Marc that you like so much, Alex?"

"No what?"

There was a soft touch of sadness in her voice. "You and I were like that once, too."

Chapter Twelve

Nathan Shoshani suppressed a yawn and glanced at his watch as the team filed into the room. It was nearly 7 P.M., which meant he was coming up on thirty-six hours without sleep. He had stayed up the greater part of the night, supervising the watch on Quinn Gerritt and his wife as their high-rolling party covered half the exclusive bars in Los Angeles and Beverly Hills. And the loss of sleep had been basically for nothing—as had most of their last week's work on Gerritt. When Nathan had returned to his apartment just after dawn, word was waiting that Moshe Gondor was on his way to Los Angeles. That had been a blow, for Gondor had been Nathan's control officer before. While he was competent and supportive of his operatives, he kept a tight leash, keeping his hand in rather than letting his men have their head. Nathan had spent the rest of the morning getting ready for his arrival, and most of the afternoon briefing him on where they stood.

Gondor entered at that moment and almost instantly the room grew quiet. Then Nathan's head came up sharply. Yaacov Shoshani, white hair in gleaming contrast to a simple black suit, shuffled in behind Gondor and took a seat in the back. Their eyes met briefly—Nathan's full of surprise and questioning, his father's veiled and noncommittal. The older Shoshani was drawing curious looks from several others in the room as well.

Gondor came forward and took a seat next to Nathan.

"What is he doing here?" Nathan asked in a low voice.

"I just found out he was here. He's been in California for better than a week. You'd better let me introduce him."

A week! And not even a call. Nathan didn't know whether to be grateful or angry. Gondor's coming was bad enough, but this? He let out a long breath, stood and faced the small group scattered around the room. "All right, let's get started. This is Moshe Gondor, who is taking over as control officer for this operation. As of today, Moshe has moved the headquarters of the operation here to L.A."

There were a few murmurs of surprise. This meant their team was in the heart of the action and was no longer on the periphery.

"He's read all of the reports, and I've briefed him on where we stand, but he'd like to get a feel directly from each of you. Then we'll talk about where we go from here." He stepped back. "Moshe."

Gondor stood and took Nathan's place behind the small table, opening a thick folder, laying out some papers, then finally facing the group. "Before we begin, let me introduce to you Yaacov Shoshani." His tone of voice left no questions about how Gondor viewed the presence of the man in the room. "Most of you know that the Prime Minister has appointed Mr. Shoshani as a civilian advisor to this operation. He is to have full access to all information and is free to sit in any planning sessions. However, he is not considered as part of the operational team. While his counsel should be considered carefully, it has no binding force."

Yaacov was nodding thoughtfully, as most of the room turned and surveyed him openly. Nathan leaned forward, staring at the floor.

"Nathan will continue as team leader. Because of the importance of this particular operation, I am reporting directly to the Deputy Director. Are there any questions about the chain of command?"

There wasn't, and the uncomfortable silence stretched on for several moments. "Okay. I want a brief rundown from each of you. Yitzhak, you begin. What about Barclay? What's your gut reaction? Can a small-time arms dealer really put together a two-billion-dollar arms deal?"

Yitzhak ben Tsur, a descendant of numerous generations of Moroccan Jews, was small and dark, lean as a greyhound and just as quick. He stood. "Well, at first I thought this assignment was going to be no big trouble. Barclay is an established and legitimate arms dealer, but he has never handled anything near this big. Mostly light stuff—rifles, mortars, a few vehicles." He shrugged. "Basically, he is a little boy playing soccer in the World Cup Championships. Except for one thing. If Gerritt Industries ties up with Barclay, it would make a tremendous difference."

"More than one thing," Gondor corrected. "While in Washington, I learned that Barclay also has some powerful support in the State Department."

Yitzhak nodded soberly. "Yes, that too. There is still much that he must do. The competition will be very fierce for this one, but I am no longer thinking that the Barclay deal will die its own death. It is going to need some help from us."

"And what of this new radar system Gerritt Industries is supposed to be developing?"

The Moroccan Israeli lifted his shoulders briefly. "We think Gerritt and Barclay are close to striking a deal. Yossi has the details on the system itself."

"Okay, thank you." Gondor turned to a larger man on the third row. Even on the streets of Jerusalem, few people would have guessed Yossi Kittelman was a third-generation Israeli. He had fair skin, flaming red hair, and a thick coating of freckles. "Yossi? Tell us about Mr. Quinn Gerritt."

Yossi stood. He too had spent the night tracking Gerritt, but either he had slept during the day or had a face that showed no weariness. "Ah yes, Mr. Gerritt. This one is harder to get to know. He has been very rich all of his life, and so he knows how to protect his privacy. There is no question but what Gerritt Industries was in serious trouble a few months ago. Then suddenly they received a massive transfusion of capital. We have not yet found out exactly where the money came from, but we are sure it came as a result of this new radar system."

He shifted his weight, not sure how much detail Gondor wanted. "As you know, many of the high tech companies engaged in weapons research for the Defense Department allow Israeli technicians to study critical new projects. But to this point, Gerritt Industries has not done that. Since this system is being developed privately and not being funded by the government, that is not likely to change."

Nathan stood and stepped forward. "Unfortunately, we did not know Gerritt was going to be a principal until he came to Barclay's office a week or two before Christmas. So we haven't been tracking him as long, and, as Yossi says, he is much more difficult to keep under the microscope."

Gondor let his gaze sweep the room. "Okay. Gerritt is critical. We will continue to place the major portion of our manpower on that connection. Anything else Yossi?"

The redhead shook his head and sat down.

"What about the two men Barclay has hired?" Gondor asked.

A couple of men in the room stirred.

"Udi?"

Yehuda Gor stood slowly. He was large-boned and seemed awkward, more like a farmer than one of the Mossad's best operatives. He said little, but when he spoke, he was listened to. He and Gondor had been raised in the same kibbutz, which accounted for the use of the nickname.

"Bringing in new men for a project like this fits Barclay's pattern," he began. "Those who know Barclay call these kind of men 'throwaways.' He uses them on one project, then dumps them. Derek Parkin came out of the law firm Barclay uses. He is very bright. His expertise is in law. He also has a reputation for being ruthless in negotiating his way through complex situations. The college professor, Jeppson, was almost certainly brought in because he's a qualified Arabist. Both have recently applied for passports, so we expect Barclay plans to use them heavily."

"Thanks, Udi." Gondor surveyed the men. "All right, anything else?" No one moved.

"You need to know that while we had great hopes that this whole problem could be solved in New York and Washington, it looks more and more pessimistic. The president is holding firm on his promise to sell the planes to the Saudis. Congressional and other pressure is not helping much. Even the Prime Minister has talked to him, but the president will not back down. As a sop to us, he told the Prime Minister that he would authorize sale of the F-22 to us as well. That could help him get it through Congress. The Iran-Iraq war, the latest penetrations of Saudi air defenses, the growing madness of the Ayatollah—these and other things have America very worried."

Gondor sorted through the papers and picked up a letter. "I have here a directive from headquarters. The essence of it is that we here in this room are to undertake every covert effort possible to torpedo the deal before it is made. That is the best way to prevent the sale without alienating American goodwill toward Israel."

Yaacov Shoshani stirred, as if he was going to speak, and Gondor paused, fixing his eyes upon him. But finally, he settled back in his chair, his face impassive.

Yitzhak raised his hand, and Gondor nodded in his direction. "We have found a way to get someone inside the Gerritt laboratories. We could sabotage the prototype."

Gondor shook his head, starting to pace back and forth as he continued. "No. At this point, we are only looking for a way to throw gravel in the gears, to let the deal fall apart naturally. If we fail in that, then we will have no alternative but to go to more direct methods."

"Sabotage is illegal."

Every head in the room jerked around to look at Yaacov Shoshani.

"If you were caught, or if the Americans found out, it would be very bad for us. It could do us irreparable harm."

111

"I said we would only resort to that if we could not find another way," Gondor snapped, openly irritated.

"Sometimes we say there is no other way, simply because the wrong way is the easier way."

Nathan groaned inwardly. Here it comes.

When the older man spoke it was almost as if to himself. "If we abandon our commitment to doing what is right and use expediency to justify such a course of action, then we become no better than those we fight against."

"Look, Mr. Shoshani! I admire your ideals, but what we need here is not preaching. We are after solutions. Do you have solutions, or just lofty phrases?"

Yaacov stood slowly. "What would you say if I told you the name of the man who came to Quinn Gerritt with fourteen million dollars?"

There was a startled intake of breath throughout the room.

"Or what if I told you the name of the engineer who designed the radar device? And that he was on the verge of selling that device to another company because Gerritt Industries couldn't meet his price, then suddenly changed his mind and signed a contract with Gerritt for one fourth the amount he had originally asked?" He removed his glasses and started rubbing them with his tie. "Tell me, Mr. Gondor, would you think those were solutions, or just lofty phrases?"

Nathan was staring. Gondor spluttered. "Well, I . . . If you really have that information. Where did you get it?"

Yaacov shuffled forward, looking at the floor as though lost in thought. "I read the reports. One of them indicated that a Mr. Theodore Wuthrich, the controller for Gerritt Industries, is dissatisfied with his boss, Mr. Quinn Gerritt."

So that was it! Nathan had flagged Wuthrich as a potential, and they had made a low-key, first contact. But so far it had produced nothing.

Yaacov had reached the front of the room and stood face to face with Gondor. "Actually, to say Mr. Wuthrich is merely 'dissatisfied' is a vast understatement. He hates Mr. Gerritt bitterly, totally, and with great passion. A possibility for revenge came as a golden opportunity. Then, with the recent financial troubles of Gerritt Industries, Mr. Wuthrich has also lost considerable income from bonuses, stock options, and so on. He is experiencing a rather acute need for some ready cash at the moment. Together, those conditions made him very easy to talk with."

Nathan was shaking his head slowly, half amazed, half irritated at himself. This was basic intelligence work. If they hadn't been running Gerritt so hard . . .

His father reached in his coat and drew out a slip of paper. "Here is the name and address of the man bankrolling Gerritt. Also, there are two other names on the list. These men were recently hired under Gerritt's specific orders to work the night shift in the shipping department of the Gerritt plant in Hawthorne."

He handed Gondor the paper. "I find that somewhat touching, don't you? That a man as important and busy as Mr. Gerritt would take the time to see that two very minor positions were filled properly."

Gondor was reading the sheet, his face flushed, his mouth tight. "What about the engineer?"

"I would like to follow up on that myself."

For one moment, Gondor opened his mouth, then his mouth clamped shut and he turned to hand the list to Nathan. "Get on these right away."

Nathan took the list, but he didn't look at it. He was staring at his father, who had turned and was walking slowly back to his seat. The older Shoshani did not notice the grudging admiration that had replaced the earlier resentment in the eyes of those in the room, including those of his own son.

Chapter Thirteen

"Daddy, is this a volcano?"

"Uh-huh." Marc was typing rapidly on his computer and didn't turn.

"Daddy! You didn't even look."

Marc turned to where his son was sprawled on the floor with the World Book Encyclopedia, and gave it a two-second look. "Yes, Matthew, that's a volcano."

"Daddy?"

"What, Son?"

"Have you ever sawn a real volcano?"

"Seen, not sawn. But no, I haven't." He turned a few pages of the book he was working with, found the reference on Saudi currency, and started to type it into the computer.

"Why not?"

"Hmmmm?"

"Were you too scared?"

Marc let out a quick breath of exasperation. "Scared of what?"

Matt sat up, the green eyes showing his own efforts to be patient. "A volcano! Is that why you never saw one? 'Cause you were scared?"

"No, Matt. Volcanos are a long ways away. I've never been there. Now, Matt, I've got to get this report written. Just look at your book."

"Oh." He turned back to the book, disappointed. He turned a few pages, then looked up at his father again. "Daddy?"

"What?"

"At breakfast you said you'd play a game with me."

Marc took a deep breath, then turned clear around. "I know, Son, but I've got to get this paper written. See if Brett will play with you."

"Brett's at Cub Scouts."

"Oh, that's right." And Mary, who was assistant den leader, had gone with him. He took a deep breath, feeling the frustration build. He had promised Alex he would have this report for him in the morning, and he was still two or three hours away from completing it.

He turned back to the computer and his books. "Look, Matt. It's still an hour before bedtime. Go out and see if Martin or Jody can play with you for a while."

"I can't, Daddy." He held up one leg. "I've got my bare feet on."

Swinging back around, Marc held out his arms, laughing. Matt was up and onto his dad's lap in an instant, grinning happily. "Well," Marc said, holding back a smile, "why don't you take off your bare feet and put some shoes on?"

"I got my shoes wet in the gutter. Mary said I had to stay in the house."

He shook his head helplessly. "What am I going to do with you?"

"Play a game with me, Daddy. Please! You promised."

At that moment, Valerie stepped into the doorway. "Hi. Your housekeeper sent her daughter over to rescue a beleaguered father."

"Valerie!" In an instant Matthew was off his father's lap and throwing his arms around Valerie's legs.

"The beleaguered father is in desperate need of rescue," Marc said, shaking his head. "You came in the nick of time."

Taking Matthew's hand, she started back out. "Come on, Matt. Let's you and I go find something to do."

"Daddy won't play with me, Valerie. Will you play a game with me?"

Marc winced at that, watching the two of them retreat down the hallway.

"Your daddy has to work, Matt. It's part of his job. That's how he earns money."

The plaintive little voice came back to him clearly—"But daddies have two jobs. One is to work and earn money; the other is to tend their kids."

Marc stared at the computer screen for several seconds, then he sighed, filed off what he was working on, and turned off the main power switch.

An hour later, Marc finished his glass of milk, put the carton in the refrigerator, and started back for the study. As he entered the hallway, he heard the soft murmur of Matt's voice from his bedroom. On a sudden impulse he turned back around.

Valerie and Matt were kneeling at the bedside, and Matt was saying his prayers. "And keep us safe when we cross the desert to go to Grampa's house this summer. And bless Jody that her mom will be nicer to her. Name of Jesus, amen."

He looked up at Valerie, who was smiling down at him, gave her an impish grin and an impulsive hug, then bounced into bed.

As she started to tuck his blanket over him, she asked, "Where does your grandfather live, Matt?"

"In Willard."

"Willard? Is that in Utah?"

"Yup."

"And you have to cross the *dessert* to get there?" There was a soft note of amusement in her voice.

"Yeah. And it's really hot. Brett says if the car broke we'd die."

"I'm sure your daddy would take care of you. And I think it's called a desert, Matt, not dessert. Do you know what a desert is?"

"Sure." There was the slightest trace of disgust at her question. "A desert is a big beach with no ocean."

Valerie's laugh filled the room, and Marc started to laugh too. He entered, shaking his head. "Where did you come from, kid?"

116

"He is a delight." Valerie leaned down. "Do I get a kiss good night?"

He threw his arms around her and hugged her tight. As she straightened and stepped back, Marc moved next to the bed. Again the little arms came up and he sat down to receive the embrace. "Thanks for playing with me, Daddy."

"You're welcome, Son." He smiled and tousled his hair. "After all, a daddy does have two jobs." He kissed him, then took Matt's blanket and spread it over him. "Now you go to sleep."

Valerie was waiting at the door, watching him with a smile. As Marc turned, there was an exasperated cry. "Daddy!"

"What?"

He pointed to two bare feet sticking out from the bottom of the small blanket. "My feet are tucking out."

"Sorry!" Marc said solemnly, returning to tuck the edge of the blanket under, then giving his son another quick kiss.

As he came out into the hall, Valerie was waiting. She was shaking her head, still chuckling softly to herself. "That's quite a boy you have there Mr. Jeppson. I wish I could have had him in my creative writing class at college," she said. "He has a gift for coining a phrase."

Marc nodded. "Earlier he told me he couldn't go outside because he had his bare feet on."

They stopped where the doorway led into the kitchen and family room. She looked up at him. "Three games of Spit and two games of Uncle Wiggly, and you didn't show one moment of impatience. I'm very impressed."

He let out his breath, shaking his head. "It's not that I wasn't feeling it."

"I'm sorry. I really came over to stop that from happening."

"I know." His face was turned in profile, and she watched as he sobered. "But Matt's right. These last two weeks since I started with Alex, all I've done is work."

"But you love it, don't you?"

That brought him around to look at her closely.

"That night at the restaurant, when you talked about Claremont, I could see the frustration in your face. Now it's gone.
Even Mom has commented on it. She says this is more like the
old Marc Jeppson she used to know. Happy, joking. She's really
pleased."

"You're right about the frustation. I still can't believe it all.
One night, thanks to a broken down old VW, Alex Barclay drops
into my life and everything changes."

And with Alex came Jacqueline Ashby, she thought, then
pushed it aside with a little shake of her head. "I'm glad for you."
She took a quick breath and started to move past him. "Well,
you'd better get going again."

Marc put out his arm, blocking her path. She looked up, a
little startled. "Matthew and Brett are not the only ones I've been
neglecting lately."

"I've noticed that too," she murmured.

"So maybe daddies have three jobs," he said. "To earn money,
to tend their kids, and to take the housekeeper's daughter out for
an ice cream cone and a long ride."

Her laugh was soft and happy. "I think I like that job descrip-
tion."

Marc stepped forward and gathered her in his arms. For a moment she was startled, then leaned forward into his arms. He just
looked down at her, his face full of wonder. Then he kissed her,
softly and with great tenderness.

When he pulled back, her eyes were shining, almost luminescent. Her lips parted, but she suddenly shook her head and laid it
against his chest.

"What?"

She looked up, but again just shook her head. This time when
he kissed her, she put her arms around him and returned it, with
the same feeling of joy and tenderness she felt in him.

"I didn't really come over with that in mind, either," she said
when they finally parted, her voice husky. He touched her cheek,
and she laid her head against the palm of his hand. Then she
straightened, put both hands on his chest and pushed him away.

"Mother should be home with Brett in about ten or fifteen minutes. Why don't you work on your report until she gets home? Then she can stay with the boys while you finish your third job."

"Do you think she'll mind?"

She managed to keep a straight face. "No, I don't think she'll mind."

Chapter Fourteen

Unlike his study at home, which was warm, comfortable, and subdued, Alex's office in the Barclay Enterprises warehouse building bordered on the flamboyant, the deliberately overstated. A huge driftwood sculpture stood in one corner, a full-grown stuffed cougar sprawled across its lower trunk. One whole wall was glass and held a small arboretum, complete with trickling fountain and stuffed birds in the trees. The opposite wall was papered with a textured burlap and held framed prints of horses, foxes, and hounds centered around a larger scene of the hunt progressing across English countryside. The desk was solid oak and massive, nearly taking the whole end of the office. A wooden mallard duck sat on one corner, opposite the phone and a picture of Ardith.

On the wall behind the desk, a plaque hung centered between a matched set of antique Derringers. It read:

Top Ten Distributor Award
Colt Arms Company
Barclay Enterprises
1984

Alex was leaning back in his chair, sipping a cup of coffee as he talked. When Marc pushed the door open and saw he was on the phone, he started to back out again, but Alex waved him in, setting down the cup. He put his hand over the mouthpiece. "Come in. I'm mostly listening anyway."

Pulling one of the brown leather chairs around, Marc sat down. A folder was on the desk in front of Alex. It was the report he had turned in the day before yesterday—a day late. He sat back, watching Alex.

The president of Barclay Enterprises was dressed casually—light-blue flannel slacks, navy-blue pullover sweater. Marc smiled inwardly, thinking of the horrified look on Mary's face when she saw his jeans, old Adidas tennis shoes, and comfortable sweatshirt. Marc had held out against her. "It's Saturday. The office won't be open. Alex said to come casual."

At that moment, the door opened and Derek Parkin stepped in. Once again Alex motioned. He took the second chair and pulled it alongside Marc.

"Hello, Derek."

"Good morning, Marc."

Marc eyed him quickly. Though Derek hadn't worn a suit either, he was *Gentlemen's Quarterly* all the way. He smiled inwardly, as he turned back to Alex. Alex and Derek spent considerable time with the men's fashion magazine. With Derek, Alex was both mentor and counselor, commenting on the style or cut of a suit, suggesting a special brand of shirt or shoes. Yesterday, he had even taken Derek to his very high-priced barber for a razor cut of his thick, dark hair. And yet with Marc, it was almost like Alex was secretly pleased that he neither cared for the latest fashions nor worried about whether he was in keeping with what others around him were wearing.

A movement caught Marc's eye. Derek carried a folder identical to the one on Alex's desk and had raised it briefly. "I finished your report last night."

"Oh?" Marc responded softly so as not to disturb Alex, still murmuring assent from time to time.

The sharp buzz of the intercom sounded. Alex leaned forward. "John, can you hold a second? Jackie's buzzing me." He punched a button, then another. "Yes, Jackie."

There was a moment's pause. "No, I'll take it out there. Tell them to hold a minute." Again there was the pop of buttons. "John, look I've got Jakarta on the line. Can I call you back? Okay, thanks."

121

He stood up. "Sorry, but this should only take a minute or two, then we'll get started." He was out the door, and in a moment they could hear him again, faintly now.

Derek leaned forward, frowning slightly. Again he held up the folder. "Is the Saudi culture really that—" He paused looking for a suitable word—"orthodox?"

Marc nodded. "King Abdul Aziz came to power with the help of a strict, fundamentalist Islamic sect called the Wahabis. That fundamentalism still dominates the country."

"So we're going to have to pray to Mecca five times a day while we're there?" he said, with obvious distaste.

Marc wasn't sure whether to laugh or be irritated at Derek's deliberate obtuseness. "If you were Muslim and didn't comply, you might get a good whack across the bottoms of your feet, but no, *Nasrani* are not required to comply with Islamic rites."

"*Nasrani?*"

"Yes, Christians. Literally, followers of the man from Nazareth."

"Oh, but all the other stuff—no liquor, the ads—all of that is for real?"

"The religious police are very conscientious about protecting their society from the corrupting influences of the West. If you bring in magazines, even *Time* or *Newsweek*, they'll go through and cut out any offensive advertisements, or black out such things as low-cut gowns."

"And they really black out the pelvic area on panty hose packages?"

"That's what they say. Anything with even remote sexual connotations is illegal."

"No smoking, no drinking, veiled women? Sounds like a great place to spend a weekend."

Marc took a quick breath. He and Derek did not work directly together much. And that was fortunate, for he found himself increasingly annoyed by the egocentric narrowness of the man. In spite of the smooth urbanity, Derek Parkin cared only for those things that fostered the position, pleasure, or patronage of Derek Parkin.

"Smoking is not banned," Marc said quietly. "Many of the Wahabis voluntarily abstain, but the Islamic religion doesn't forbid it like it does drinking liquor."

"Who's smoking and drinking liquor?" Jacqueline Ashby was standing at the door. She held a tray with a coffee pot and two cups. There was also a glass of ice and a can of Seven-Up.

"Oh, hi, Jackie," Derek said, standing. Marc followed suit. She smiled, noticeably more warmly at Marc than Derek, then set down the tray. She took the coffee pot, poured two cups and turned to Derek.

"Black?"

He nodded and reached for the cup.

"And how about your Seven-Up, Marc? Cream and sugar, or would you prefer it black?"

He grinned good-naturedly. "On the rocks is fine, thanks."

She handed him both the glass and the can of pop, then picked up the pot again and refilled the cup Alex had left on the desk.

"So who's smoking and drinking?" Jackie asked again, taking a third chair.

"We were just talking about Marc's report."

She nodded. "That was very well done, Marc. I found it fascinating."

"Thank you." He was pleased by that. In addition to being an attractive woman, Jackie was quick, astute, and did not pass around compliments cheaply.

"If you do have to go to Riyadh, I'm glad I won't have to go. Any place where it is illegal for a woman to drive a car, or even ride in a car with a man other than family members, you can leave me out."

She had said it in fun, but Marc felt himself going on the defensive. He had always loved the Arabic culture, and in the last three weeks had become especially intrigued by the Saudis and what they had accomplished. "It's not that bad. The status of women has gotten a lot of bad press, but in a way they are more protected than exploited. And great strides are being made. Several of the women of the royal family have done a lot for them in terms of education, work opportunities, that sort of thing."

She sipped her coffee. "Do they really have banks just for women that are staffed solely by women tellers and clerks?"

"Yes. It is forbidden for women to come in direct contact with strange men. That's one reason why they wear veils. A male doctor may examine a woman patient, but only with another woman in the room. That's true if she is fully dressed and getting only an eye exam."

"And you call that progress?" Derek exclaimed.

Realizing that he was on the verge of becoming evangelical, Marc deliberately caught himself and shrugged. "That's an interesting question. The Saudis want our technology and twentieth-century advancements, but they're leery of some of our other exports."

"Like what?" Derek demanded.

"An overpermissive society that breeds insolent, irresponsible children. Media that is obsessed with sexuality and promiscuity. Men who are steeped in alcohol, immorality, and self-indulgence." Derek flushed at that, but Marc went on steadily, almost as though to himself. "Alcoholism, drug abuse, child and spouse neglect, armed war in the streets of every city. Actually they're anxious to leave quite a few things strictly to us Americans. I guess that does make them sound a little primitive."

"Hear, hear!" Alex said enthusiastically, pushing the door open.

Marc looked up, startled.

Alex moved to his chair and sat down. "You're one hundred percent right, Marc. And if we are going to work with the Saudis, we've got to remember that difference between them and us." He raised one eyebrow as he looked at Derek. "If we don't, we could lose everything."

"I never said they were primitive," Derek said sullenly. "Archaic is a better word, I think."

Marc bit back a retort, opened the can of pop, and poured it over the ice, aware that Jackie was watching him with open interest. Finally she turned to Alex. "Well, whatever it is, primitive or archaic, I think you got the right person to help us deal with it."

"I agree," Alex said, nodding. "And with that, let's get on with it. Jackie knows why the Saudis are of such peculiar interest to Barclay Enterprises right now. I think it's time we bring you two up to date on what is starting to shape up."

"Excuse me."

The man and woman bent over in the flower garden straightened and turned around. Their seventeen-year-old daughter playing with a pure white Persian kitten on the lawn nearby also looked up.

"I . . . I seem to be lost." He had a deeply lined face, a thick head of white hair, and spoke with a pronounced accent. His black suit was definitely not American.

The man working in the yard smiled encouragingly and stepped carefully out from among the flowers. "What are you looking for?"

"I think I got on the wrong bus." It was said hesitantly, almost apologetically. The stranger took a watch from his vest pocket and squinted at it. "Oh, dear. I think I am not going to make it."

Jonathan Taggart, engineer and chief designer of the VSM-430 radar system, set down his hoe and walked over to the man. "Where is it you were going?"

"To synagogue. It is Shabbat."

"Which synagogue?"

"Temple Beth El."

Taggart wrinkled his face, perplexed. "Temple Beth El?" He turned to his wife. "Mildred, do you know of a synagogue in town?"

She shook her head slowly. "I don't remember seeing one."

Charlene now moved to join her mother, stroking the kitten gently. She also shook her head.

"I have the address here." The old man took out a slip of paper and handed it to Taggart.

"But this is in Long Beach! You're in Cypress. Long Beach is fifteen or twenty miles from here."

The old man smacked his forehead. "Oi vavoi! I thought it did not feel right. But the city is so big. I could not tell. I . . . Could you show me where to catch a bus? The services start at ten."

Taggart shook his head slowly. "I never ride the bus. I don't know the schedules at all. And to get to Long Beach?" He turned to his wife. "Do the busses here even go to Long Beach?"

Mildred came over to stand next to her husband, and laid her hand on his arm. "Why don't we take him, Jonathan? It's already nine thirty."

"Oh, dear lady, I did not mean to ask for that."

"No," Taggart said, brightening. "Mildred's right. We'll take you. Even if we could find a bus, you'd never make it in time."

"But such an imposition. It would not be right."

"Nonsense," Mildred said firmly. "We'd be delighted. It's a beautiful Saturday morning. The ride will be delightful." She looked to her daughter. "Charlene, would you like to go?"

"I've got cheerleading practice at ten, Mom."

"Fine," her father said. "We'll be back in a little while."

"This is most kind," the old man said. "Most kind. I had heard that Americans were so full of—how do you say it? Hospeet-al . . ."

"Hospitality?"

"Ah yes, hospitality."

"We're happy to help. Are you from Israel?"

The old man was instantly surprised and pleased. "Yes, how did you know?"

Taggart grinned. "The synagogue helped."

"But of course." He bowed with great grace and dignity.

Taggart held out his hand. "My name is Jonathan Taggart,

and this is my wife, Mildred, and my daughter, Charlene."

Again there was the slight bow, which was somehow both quaint and stately at the same instant. "My name is Yaacov—Jacob in English. Jacob Shoshani."

Alex leaned far back in his chair, his mood expansive. "I guess the primary question is, why should Saudi Arabia work with us anyway? Obviously they know where to purchase jet fighters."

"I was wondering that myself," Derek said. "Surely Northrup or General Dynamics, or whoever, would be happy to deal directly with them and save the commissions."

"For sure!" Alex took a sip of coffee, enjoying his role as instructor. "There are various names given to what I do. Some call me a middleman, others say we are agents or sales representatives. I like to think of myself as a marriage broker. But whatever the name, we become critical in a contract such as this for a couple of reasons. One of the most obvious is that governments are very big entities. They move slowly. There is a horrendous amount of bureaucracy and red tape."

He began drumming his fingertips together slowly. "Another reason is, though at first it may seem to contradict what I just said, governments are in some ways very much like children. They are naive in the ways of the world. They can be ripped off like any individual. Worse, because of the size of the purchases involved. So the middleman becomes a protector to them, helping them negotiate the shoals of shallow water.

"A third reason. Remember the Lockheed scandal of a few years ago?"

Marc looked a little puzzled, so Derek broke in. "Lockheed executives were paying huge sums of money in bribes to get orders in foreign countries."

"Oh, yes."

"It wasn't just Lockheed," Alex continued. "Everybody was doing it. When all of the dust and fooforah settled, Congress had passed the Corrupt Foreign Practices Act, outlawing all such practices. Today, an executive of a corporation can end up in jail if he tries to influence the sale of his products through illegal payments."

He took a deep breath. "Now, you need to listen to this part very carefully so you understand the fine line we have to walk. A bribe is one thing, but a 'commission' is something else again. What many Americans would call a bribe is really a way of life in most of the world. Everyone has their hand out for a piece of the action. I call them the five-percenters. Everywhere you go—Latin America, the Orient, the Middle East—anyone who helps wants a cut of the action. It's part of the culture, and I'm sure Saudi Arabia is no different."

Marc was nodding. He had seen it in South America, but the Middle East had raised it to an art. Someone had once said that the favorite biblical passage in the Middle East was, "I was a stranger, and ye took me."

"If a corporate executive or a government official pays someone a commission," Alex was saying, "it may be interpreted under the Foreign Corrupt Practices Act as a bribe, and then the man's in trouble."

"But a middleman is different," Derek finished for him. It was not a question. Derek had followed the discussion perfectly.

"Right. We've got to be very careful, and I want it perfectly clear. We will not be bribing anyone. But I expect to pay out something like three or four million dollars in commissions before we're through."

Jackie did not seem at all surprised at the figure, but both Marc and Derek were suitably impressed. "Another way to look at it is this: An agent becomes an arbitrator between life-styles. In the Middle East the payment of commissions is a life-style. In America it is not. Both parties know the realities of life, but can't change—or won't. So I become the arbitrator between the two life-styles. That's why I call myself a marriage broker.

"This deal is a case in point. Here we have two parties who want a marriage—namely the sale of sixty high-performance jet aircraft. But there are obstacles. Some years ago, the Saudis passed a law against paying commissions on the purchase of military hardware. But they know this deal is so hot and so sensitive, normal channels will fail. America on the other hand, also has a problem. No executive of the aircraft company can pay the necessary 'grease money' required to make things work. And yet they know that without it, the deal will bog down completely. So, both governments say, 'We want the marriage badly. We'd better get a broker.'"

"And brokers have to be paid," Jackie concluded for him.

"That's right," Alex added with a beatific smile, "and if so, why not let it be us? The challenge will be to bind the Saudis to us and no one else. We're not the only ones who'd like to sew this one up. So we've got to put together a package that the Saudis can't get anywhere else." He turned to Derek. "Do you have your passport yet?"

"Yes, it came last week."

"Good. I want you to fly to Jakarta day after tomorrow."

That surprised everyone but Jackie. "Jakarta?" Derek echoed.

"Yes. I think we've found a way to leverage the Saudis to us. If this Gerritt Industries radar system proves to be all they're claiming it will be, that will be our biggest selling point. But every other thing we can do will put it in concrete."

"So what's coming down in Jakarta?" Derek asked.

"A few months ago, I worked a deal in Indonesia. I didn't make a dime on it. In fact I nearly lost my shirt. But it was a great favor to a very important general."

He saw the look on Marc's face and smiled. "Everything was perfectly legal. The president had given the army a certain percentage of the oil being pumped from one oil field. The general needed money, not oil. So he called us for help in marketing it. Oil is not my line, but I decided to do him a favor." He grinned more broadly at Marc. "Remember the lecture at UCLA?"

Marc had already been thinking about that very thing. "How one goes about selling widgets and all that?"

"Exactly! Well, Mr. Indonesian General is now in the market for some widgets."

Jackie turned in surprise. "The arms deal is going through?"

129

Alex nodded smugly.

"But I thought they couldn't get the funds."

"They can't."

She waited, knowing Alex well enough to sense when he had pulled off another coup.

"The army is willing to pay off one hundred percent in a counter-trade transaction." He turned to Derek and Marc. "That's what common folk would call bartering."

"What's the product?" Jackie asked.

"Bauxite ore."

She sat back, nodding with understanding. "Very good."

Marc and Derek were still baffled, and Alex laughed out loud. "So what does Barclay Enterprises want with several thousand tons of bauxite?"

"The thought had crossed my mind," Derek said.

"Do you know what bauxite is used for?"

"It's used in making aluminum," Marc answered.

"Right." He paused, savoring the moment. "A couple of months ago I heard that several companies, including Reynolds and Kaiser, have been asked to submit preliminary proposals for building an aluminum foil factory in the Middle East. In Jeddah, as a matter of fact."

Marc sat back. The complexity of it all was almost breathtaking. And Alex thrived on it. He was a master at it.

"If we could promise a cheap source of ore, we could make a few bucks on the side and at the same time get one more peg nailed down around the Saudi tent."

"That's great, Alex," Jackie said, almost as pleased as her boss.

"I know. That was good news at the right time." Suddenly he was all business. "Derek I want to brief you on exactly what has to be done in Indonesia. The groundwork is all laid, but there will be contracts to write and get signed, details to work out. That's where you really shine." He swiveled in his chair. "Jackie, I want you and Marc to put some real thought into Gerritt. I don't want him slipping out from under us."

"Gerritt?" Marc asked. "I thought you already had an agreement with him."

"Oh, we do. But if that prototype performs next Monday like he says it will, Quinn Gerritt will move from starving industrialist with hat in hand to the hottest item on the defense industry circuit. Right now, he needs us. We're a guaranteed market for his product, and that keeps his financing secure. But once he's got a pocketful of chips, you can bet he'll start looking to see if there are any other games in town."

"But haven't you signed a contract?"

Alex hooted. "Sure I have. But to a man like Gerritt, a contract is like a napkin at the dinner table. You use it so folks will think you're polite, but once the food is served, you forget the paper and go for the meat."

"Then maybe somebody ought to teach Gerritt what table manners are all about."

It was said so calmly that for a moment Alex just blinked. Then he recovered and leaned forward. "Are you serious?"

Marc nodded, meeting Alex's gaze.

Derek snorted in disgust, and Marc caught Jackie's quick glance of warning. He ignored both of them. Alex sat back, his expression still incredulous. "Without Gerritt's radar system, we've got nothing with the Saudis. The whole deal goes down the tubes."

"So you let Gerritt do whatever he wants?"

"Look!" Alex exploded, "I don't like Quinn Gerritt any better than you do, but I'm not about to lose the biggest opportunity of a lifetime just to make some point about who's right and who's wrong. There's too much riding on this one."

"It's your game, Alex," Marc said evenly.

"What's that supposed to mean?"

"You hired me to help you deal with the Saudis, not tell you how to run your business."

"I was beginning to wonder," Derek murmured.

Alex spun around. "That's enough, Derek!" Then he was back to Marc. "It's my game, but I'm doing it all wrong, right?"

"I didn't say that, Alex. I simply said that I don't think you have to take Gerritt on his terms."

Alex threw up his hands, but Jackie cut in smoothly, smiling kindly to ease the sting of her words. "Aren't you being a little naive, Marc? This isn't a class on ethics where you can debate what ought to happen. This is the real world."

"You'd better believe it!" Alex said, jabbing his finger at Marc. "Sometimes what ought to be and what you'd like to be gets bulldozed under by what is. Sometimes you have no choice."

"I guess that's where we differ. I think there's always a choice."

Chapter Fifteen

The pull out of Redlands, up and over Beaumont Pass, is not particularly dramatic, but enough that the thunderous roar of the six diesel locomotives shattered the quiet before dawn of the late January morning. A hundred and twenty-six cars were strung out over a mile behind the engines in a serpentine trail of black and silver, glinting dully in the moonlight. Formed the previous day in the sprawling Southern Pacific yards at Colton, every car was loaded to capacity. Even with eighteen thousand horsepower pulling it up the grade, the speed had dropped to less than twenty miles an hour.

Two men lying flat in the brush alongside the track felt the train before they heard it. A powerful, throbbing vibration pulsed through the ground. Both men were nearly invisible, even in the light of the half moon. Their faces were blackened, and dark caps and clothes covered everything else. The smaller of the two men came up into a low crouch. He was motionless for almost a full minute, then gave a low grunt of satisfaction. Three quarters of a mile away the swinging beam of the lead locomotive had rounded the hill.

The second man pulled a walkie talkie up. Though they were several miles from the nearest dwelling, he still spoke in a low murmur, and he spoke in Hebrew. "We've got it in sight. Is this the one?"

The radio crackled softly. "Affirmative. We have visual confirmation on the engine number."

The radio was clipped onto a belt. Canvas bags set to one side were lifted and quickly tied to the belts as well. There was a quick, last minute check of equipment. Gloves were pulled on. Then they moved deeper into cover as the first rays of the engine's searchlight caught the tips of the sagebrush.

They let all six engines lumber past them, the deafening roar and stench of diesel fuel filling the sagebrush and the air. Only after the engines had passed did they come up, peering at the box cars towering over them, both of them counting as the cars rocked slowly past. The thirty-fifth car was the first of a whole string of flatcars carrying truck-trailers piggy back. Still they didn't move.

"Forty-six!" the lead man yelled suddenly. "Let's go."

They were up and running. Twenty miles an hour seems pitifully slow for a moving train, but for a running man it can be fatally fast. The smaller man grabbed the steel ladder and swung up. His partner missed the car behind, nearly stumbled, caught himself, then dropped back slightly. He looked over his shoulder, gave a sudden burst of speed and swung up onto a flat car two back from the first man.

He was still hunched over gasping for breath when the first jumped the gap between the swaying cars and ran to his side.

"You okay?"

"I'm fine. Let's go."

The second man reached in his bag and pulled out a powerful flashlight.

"If I counted right, this is car fifty-three or fifty-four. We want sixty-one."

They moved swiftly down each flat car, leaping the gaps between cars easily. They started checking registration numbers on the truck trailers on the sixth car back and found what they were looking for three more beyond that.

Each knew exactly what to do. They circled the trailer working swiftly. Small globs of plastic explosive were slapped around the half-inch steel eyelets where the chains holding the trailer were snubbed down tight. Bolt cutters snapped the locks on the back of the trailer, and the doors were swung open to bang free. A small sledge hammer battered away the chocks beneath the wheels.

"Ready?" They had moved one full car away. The smaller man held two wires and a square battery. The second man grabbed onto a rail and leaned far out, peering forward into the night.

"All clear!"

The wires touched the terminals on the top of the battery. There were four flashes and a muffled explosion. Both men darted back to the trailer. The chains were swinging loose now, doing a slow dance in rhythm to the swaying of the train.

"Let's go!"

They moved to one side, watching ahead. The first man's arm raised up to point. "There's the crossing!" They turned their heads so the flashing red semaphores would not destroy their night vision. As it passed, they jerked back around. A pair of headlights, back fifty or so meters from the crossing, flicked on, then off again.

The man in the rear tapped the other on the shoulder. "Watch yourself."

Canvas bags were dropped over the side, then they leaped, one after the other, out into the night.

Some fifteen minutes later, as the engineer passed the point where Highway One Eleven leaves Interstate Ten and angles off toward Palm Springs, he had all hundred and twenty-six cars over the top of the pass and pushing at his back. He laid on the whistle as they rocketed past a crossing at close to seventy miles an hour. The first of the engines laid into the sharp curve that turned the line into the long, flat run to Indio. One after another the cars behind followed suit.

As car sixty neared the curve, the chains on the trailers snapped tight with a sharp crack. But the sixty-first trailer had no such restraint. There was a screech of metal as the prop beneath the front of the trailer tore loose. Forty thousand pounds of trailer and cargo careened sideways, then hurtled off the flat car. Six tamarisk trees lining the track, planted to hold back the eternally blowing sands of the desert, were sheared off like twigs beneath the blades of a power mower. The thin aluminum shell of the trailer exploded, and as the nose of the trailer hit the earth, boxes and crates flew in every direction.

The caboose flashed by the clouds of dust and the shattered truck a few seconds later. There was a quick impression of a startled face at the window, followed almost instantly by the shriek of metal against metal as a thousand steel wheels locked against brake shoes and the mile-long monster fought to bring itself to a halt.

The wind off the pass quickly cleared the dust and the fine layer of sand particles from above the wreckage. In the moonlight the carnage was everywhere. Here and there, amid the smashed boxes, which carried the red and white circular logo of Gerritt Industries, small cloth bags could be seen. Some had split open, and a fine white powder trickled out to mingle with the sands of the Mojave Desert.

Rod Bigelow came out of the diner next to the truck stop in Tucamcari, New Mexico. He stopped for a moment, took a deep breath of the frosty morning air, then headed for the line of eighteen wheelers. He popped a piece of chewing gum in his mouth, considering the day ahead. He could easily make Tulsa by nightfall, maybe even push on to Springfield. Then the run on into St. Louis would be an easy half day.

He came around the cab of his White Freightliner, whistling softly. He had started it idling before he went in for the shower and breakfast, and it was ready to roll. But his whistling died instantly as he saw the man waiting at the door of his cab. He stopped, wary, but before he could move, someone stepped in quickly behind him, and he felt a sharp jab against his neck.

"We don't want to hurt you. Get in."

As they climbed up and into the cab, the muzzle of the pistol was kept firmly against the back of Bigelow's neck. He slid over beneath the wheel, and the man climbed up into the sleeper behind him. The second man moved without haste across the parking lot to a blue Ford sedan.

"Just follow him."

Bigelow licked his lips. He had heard too many stories across the country. Truckers disappearing, cargos hijacked. "Hey, man. I don't want no trouble. Just tell me what you want."

"You've got nothing to do with this," the voice behind him said easily. There was an unmistakeable foreign accent. "You just happened to draw the truck carrying what we're after. Just stay cool, and you'll be on your way in an hour."

The sedan turned off the Interstate twenty-three miles out of town, taking a small two-lane highway headed south toward nowhere. Again Bigelow felt a sudden clutch of fear. His jaws worked rapidly, chewing the stale piece of gum like it was the one thing that could pull him through this safely.

Ten miles down the road, the blue Ford pulled off the road into a wide graveled turnout. Bigelow's heart fell. They hadn't passed a single car going either direction.

"See that tree over there?"

Bigelow's head turned, feeling the pistol move with him.

"Just lean against that tree and keep looking south. Do that, and we'll be out of here before you know it." The cold pressure against his neck was gone.

Bigelow climbed down, wanting to turn around to get a clearer look at the man with the gun, but he didn't dare. He moved swiftly to the tree and leaned into it. There was a murmur of voices then a sharp snap, followed by the creak of doors opening. He sneaked a quick look beneath one arm. A large carton hurtled out and hit the ground with a crash.

"Keep your eyes away from the truck!"

Bigelow's head snapped around, and he concentrated on the horizon with studied intensity.

There was a second crash, and then a third. He heard the

tearing of cardboard, footsteps, something heavy being tipped, then all fell quiet. He strained to hear, fought the temptation to look again, cursed his impulse to drive on to Tucumcari instead of stopping in Albuquerque last night as he had first intended.

Suddenly, car doors slammed. The engine of the Ford roared, and Bigelow spun around as the car fishtailed across the gravel, hit the pavement with a screech, and disappeared rapidly toward the north.

The trucker swore, darted to the cab of his truck, and grabbed the CB. Then, suddenly curious, he set the microphone down and walked around to the back of his trailer.

They had ripped open three cartons, all bearing the markings of Gerritt Industries. Boxes of small appliances lay scattered on the gravel. He started to turn, then spun back around, pushing one of the smaller boxes with his foot. The top had been torn open and inside, packed around a hand mixer, were three long, cloth bags. Each had been slashed open. White powder had spilled out onto the gravel. Bigelow knelt down, touched the tip of one finger to his tongue, touched it to the powder, then brought it back to his tongue.

He gave a low whistle, swore again, and darted around to grab the CB microphone.

It was late that same night that a soft knock sounded on Nathan Shoshani's apartment door in Los Angeles. Surprised, he walked over and looked through the peep hole. There was a soft exclamation, part surprise, part exasperation. He unlocked the door, opened it, and stepped back. "Hello, Papa."

Yaacov nodded, sweeping off his black felt hat. "I'm sorry to be so late, but . . ." He left it unsaid, and came inside.

"I just got home a little while ago." He waved in the direction of the table, covered with dishes. "I still have some fish and some chilled wine. Would you like something?"

"No. Thank you." There was a gentle smile as he looked around the apartment, most of which was in the same state as the kitchen. "Sarah should visit you for a week, maybe?"

Nathan nearly flared, then realized he was tired. His father was only trying to make conversation. "Come in, Papa. Sit down."

"I cannot stay." The hat was twirling round and round in his hands.

"What is it?"

"I read the reports this evening."

With a sigh, Nathan sat down on the couch. "Please, sit down."

His father nodded absently and took a chair across from him.

"Let's get it over with."

"What if that trailer truck had come off the train in a city or at a busy crossing? People could have been killed."

There was a deep intake of air, then a long exhale, as Nathan fought for patience. "Papa, we chose that train because we knew it would be crossing the desert early in the morning. And we knew exactly where that track curved and how fast the train would be going. We did not leave it to chance."

"And the truck driver in New Mexico? What if he had tried to resist?"

Nathan threw up his hands. "What if? What if? You can spend your life asking what if? The point is we ran two very tightly planned operations today and had perfect success with both. Because of our little 'accidents,' the police called in the federal narcotics people. They found drugs in six other shipments coming from Gerritt's plant in Hawthorne. I just came from Gerritt's house. He had four visitors tonight. All of them are federal agents."

"And so you violate the law to gain success?"

Nathan slammed his fist against the couch. "Do you want the Saudis to have the planes?"

"Expediency, always expediency. You violated the law!"

"Abraham told the Egyptians that Sarah was his sister in order to save his life. Wasn't that expediency?"

Now it was Yaacov who flared. "So my son quotes me from

139

the Bible now? My son, who hasn't read Torah in ten years? My son who can't be bothered with morning prayer, or synagogue?" He looked up at the ceiling. "Oi! And he uses Torah to justify crime."

Nathan shook his head wearily. "Papa. The point is, we have brought Gerritt into a dangerous position. Not only is he under investigation, but he will also have to account to the men who put up the money for him."

"You think you will stop Gerritt in that way?" Yaacov cried angrily. "He did not know what those men in his plant were doing. He did not want to know. They can prove nothing to convict him. And Mr. Andrew Hadlow will not be hurt either. You are like a horsefly buzzing around the horse. You may sting him slightly, but he will flick the tail and shoo you away. For that you break the law and risk innocent people's lives."

Nathan stood, too tired to fight. "It's time for us both to go to bed, Papa." He started for the door, then turned back slowly. "Gondor called the Deputy Director today. You will be asked to turn over the running of the informant in Gerritt Industries to us. And the radar engineer. You will have to leave him to us as well."

Yaacov stood also, the fire gone out in him as well. "Yes, your Moshe Gondor called me to gloat. You think I refuse to turn them over to you just to be difficult, don't you?"

"I—"

"Don't you? And yet you and Moshe both know that one of the primary rules of intelligence is to protect your sources. If you switch controls too early, the rabbit will flee."

"You could help us make the transfer. You are not part of the operating team."

Yaacov moved past his son and opened the door. "I am now."

Nathan's head came up. "What do you mean?"

"I'm afraid I pulled rank on your Moshe Gondor. I called the Prime Minister and explained why I have not turned these two men over to you. He agrees that things are still too sensitive to risk losing them. Along about now, Gondor should be receiving a telephone call. You will be ordered to leave Wuthrich strictly to me. Also, Mr. Taggart, the engineer."

He put on his hat and opened the door, ignoring the look on his son's face. "*Erev tov, Nahtan,*" he murmured in Hebrew, and left.

Chapter Sixteen

It was one of those cases where people were watching people who were watching people who were watching people. The first watcher was Jacqueline Ashby. She stood next to Marc in a small circle standing in the family room of the Barclay home. Her eyes never left his face as he told the story of his first experience riding a camel when he was in the Peace Corps. He had the whole group rocking with laughter.

Valerie Robertson sat in a chair across the room, sipping a glass of ginger ale. The cocktail party swirled around her. People would smile down at her politely, and she would return the smiles. But she was watcher number two, and she was watching Jacqueline Ashby. The story was hilarious, and she found herself smiling at Marc as he told it. But primarily her focus was on Jackie. Elegant, beautiful, charming Jackie. Jackie, whose eyes were sparkling with delight as she watched Marc talk. Jackie, who would lay her hand on Marc's arm when she laughed, letting it linger there for a moment or two.

Valerie looked down into her glass, chiding herself for her pettiness. Marc was not encouraging Jackie in any way. In fact, he was so caught up in the telling of the story, he seemed unaware of either her touch or the rapt attention she was giving him. Valerie looked away as Marc finished and Jackie slipped her arm through his. The chiding of herself had not helped in the least.

The third watcher was Ardith Barclay. She had brought out another tray of canapes and had started to transfer them to the dishes on the table when her eyes lifted and caught the expression on Valerie's face. Ardith turned slightly to see what Valerie was staring at. Her expression softened as she looked back in time to see the quick frown and the averted head.

She finished quickly, set the tray aside, then moved over to Valerie. "Did you know that I hate these parties?" she asked with a smile.

Valerie looked up, then smiled. "They must be a tremendous amount of work for you. How often do you have to do this?"

The older woman shrugged. "Much of what Alex does takes place in informal settings like this. So I do it. But I'm much happier with a book and some classical music."

"Well, you'd never notice it," Valerie said warmly. "You're always such a gracious hostess."

Ardith was pleased, knowing it was said sincerely. "Thank you."

"Can I help you do something?"

For a moment, Ardith started to shake her head, then remembered the expression she had seen. "Well, I was going to get some more drink stirred up for the punch bowl."

Valerie was up. "Then let me do it. I'd love to be doing something."

Suddenly Marc was at her side. "You'd love to be doing what?"

Valerie turned in surprise. "I was going to help Ardith fix some more drink."

Marc took her elbow. "Good idea. I'll help too."

Over Marc's shoulder both Valerie and Ardith saw the sudden narrowing of Jackie's eyes as she saw Marc take Valerie's arm. She turned away quickly and walked over to join another group. Ardith felt a certain sadness, for she thought a great deal of her husband's secretary, but then she smiled up at Marc. "I shouldn't really let the guests do this, but Janet's in the kitchen. She can show you what needs to be done."

As they moved off, Ardith watched them go, her face thoughtful. At that point, Alex, who had been the fourth

143

watcher through it all, disengaged himself from the couple he was with and joined his wife.

"Sweet couple," he commented.

She cocked her head with a serious expression. "Them or us?"

He slipped his arm around her waist. "Well, you know we are. I was thinking of them." He watched Marc and Valerie through the door of the kitchen getting instructions from the maid. "I'm not as hopeful as I was for Jackie anymore. Those two seem to be getting pretty serious. But Valerie is a sweet girl."

"I'm sure she would be flattered to hear you say that."

"What's that supposed to mean?"

"You know that I think a lot of Jackie. But Valerie is more than a sweet girl, Alex. She's a lovely woman in her own right."

"Of course. I didn't mean otherwise."

"She's better for Marc than Jackie."

He gave her a sharp look. "And when did you come to that conclusion?"

She ignored that. "How is Marc working out for you?"

"Terrific! He keeps surprising me." He paused, frowning slightly. "He tends to be a little naive about some things, and he certainly speaks his mind now."

"But?"

"But he is also quick to learn and shrewd at sensing what needs to happen. I don't know, Ardy. He's an unusual young man with some real promise. I'm finding myself more and more impressed with him."

"Maybe that's not so good."

That really took him back, and he turned so he could look at her fully. "What do you mean by that?"

"Marc's been with you almost a month now. You're working him pretty hard."

"No more than me!" he retorted. "Or Derek and Jackie, for that matter."

"Derek and Jackie don't have two little boys at home who need a father."

"Ardith, what has gotten into you? You've never given a hoot who I hired or what I did with them."

She didn't look at him, just finally shook her head. "Don't burn him out, Alex. Not this one. Okay?"

She left him staring after her as she crossed back over to the table, picked up the tray, and headed for the kitchen.

Marc kissed Valerie, then sat back, fingering the wheel of the Volkswagen. They had driven home from the party in Palos Verdes with long lapses of silence. Now Marc was again quiet, his thoughts far away from her.

She watched him for a minute. "What?" she asked softly, noting the sudden creasing of his eyebrows.

"Alex is going to have us work tomorrow again."

"I know." She turned to look out the window. "I heard him telling Jackie."

"Look, I'm sorry, Valerie. This is the fourth Saturday in a row, but Derek is back from Jakarta and needs to report. And this delegation of Saudis coming to Washington on the fourteenth is critical. I've never seen Alex so nervous."

"I know." She turned back. "Mom's got an all-day meeting downtown tomorrow, but I can take Brett to soccer. And then I'll go with them to the party at the church."

"I should be home by four. Couldn't we go after that?"

She shook her head. "My Aunt Edna is coming over in the evening. And the party only goes until dark."

Marc's face fell. "That's right." He took a quick breath. "Valerie, once we get this Saudi deal put together, things should lighten up."

She reached out and took his hand. "You don't have to justify anything to me. It's the boys that will be disappointed."

"I see," he said soberly. "Just the boys?"

She sighed. "You know I will too. I was looking forward to being with you."

"Look, let's plan on something for Monday night. We have to

be to Edwards Air Force Base by nine o'clock for the demonstration of the prototype, but it shouldn't take more than an hour or two. I think I can be home by three or four. Let's take the boys out to McDonald's, then go to a movie."

"That sounds fun. And that will help ease tomorrow."

He moved back over to her, and she laid her head on his shoulder. For several moments they were both quiet, then she looked up at him. He was looking out the window, seeing nothing.

"Tell me what you're thinking," she said softly.

He glanced at her quickly, then turned back. "I was thinking about Alex Barclay."

"What about him?"

"Remember what you said about him, that he always seems to want people to know how much money he spends on things?"

"Yes."

"I used to think that was what made him tick. The money."

"And now?"

"It's not the money. That's just a nice side benefit. It's the deal."

"What do you mean, it's the deal?"

"To Alex, the deal is everything. There's something about putting it together, through all the challenges, with all the risks. It's what drives him."

"I think I know what you mean."

He kissed her, then pulled her close, burying his face in her hair. "And do you know what is scary?"

"What?"

"I'm starting to know exactly how he feels."

When the doorbell rang, Quinn Gerritt looked up in surprise. After the party at Barclay's, Jessica had gone straight to bed, but he had stayed up to pore over the papers on the prototype. Jessica stirred, then turned over as he put down the book. "Who's that?" she mumbled.

146

He shook his head, glancing at the clock on the lamp table. It was nearly midnight. "I don't know."

As he stood, Jessica came fully awake. "Quinn, be careful."

He laughed that off. "Maybe it's a burglar. I'll take a gun down and see what he's got. We could use the cash."

But in spite of his outward amusement, Gerritt padded through the massive living room without turning on the lights. At the intercom system, he stopped and pushed a button, just as the bell rang again, more insistently. "Yes? Who is it?"

"Gerritt, this is Arthur Hadlow."

As Gerritt ushered the small, dark man into the living room, there were no apologies for the hour, no inquiries as to whether he had been asleep. He sat down on the couch, watching as Gerritt turned on two lamps.

"Can I get you something to drink?"

"No."

Gerritt shrugged and took a chair facing Hadlow.

"You know why I'm here."

There was the briefest of nods. "I thought you might come."

"You caused us a significant loss yesterday, Mr. Gerritt."

"I caused you a loss!" Gerritt blurted. "What about my loss? I had four federal narcotics agents here last night."

"Can they tie the hiring of those two men directly to you?"

Gerritt shook his head. Only he and Theodore Wuthrich knew about that, and Ted wouldn't implicate himself. "You should have told me why you wanted those men hired." There was an accusing note in his voice.

"As I remember," Hadlow said dryly, "you didn't ask." He leaned forward, his voice still bland and expressionless. "On Monday morning, you will find that all of your funds are frozen."

"What!"

"When you get things in your organization under control, let us know."

"You can't do that! We show the prototype Monday. We'll need massive amounts of cash to take it into production."

Hadlow could have been discussing gardening across the back fence for all the emotion that was in his voice. "My people are not happy, Mr. Gerritt. You cost us two men and eleven million dollars in street value."

"How do you know it's my problem? Somebody in your organization could be the leak."

Hadlow shook his head. "If it were somebody in my organization, the cocaine would have disappeared. It wouldn't have been spread out in the sunshine for the whole world to see. Someone is trying to destroy you, Mr. Gerritt, not get our coke."

"But why?"

"When you find that out, the funds will be released."

"But you'll ruin everything!" Gerritt's voice had gone hoarse. "We've got to go into production this week, or lose the deal."

Hadlow stood. "If you were to seek other financing, we would assume you weren't happy with our relationship."

Gerritt sagged back, a sickness twisting his stomach. Hadlow moved to the door, then stopped and turned. "There is one other possible option."

Gerritt shot up. "What?"

"We have a replacement shipment waiting in Columbia. If we could find someone who could bring that into the country . . ." He lifted his palms.

"Are you crazy? The feds are watching me now."

"A man with a large organization and many contacts would be foolish to do everything himself. Especially if he has high exposure."

He opened the door and stepped out. "Good night, Mr. Gerritt. My best to your wife."

Chapter Seventeen

The sky in the Los Angeles basin had been gray and overcast when Alex, Derek, Jackie, and Marc had left the city, but by the time they reached Edwards Air Force Base, the high deserts were cloudless, and the air temperature stood at a delightful sixty-nine degrees.

General Taylor Canning and a staff sergeant walked them into the pilot's ready room, and two men in g-suits and full flight gear stood. The nearest saluted the general smartly. Canning returned the salute, and then turned to the group behind him. "This is Colonel John Talbot, our senior test pilot." Talbot nodded. He was just starting to gray and had a quick, easy smile.

Canning motioned to the other man. He was slightly shorter than Talbot, with olive skin, a neatly trimmed mustache, and jet-black eyes. "And this is General Sayeed Amani, commander-in-chief of the Royal Saudi Air Force."

Marc gave a deferent nod of his head. *"Is-salaam 'alaykum."*

The dark eyes widened slightly. *"Wa-'alaykum is-salaam."*

"Ahlan Wa Sahlan. Welcome to America."

General Amani smiled, white teeth flashing. "Your Arabic is excellent."

"As is your English."

Canning watched the interchange, pleased. "This is Marc Jeppson, one of the associates in Barclay Enterprises. And Derek Parkin, another associate." They shook hands quickly, then Canning touched Jackie's elbow. "And this is Jacqueline Ashby, Mr. Barclay's executive secretary."

Amani and Talbot both inclined their heads, the admiration clearly evident in their eyes.

"And this is Alex Barclay, president of Barclay Enterprises."

Alex nodded and gripped the other's hand firmly. "General. Welcome." He also shook hands with Talbot. "Colonel."

Talbot turned to Alex. "I understand you're going to be flying back seat with the general."

That brought both Derek and Marc up in surprise. Alex just nodded. "Yes. I'd like to see what this little system of Gerritt's can do."

Canning turned. "Sergeant. Show Mr. Barclay where to suit up. Then have someone bring him out to the flight line."

"Yes, sir."

They moved off, but at the door Alex turned back. "Jackie? Tell Gerritt I want to talk to him after the test. In fact, you can take the car back. He and I can have lunch."

"Okay."

Canning watched them go, then turned back to the group. "You can watch everything from the control center. We've got it wired so you'll see exactly what Colonel Talbot and General Amani are seeing on their HUD's—Head Up Displays—as well as what ground control is feeding into the system. They'll be flying what is known as a DACT mission first. That's an acronym for Dissimilar Air-to-Air Combat Tactics. It means Colonel Talbot will be flying a different plane—the McDonnell Douglas F-15— and will be the 'enemy.'"

Talbot grinned. "I'll be simulating a Soviet pilot in a MIG-22. Since the Barracuda is the test platform for the new radar system, the General will fly that, see what he can do." The good-natured challenge in the Colonel's voice was obvious.

Amani laughed softly. "This system had better be good. Colonel Talbot has a reputation for being one of the most cunning 'enemy pilots' in California."

"After we test the air-to-air capability," Canning went on,

"we'll try some ground targets. The people at China Lake Naval Weapons Center up north of here have laid out some simulations that will test the mettle of the system."

The sergeant returned. "About three more minutes, sir."

Amani and Talbot picked up their helmets.

"*Fi Aman Illah,*" Marc said, as the two men turned and started for the flight line.

The Saudi turned back, obviously pleased. "I shall need it. *Shukran.* Thank you."

As they started down the corridor, Jackie increased her pace and fell in step with Marc. "What did you say to him?"

"Well, really it's just 'good-bye,' but literally, it means 'Go in the care of God.'"

"If the colonel's as good as they say, he'll need some help," Jackie said.

"He is," Canning said. "Talbot's the best."

Marc turned to Jackie. "I didn't know Alex was going to fly with them."

"Oh, yes. When they granted permission, he was elated."

Canning gave a short laugh. "Didn't you know? Alex flew jets in Korea. He maintains a commercial pilot's license."

"We lease a Lear Jet," Jackie added with a nod. "Alex flies it most of the time."

Marc just shook his head, and they fell silent as the sergeant led them through the long corridors. Alex Barclay was full of surprises. How much more was there to the man that he had yet to learn?

"Radar confirms a definite kill." The triumph in the voice of General Amani was evident even through the overhead speaker in the control center.

"That's a roger here, too, General," the fire control officer for the tracking center said into his headset. "That's four for four."

"Very impressive," came the laconic voice of Talbot. "I'm glad this system belongs to us."

"Gerritt?" It was Alex's voice.

Gerritt stepped forward. "This is Gerritt."

"You've got yourself a winner!"

A faint smile pulled at the corners of his mouth. But it was Jonathan Taggart who was beaming. Marc leaned over and shook his hand. "Congratulations, Mr. Taggart, you've designed yourself quite a system there."

"Thank you."

"Control? This is Dolly Leader." Talbot was all business again now. "Do you wish further DACT testing?"

The fire control officer turned. "What do you say, Mr. Gerritt?"

Again Alex's voice was heard. "What do *you* say, General Amani?"

The deeper voice of the Saudi came in almost instantly. "I'm satisfied. Let's proceed."

"Roger, Dolly Leader. China Lake? Do you copy?"

A new voice came on. "We copy, Edwards Control. We're standing by."

"Proceed with phase two, Dolly Leader."

As the speaker continued to chatter, Taggart stepped to the large computer display in front of them and picked up a pointer. The glass prism display feeding from the ground control at China Lake showed the images of more than a dozen vehicles. Four were tanks; two were missile launchers; the rest, trucks and jeeps. A jagged line ran clear across the screen in front of the vehicles.

"A jet fighter has two basic functions," Taggart began, "airborne intercept and ground attack. You've just seen what the system provides in the air intercept category—complete flight envelope coverage, head-on attack capability, fire-and-forget missile control for up to eight missiles simultaneously. The VSM-430 system has included some significant improvements in this area, but basically that is all they are, improvements. Most current radar systems have all those capabilities. We have just refined them somewhat."

He tapped the screen with the pointer. "But what is significantly different is that we have combined the air intercept potential with greatly enhanced ground attack capability. The technology utilizes what we call a millimeter wave radar seeker. This has the ability to seek out, detect, identify, lock on, and track tactical military ground vehicles."

The tip of the pointer touched the images one after another. "Here you see a typical ground emplacement." The pointer traced the jagged line. "They are in excellent concealment behind a steep ridge. You'll also note they have surface-to-air missile capability." He tapped the two long, slender shapes pointing into the sky.

"The SAMs are, of course, controlled by ground radar systems that can lock on and track high-performance jet aircraft. Thus, the attack capability of the fighter is jeopardized by the counterattack capability of the ground forces."

"Approaching China Lake Naval Testing Center." Talbot's voice interrupted the lecture, causing Taggart to talk faster.

"Millimeter wave radar technology is not new, nor is the hardware we've developed dramatically different. What we have accomplished with the VSM-430 is an innovative use of the data gathered by the seeker device. And we've greatly enhanced its ability to screen out other ground clutter that can deceive the radar tracker."

"Edwards Control, this is China Lake Ground. We're patching in the video of the target area."

Marc and the others swung around to where six television monitors were mounted in a bank against one wall. Vivid color pictures sprang to life, each focusing from a different angle or distance on the various vehicles. The same images that were just computer graphics on the prism screen now leaped into life. The tanks were dug in with camouflage netting. The missile carriers were in similar concealment. A jagged and rocky ridge, bare of vegetation, could be seen in the background.

"China Lake Control, this is Dolly Leader. We are on station and standing by."

"Roger, Dolly Leader. Proceed to designated coordinates and stand by for your approach run."

"Proceeding as directed, China Lake." Then Talbot's voice became less official. "General, I'll stay right in your six o'clock until you launch the missiles and break off. I'll follow the missiles in to the target area with the cameras rolling."

"Roger, Dolly Leader."

The designer of the VSM-430 turned to an airman. "Could we get the radar display from General Amani's plane on one of the monitors please?" Almost instantly the far screen went blank, then filled with the images from the radar tracker. Taggart turned back to those watching the demonstration and pulled up a chart that had line drawings of tanks and a missile carrier nestled behind a ridge. The simplified outline of a jet fighter was in the far upper left corner, with arrows diagramming the attack run. He swung up the pointer again.

"What you are about to watch is drawn in this diagram. General Amani's F-22"—he tapped the drawing of the fighter—"carries two rocket pods under the belly. Each pod holds twelve WASP antitank missiles. The VSM-430 system allows the pilot to make his attack run with no inherent restraints on either the approach or escape. In other words, there are no required altitudes, speeds or other limiting factors. It allows for a low-altitude, high-speed launch from a large standoff range. That means he can launch and break off before he even enters the range of the SAMs."

"And the radar can tell the difference between a truck and a missile launcher from that distance?" Marc asked, a little bit awestruck.

"That's what we're hoping," Gerritt said shortly.

"Hope nothing, Mr. Gerritt!" Taggart snapped. "That is exactly what the VSM-430 will do, and with great precision. The system sets target priorities and specific attack modes prior to launch. Once launched, the missiles will climb or descend to search altitude. Digital processors in each missile control all flight- and target-search functions. Once the target is selected, the missiles lock on, arm a contact fuse, and make a diving attack on the selected target."

"China Lake?" Jackie had raised her hand, but Talbot's voice over the speaker caused it to drop again. "This is Dolly Leader. We are at our coordinates."

"Begin your attack run, Dolly Leader."

"Watch the tracking screen," Taggart said excitedly. "I'll tell you when to watch the video."

"Roger, China Control. Okay, General. Here we go."

"Dolly One to Dolly Leader." The general's voice was calm, unhurried. "We'll take it in the weeds. Here we go."

"In the weeds means on the deck," General Canning supplied. "Very low altitude."

A radar tracker behind them sang out, "Dolly One is dropping fast. He's under a thousand feet. Speed, Mach one point four."

"One point four!" Gerritt said. "He's not holding her back."

"Good," Canning said in a clipped voice. "Go for it, General!"

"I have the ground targets on my HUD," Amani said.

The monitor duplicating Amani's Head Up Display in the cockpit now showed the images of the vehicles hidden behind a ridge several miles in front of him.

"No joy."

"That means he has no visual sighting of his target," Canning said.

"Lock on." Amani's voice was almost like that of a computer's now. "Six seconds to launch."

The tension in the room heightened visibly.

"Missiles away! Jinking hard."

"He's breaking off the attack, pulling away sharply." Even Canning was getting a little excited.

"Six missiles on their way."

"Watch the target! Watch the target!" Taggart yelled, but it was unnecessary instruction. Every eye had already swung to the other video monitors.

"There they come!" Gerritt shouted, pointing to the wide angle shot. Six smoking trails were coming in with blurring speed.

And then it was too fast to see it all. There was no sound with the video, but the effect was almost as dramatic. A black streak homed in on the lead tank. The turret disappeared in a flash and a burst of smoke. On another screen, Marc saw one of the dummy missiles on the SAM launcher hurtle end over end as the WASP from the F-22 hit it just above the tracks. And then the five screens were filled with fire and black smoke.

"Dolly One, this is China Control. We have confirmed hits on six out of six of the designated targets."

Jonathan Taggart leaped into the air. "All right!"

Chapter Eighteen

"So that's it. I think all the essential elements are in place now." Though a few hours had passed since the test, Alex was still so keyed up from the success of the testing and from his luncheon with Gerritt that he couldn't stay seated for more than a minute or two. He was up again, and Marc, Jackie, and Derek had to swing around in their chairs to watch him as he paced. "I haven't dared hope we could really pull this off, but I think we can. I think we can."

"General Amani seemed very impressed," Marc offered. "I think what he said afterward went far beyond mere Arab courtesy."

"I do too." Alex beamed happily. "And Gerritt is absolutely elated."

"He should be," Jackie said. "This will put Gerritt Industries back into the black and then some."

"Yes, and then some is right. So we have our radar system. Derek's got the Jakarta deal on its feet. I think we're ready to lay out the whole thing for the Saudis. Amani will go back and confer with the powers that be."

"Will he be part of the delegation that comes to Washington?" Marc asked.

"Yes. Which will be in our favor." Alex moved back around behind his desk and sat down, giving them each a long searching look. "I really think we're going to do it!" he said again in wonder. Then suddenly, he was all business. "Well, we got an early start this morning. Let's call it a day, and hit the ground running tomorrow."

They stood. "Thanks again to all you," Alex said. "I think we've got ourselves one heck of a team."

They started to move to the door, and Alex stood up to see them out. Jackie was first with Marc and Derek right behind her. As Marc passed, Alex touched his arm. "Oh, Marc. Could I see you for a minute or two?"

"Sure." Surprised, he moved back to his chair.

"Jackie, if you'll lock up the front, Marc and I will go out the back and do the warehouse."

"Okay."

Alex shut the door, which was the second surprise. Alex rarely shut his office door. "Well," he began as he pulled a chair alongside Marc and sat down, "what did you think of that little demonstration today?"

"As the kids would say, it was awesome. Almost disturbingly so."

"Why disturbingly so?"

Marc considered that. "When I was teenager, I got to sit in an M-60 tank once. I can remember thinking, 'Now, if I had to go to war, this is where I'd like to be.'" He took a breath. "Watching those tanks go up today, with absolutely no chance to defend themselves . . . I don't know, it was kind of sobering."

"Yes. This high-tech warfare is really something."

Marc was looking at the derringers on the wall, absently. "Does it ever bother you?"

"What?"

"Knowing you're dealing in death."

For one second, anger flashed, then suddenly Alex threw back his head and laughed. "Marc, do you know what the difference between you and Derek is?"

Now it was Marc that was caught off guard. "No, what?"

"Well, in the first place, the ethics of arms sales would never have crossed his mind. And second, if it had, he would never have asked that question of his boss, who makes a living selling arms."

Marc's face flushed. "I didn't mean it that way."

"Yes, you did. And I find that quality in you admirable. Sometimes it startles me, and often I don't agree with you, but I know I can trust what you're saying." Suddenly he sobered. "And that's not true of very many people I know."

"I . . ."

Alex cut in. "No, I mean it. It's what I like most about you. I believe in integrity, but you also know that part of me is a crafty old coyote that watches every word he says."

He went on quickly, cutting off Marc's attempts to extricate himself. "Don't change, Marc. It's one of your strongest qualities." He paused, still chuckling to himself. "But, to answer the question . . ."

He sat back, the lines around his mouth and eyes deepening. "Well, believe it or not, I have thought a great deal about that. But before I answer it, let me tell you a little bit more about middlemen."

Marc nodded.

"Basically, there are three kinds of people who become marriage brokers in this business. First, there are the flakes. The money to be made attracts them by the hundreds. They take the money from investors, promising returns of one or two thousand percent. Then they fly to Europe, move into five-hundred-dollar-a-night suites and blow everything."

"I can believe that."

"The second kind is in it for profit. This guy can deliver, because he's got high-level entry. Probably the most famous of this type is Adnan Khashoggi. He is a multibillionaire, and it was commissions from arms sales that got him started. Over a ten-year period, Khashoggi made commissions of six hundred fifteen million dollars. That's over sixty million a year!"

Marc gave a low whistle. Sixty million a year! Alex had never said what this deal would involve, but if it was even half that . . . No wonder he was elated with the day's success.

"But there is a third kind of broker," Alex was saying. "These are not as common, but they are the most important. Most are not highly visible like Khashoggi. The world never knows who they are. They just stay in the background making things happen. Of course, they're interested in making a profit too. But it's more than that. Theirs is a different kind of commitment. Take the Jakarta deal I told you about. At the time I handled the oil for the general, I actually lost money. It was a royal pain in the neck and took about three months of solid hard work. Most brokers would have said, 'No way!' So why did Barclay Enterprises take it on?"

It was not a rhetorical question, and Alex was watching him closely, waiting. Marc considered the question. "Well, I suppose partly to create leverage."

"Yes, that too, but there was something else as well. The president of the United States called me personally. Officially the government didn't want to get involved, but neither did they just want to turn their backs on the Indonesian request. So Alex Barclay got a call directly from the president of the United States. And why did he accept the job when he knew it would be a royal pain? Because believe it or not, he's a bit of a patriotic slob, and when the president directly asks him to help, he does it."

Marc studied Alex's face as he talked. He suspected that maybe the idealism didn't burn quite as brightly as Alex was saying. He also sensed that the profits weren't quite as unimportant as he was suggesting, but there was no question: idealism was there, and the profit motive was secondary. It was an insight into Alex that was revealing.

"Now," Alex went on. "You think I've forgotten your question in all this rambling, but I haven't. You question whether the sale of arms is ethically acceptable. I answer that with a resounding yes! Let me give you an actual example. I can't tell you the details, but recently I was asked, again by the president, to arrange for the sale of some rifles to anti-Communist guerillas in a country that has already gone over to Communism. Because of political sensitivities, the sale was officially illegal. I could have been sent to prison, ruined both financially and professionally. I made less than ten thousand dollars on the deal. That doesn't even cover my overhead. So again I ask, why should I take on a lousy deal like that?"

"To help the country?" Marc supplied.

"Yes. But in this case there was more. I happen to strongly believe that if we don't stop the Communists, eventually they will take over the world. So I sold the guerillas sixteen thousand rifles and four million rounds of ammunition. That's a lot of death, Marc. A lot of death!"

"And yet, what it prevents . . . "

"Exactly. Arms can lead to war and death, but they can also prevent it. Take the very case we're working on. As you saw today, the F-22 Barracuda is the ultimate killing machine. If we sell it to Saudi Arabia, we have greatly enhanced their ability to destroy."

"Yes."

"But you know the Ayatollah Khomeini would give up his beard and mustache if he could overthrow the Saudis and take control of the Islamic holy places. He also knows one of his defecting pilots got in right over the oil fields a few months ago without being stopped. So he starts thinking about the odds. If he tries that, we're talking about an Arab blood bath in the Middle East."

"At least! Maybe World War III."

"And what effect would sixty F-22s have on his temptation to launch an attack against the Saudis?"

"I think the word is deterrent."

"And who is going to bring about all this peace in the Middle East and prevent World War III?"

"Alex Barclay," Marc laughed.

"No, no! Not just me. It's Alex the marriage broker and his conscience, Marc Jeppson. Not bad, huh?"

Marc threw up his hands. "All right, all right. I should have learned in that lecture at UCLA not to try and debate with you."

Alex leaned back, savoring the moment, and the warmth and bonding between them was palpable. He was lost in his thoughts for several moments, and Marc waited, still a little puzzled about the whole conversation. Finally Alex took a deep breath and leaned forward again. "The big question is Mr. Quinn Gerritt."

"But you said you felt really good about your meeting with him today."

"I did, but like I said the other day, he's got success in his pocket. Now we've got to find a way to bind him to us and us alone."

Marc hesitated for a moment, then took a quick breath. "I have some ideas about that. I was going to talk them over with Jackie, then make some recommendations."

"Let's hear them."

"Well," Marc smiled, a little sheepishly. "I've been trying to think like Alex Barclay. How do we get leverage with Gerritt?"

"Ah," Alex sighed, feigning sadness, but actually deeply pleased, "the corrupting influence of the coyote. But Quinn Gerritt is a challenge. If I'm the coyote, then he's the wolf."

"Good comparison. Anyway, I asked myself, what is it Quinn Gerritt needs? And what can we do to fill those needs?"

"Astute question. What did you come up with?"

"This may seem pretty far out, okay?"

"Okay."

"For the longest time I couldn't come up with anything. Then it hit me like a hammer. What does Quinn Gerritt want and need more than anything else right now?"

For a moment Alex was silent, then suddenly his eyes widened.

Marc nodded. "Money!"

".And lots of it!"

"The VSM-430 will probably turn that around, but not for a while, right?" Alex nodded, and Marc went on slowly, thinking it through as he went. "Our problem is, we offer him a chance for a major sale of his system, but it's not an exclusive chance. Another middleman could come in and set up the sale of the Barracuda's using Gerritt's system too."

"Exactly! And that's what's giving me ulcers."

"So what if you make him an offer no else does."

Alex slouched down deeper into his chair. "Go on."

"Remember what you said about the five percenters? Well, make Quinn Gerritt one of them. Suppose you make him a limited partner, or a consultant, or whatever. Pay him five or ten percent of whatever you make. That could be several million dollars. But it would not be part of the profits made by Gerritt Industries, which will have to go toward paying off his rather substantial debts. We would pay the commission directly to him as one of our sales agents."

"That's a hefty cut," Alex said, but he was not so much protesting as thinking out loud.

"True, but you set him up as our agent on one condition: you become his agent for the sale of the radar system to other users. He's got to pay those commissions to someone. So he's out nothing. I'll bet you could recoup whatever you pay him in the long run."

For almost a full sixty seconds Alex just watched him through half-closed eyes, his face impassive, his body motionless. Finally he stirred, then rose from his chair and walked over to the driftwood sculpture and the cougar. He stroked the fur absently. Suddenly he turned around. "It will work. I know it will. We're talking Gerritt's language."

"And everything is perfectly legal and above board."

"There is one other thing that will help. Gerritt needs a favor."

"What?"

Alex glanced at his watch. "Actually, that was what I wanted to talk to you about. Can you spend some time tonight? This is pretty urgent."

Marc's face fell. "I promised the boys we'd go to a movie."

Alex frowned. "I don't mean kind of urgent, Marc. This is very urgent. It could be the key to turning Gerritt. Look, if it would help, I could call your boys, explain things."

Marc hesitated, then shook his head slowly. "No, I'll call. How long will we be?"

Alex pursed his lips, then moved behind his desk and sat down. "Probably late. Let me ask you one question first, then I'll go lock up the warehouse while you call home."

"All right."

"I can't remember who it was now, but someone told me that you speak fluent Spanish. Is that right?"

Valerie's voice was flat and lifeless. "I knew when the phone rang that it would be you."

"Val, I know I promised. I tried to tell Alex, but he's got to get back with Gerritt tonight. And a lot has to happen in the meantime."

"Gerritt! What has he got to do it?"

"His copper supplier in South America just fell through. That puts his whole appliance division in jeopardy. He wants us to try and pull it out of the fire."

"That's fine, Marc. The boys are all dressed, but I'm sure they'll understand."

"Valerie!"

"Well, what am I supposed to say? That's wonderful, Marc? I'm happy that Alex has such confidence in you?"

"Val, this could tie everything together. I don't know what else to do. It's got to happen tonight."

She sighed. "I know, Marc. I'm sorry. I didn't mean to pressure you. I'll take the boys."

There was a long pause. Then, "There's one other thing."

"What?"

"Alex wants me to go to Bogotá for him."

"Oh." Now the silence became heavy over the phone.

"We leave Wednesday morning. He needs someone who can speak Spanish."

"We?" she said slowly.

"Yes, he wants Jackie and me to go. He's got to be in Washington."

He paused, but she remained silent.

"It should only be for three or four days."

"So you'll be gone Saturday?"

"Probably, why?"

"Well, I'm sure you have more important things to worry about, but you did promise Brett you would be here to help him with the pinewood derby for Cub Scouts."

"Oh, that's right!"

She waited, her mouth drawn into a tight line.

His voice was so soft she almost didn't hear him. "I totally forgot."

"You'll have to tell Brett. He's been so excited about this."

"Valerie, I . . . " His voice trailed off. "I'm sorry."

She softened a little, but her voice still held a touch of hurt. "It's not me you need to apologize to."

"Yes, it is. You too."

"I'd better go, Marc. We're going to miss the show."

"Valerie, I really am sorry."

"I know." There was a brief pause. "Good-bye, Marc."

She hung up the phone and turned. Her mother was watching her, shaking her head slowly and sadly.

Chapter Nineteen

Although Bogotá, Colombia, is only three hundred fifty miles north of the equator, it sits on a high plateau at more than eighty five hundred feet above sea level. At one forty A.M. on the tenth of February, the air was crisp and cool, almost biting. It had rained earlier, and the tires of the Toyota pickup hissed softly on the wet concrete as the pickup pulled up to one of the back gates of Bogotá's international airport. The headlights of the truck went out.

The guard came out slowly from the small booth, holding a paper in his hand. He checked the license plate, then the paper, then moved to the gate and pulled it open. As the truck drove away, he slid the gate shut again and went back inside to his magazine and heater. He had been paid handsomely to do just that and nothing else.

The tie-down area for the small private planes was not very well lighted, but through the magnification of the binoculars, the silver gray Lear Jet, registered to Barclay Industries of El Segundo, California, clearly stood out. So did the blue Toyota pickup as it pulled up alongside the sleek aircraft.

The man with the binoculars was a hundred yards away, sitting in the driver's seat of an unmarked panel truck. He leaned forward, suddenly intent. Without lowering the glasses, the man reached across and elbowed his partner, who was slouched down and snoring softly. He was instantly awake.

"Look!" his partner said softly in Hebrew, and handed him the binoculars.

Moshe Gondor was angry and made little effort to hide it. "Come on, Mr. Shoshani! What do you think those two men were doing in Barclay's aircraft at two in the morning? Stocking the refrigerator?"

Yaacov's head came up slowly, his eyes glittering. "You have an annoying habit of hearing only what you want to hear, Mr. Gondor."

Gondor blinked in surprise, as did Nathan and Yehuda Gor. To this point, Yaacov had maintained the sleepy, good-natured, old-man demeanor, nodding slowly, speaking in a patient voice. Nathan knew very well it was not the real Yaacov Shoshani, but the sudden attack caught Gondor completely off guard.

"I think the two men were removing panels inside the cabin and hiding fifty or sixty kilos of cocaine," Yaacov went on. "I have no question about that."

They were in Gondor's apartment in Westwood, which was now the team's operating headquarters. Gondor had received the report from Colombia around four A.M. California time and had called a meeting for six. He had not called the older Shoshani, but somehow he had arrived just the same. That, and the interrupted sleep, left Gondor's temper short.

"Then what are you saying, Mr. Shoshani?" he snapped.

"Marc Jeppson and Jacqueline Ashby had no idea that those drugs were being planted on their plane. You know that as well as I do."

"Did I ever once suggest I thought they were in on this?"

"Yet all you do is to call the federal drug people and give them an anonymous tip about a planeload of cocaine."

"I have one interest and one interest only, and that is to halt Barclay's deal with the Arabs."

"But these two are innocent! This could ruin their lives. All you have to do is tell the Americans what we know. It is Gerritt we're after, not these two."

"You know that we have the strictest instructions not to give the Americans the slightest indication Israel is tampering with this affair."

"Jeppson and Ashby are one half of Barclay's total team," Nathan broke in. "Eventually they will be proven innocent. But if they are arrested, it can only help our cause by delaying Barclay."

Yaacov turned on his son. "You too, Nathan? You would play with people's lives like players on a chess board?"

"I don't like it," Nathan answered, "but if you're in the game, you take the knocks along with everyone else. And Jeppson and the woman are in the game."

"Your Sarah works for a businessman, just like Jacqueline Ashby. Suppose it were her, Nathan, who had been used as an innocent dupe. Would you be so calloused then?"

Gondor had just lit a cigarette and taken a deep draw on it. He grabbed it from his mouth and waved it angrily in Yaacov's face. "Nathan's wife is not involved in the sale of jet planes to our enemies!"

Yehuda Gor, who had remained silent through it all, now spoke. "Gerritt is the key, and he acts increasingly desperate. If the Americans do arrest these two people of Barclay's, they will tell them that they were in Colombia for Gerritt. Gerritt is already under suspicion. It is Gerritt we are after."

Gondor nodded firmly. "Barclay is the only agent close to a contract with the Saudis. If we can delay this, that will give our people in Washington more time to overturn the sale once and for all."

"And in the meantime our clandestine actions ruin the lives of people."

"By this weekend the listening devices will be planted in Gerritt's home and office. We'll also have Barclay and his people covered. If we can find a way to put the drug people directly onto Gerritt, we will. Knowing the drug people as we do, they'll likely let Jeppson and Ashby walk away from the plane anyway, put a watch on it, and see who comes to get the drugs."

"You hope," Yaacov said softly.

"Yes, we hope!" Gondor shot back. "We have no desire to see these two hurt, but we have our instructions. The sale of the planes must be stopped. And right now, it is up to us to do so."

By six o'clock that same evening, the large hall was full. Almost everyone had crowded around the four highly polished, parallel wooden tracks that were set up near the stage. There were half again as many children as adults, and many of the boys were in Cub Scout uniforms. The sound level was deafening, and the official starter for the pinewood derby races had to shout to make himself heard. "All right, let's hold it down a little. We're ready for the next heat."

His plea had no effect on the noise, and with a shrug he looked at the clipboard, then yelled: "Darrin Warner, Kevin McInnes, Seth Anthony, and Brad Armstrong." He looked around. Three boys in Cub Scout uniforms stepped forward with their fathers. "Darrin? Where's Darrin Warner?"

A muffled shout from behind the crowd was heard, and another boy in a blue uniform pushed his way to the front, with his father trailing close behind. As they passed Brett Jeppson, he saw that Darrin's car had been shaped into a sleek, Corvette-looking shape. It was painted metallic blue and had neatly stenciled, white racing stripes. As Darrin reached the track and handed his car up to the starter, Brett saw the underside of the car. Just in front of the rear wheels there was a round hole that gleamed with the dull sheen of metal.

Valerie saw the look on his face. "What's the matter, Brett?"

"See, I told you. Did you see Darrin's car?"

She shook her head.

"They drilled a plug out of the bottom and filled it with lead. You gotta do that, Valerie."

Valerie put her arm around his shoulder. "Brett, we didn't have anything to drill the hole with. And we don't have any lead."

He pulled away from her. "It doesn't have to be lead. It can be pennies or nails. Anything to give it weight."

"I'm sorry, Brett. I'm sure it will be all right."

Mary touched his shoulder. "Your car looks very nice, Brett."

He glanced down in disgust. The back end was still square, the nose rounded like the front end of a lawn mower. The only paint they had been able to find was the pale yellow latex his father had used to paint the bathroom some months before. Even the numbered decals weren't on exactly straight. Brett dropped the car closer to his leg, so no one could see it.

The official had the four cars now and set them on the track. They rolled forward to rest against the starting gate. Brett edged forward to see better.

"We'll run two heats. The winner of the first heat will drop out for the second. The winner of both the first and second races will compete in the final 'Race of Champions.'"

There was a momentary drop in the noise level, then a shout went up as the starting gate was raised and the cars shot down the incline. Darrin Warner's blue Corvette flashed ahead, hit the level stretch, and coasted to a stop a good two feet further out than any other car.

Seth Anthony's car easily won the second heat. There was brief applause, and then the man consulted his clipboard again. "Josh Morgan, Brian Keebler, Brett Jeppson, and Kyle Carver. Let's have the next four."

Mary pushed gently on his back. "Okay, Brett. That's you."

He held his ground, dropping his head. "I don't want to."

Valerie leaned over, putting her arm around him. "Brett. It's your turn. You've got to go up there."

"I don't want to race."

At that moment, Matt pushed in to stand beside his brother. "Brett, they called you."

"Brett Jeppson," the official called again, more loudly this time.

Valerie gave him a little shove, and he took a deep breath,

then stepped forward to hand the car to the offical without looking up.

"Same rules apply to this heat. The two winners will compete in the finals."

The starting gate went up. Brian Keebler's car shot forward into the lead, the other three close behind. To that point, Brett's yellow lawnmower was holding its own, but as it hit the bottom of the incline, where the track leveled out, the front end was too long, or perhaps the wheel base was not aligned properly, because the car bottomed, jerking the front end to one side. The left wheel hit the side of the track, and the car ground to a halt several feet short of where the others had come to rest.

Brett felt a hand on his shoulder. "What happened, Son?" An adult den leader was at his side. He picked up the car, spun the wheels. "Hey, don't worry about it. Let's try it again."

"Okay," cried the starter, "bring them up here for the second heat. Winner drops out."

Brett felt his face burning with shame, and he didn't even look up this time as he heard the quick hush, the sudden shout, and the sound of the cars on the track. As several disappointed "ohs" sounded in his ear, he looked up, then blindly reached out and grabbed his car. It had been an instant replay of the first heat, and his car sat far back from all the rest.

"It's all right, Brett," Matt said loyally as he rejoined Mary and Valerie. Brett just stared straight ahead, dimly aware of the looks of the other boys and the murmured attempts at comfort from the adults. Valerie, close to tears herself, put her hand on his shoulder. He jerked away.

"Brett," Mary said kindly. "It's all right."

He whirled around, tears streaming down his face. "It's not all right!" he whispered fiercely, aware that others were turning to watch. He ducked his head and pushed through the crowd.

"Brett!" Mary called after him.

"It's all right, Mom," Valerie said. "I'll go talk to him. You stay with Matt."

She found him in the back hallway, shoulder against a doorway, staring at the floor. "Brett," she called softly, moving slowly toward him.

"Leave me alone!"

She stopped a few feet away. "Brett, I'm sorry it didn't go better. Let's see if we can fix it. I'm sure they'll let you try again."

He spun around. "I won't race this stupid car!" he shouted. "It's a dumb, stupid car!"

Valerie flinched. "Brett, that's not true. It didn't win, but—"

"I didn't want to come! You made me come!"

Suddenly he whirled and threw the car against the wall with all his might. It shattered, spraying pieces across the hall. A black plastic wheel bounced twice, then rolled several feet down the polished tile.

"I didn't want to come with you!" he shouted, crying openly now. "I wanted to come with my dad!"

It was nearly eleven-thirty when Marc slipped through the garage door and into the kitchen. As he set down his bag, he noticed the light in the living room was on. Surprised, he crossed softly to the entryway and into the other room. Valerie was sitting on the couch watching him steadily.

"Hi," he said. "I didn't expect to find you here."

"I told Mother to go home and sleep."

He came over and sat down beside her with a weary sigh. "I'm sorry we're so late. We left early this morning so we could get back, but then we had to wait two hours to refuel in Guatemala, and it took almost three hours to clear customs in L.A."

"How was the trip?" Her voice held little life.

"Kind of odd, actually. We got the job done, but it wasn't nearly as critical as Gerritt led us to believe. But it went well."

"Good. I'm glad you're home." She stood. "I'd better go."

He looked at her closely. "Let me run you home."

"It's only a couple of blocks. I'll be fine."

"Don't be silly. I'm not going to have you walking out this late at night. Come on."

He stopped for a moment, fumbled in his bag, then led her out to the car. The Volkswagen was gone now, but in its place Marc had a Chrysler LeBaron convertible, another company car from Barclay Enterprises. He was glad, for he didn't want bucket seats between them tonight.

Valerie was quiet the short distance to her home, and when he pulled into the driveway and turned off the engine, she immediately reached for the door handle. "Thank you, Marc. Good night."

"Valerie!"

She didn't open the door, but neither did she turn around. "What?"

"What's the matter?"

"Nothing. It's late. I'm very tired."

"I know. I really am sorry we were so late." He reached in his jacket pocket and pulled out a small box. "I brought you something from Bogotá."

Finally she turned around to look at him. He reached across and set the box in her lap. She took it without looking up, unwrapped it slowly.

"It's a tiny replica of one of the artifacts in the Gold Museum in Bogotá."

"It's very lovely."

He sat back. "Well, I'm glad you're able to contain yourself."

Her head snapped up, and for several seconds her eyes locked with his, bitterness tightening her mouth. Then she suddenly shook her head and looked away, but not before he saw the glint of tears in her eyes and the quiver in her lips. He moved over and touched her arm. "Valerie? What is the matter?"

She shook her head. "I need to go in, Marc."

He took her hand. "No, not yet. I want to know what's wrong."

She turned then, brushing angrily at the streaks on her cheeks. "You don't even know?" she cried.

He blinked in surprise. "No. What?"

"You think about it a minute."

He did, then suddenly understanding dawned. "Is it Jackie?"

Valerie just stared, then laughed bitterly. "Did you have a wonderful trip together?"

"Valerie," he said softly, "I don't have any say in who Alex sends. Jackie is a charming and lovely woman, but—"

"It isn't Jackie," she snapped. "So don't worry about trying to explain things to me."

"Then what?" he demanded in exasperation.

She whirled, her eyes blazing. "Why don't you ask how Brett did in the pinewood derby? Did that even cross your mind?"

Marc felt like he had been kicked in the stomach. "Oh!" He put one fist to his forehead and banged it softly. "I totally forgot."

"Good! That will make Brett feel better."

"Valerie, I'm sorry. I was thinking about it this morning, hoping we'd get home in time, but the day has been such a nightmare since. I . . ."

She was looking out the window, fingering the necklace and tiny gold figurine without looking at them.

"How did he do?"

"He got the 'Safe Driver' award."

"The 'Safe Driver' award? Is that good or bad?"

She opened the door, suddenly very weary. "Why don't you ask him tomorrow, Marc? That is assuming you're going to be home long enough to see him."

He sat back, took a deep breath, and started running his hands slowly over the steering wheel.

Valerie started to get out, stopped, and turned back half around. She sniffed back the tears. "I'm sorry, Marc. I know you're tired too. Let's just talk about it tomorrow."

Marc nodded, not looking at her. She raised one hand, as though to touch him, hesitated, then let it drop again. "Thank you for the necklace, Marc." Then she shut the door and walked slowly into the house.

•　　　•　　　•　　　•　　　•

Marc tiptoed quietly into Matt's bedroom, picked up a dump truck, and set it on the toy chest. One hand was tucked under the tangled blond hair, the other was entwined in the small blanket that was Matt's inseparable sleeping partner. Marc pulled the covers up and placed them across his son's shoulders softly, then tiptoed out again.

The moment he entered Brett's room, he knew his older son was still awake. There was no movement, but the thin body was rigid, the breathing shallow and controlled. Marc walked over and sat down on the edge of the bed.

"Hello, Son."

There was neither answer nor movement.

"Valerie told me about the derby."

Silence.

"I tried to get back. We left real early this morning from South America, but we had several delays in flight. I'm sorry, Brett. I know I promised I'd be there."

Still nothing.

"Who had the fastest car?"

The shoulders moved slightly, and Marc waited. Finally, "Darrin Warner."

"What did they give him?"

"A gold trophy."

"Valerie said you got an award."

No answer.

"Can I see it."

"I threw it away."

Marc sighed wearily. "I understand." He laid his hand on Brett's shoulder. "One of those they give just to try and make a guy feel good."

There was an almost imperceptible nod.

"Look, Brett. I know that saying I'm sorry isn't much better than getting the 'Safe Driver' award, but I am, Brett. I'm going to make it up, too."

He stopped, but again Brett did not respond, and after several seconds he went on. "I've been gone a lot. It's been hard on you guys. But I'm going to change that."

"Does that mean you won't be going to Washington, D.C., on Monday?"

Marc winced. "No, Brett. That's one I just can't get out of. But when I get back, we'll go over to Puddingstone Reservoir and do some fishing. How would that be?"

"You can take Matt. I don't want to go fishing."

"What?" Marc teased. "Is this Brett Jeppson I hear talking? The Brett Jeppson who can cast a line farther than any kid I know?"

There was no answer.

"Brett?"

Nothing.

"I brought you and Matt something from South America."

Nothing.

"We'll talk about it in the morning, okay?"

Nothing.

Marc stood, leaned over, and kissed his son on the cheek. "Good night, Brett."

He waited for a moment, and when the silence became too heavy to bear, he turned and walked slowly out of the room.

Chapter Twenty

The old man standing next to Marc in the Smithsonian's National Air and Space Museum gazed upward, where the fragile "Wright Flyer," the plane flown by Orville and Wilbur Wright, hung a short distance from the sleek, rocket-like X-15, the first aircraft to fly at six times the speed of sound.

"The old and the new, the new and the old," the man said in a heavily accented voice. "It seems impossible that they come from the same generation."

Marc nodded, taking note of the man for the first time. He was lean, but with a kind face and wise eyes. His hair was completely white, and he wore a slightly rumpled black suit and a black Homburg hat.

"My grandfather was born in 1903," Marc said. "His life spans the first powered flight to the space shuttle."

"He is still alive then?"

"Yes. He still runs his farm in a little town in Utah."

"Utah," the older man smiled. "I was there not long ago. In Salt Lake City." He held out his hand. "My name is Yaacov Shoshani. I am from Jerusalem." He smiled, with a sparkle in his eye. "That is in Israel."

Marc laughed. "I know." He shook the other's hand, which had a surprisingly firm grip. "My name is Marc Jeppson."

"I am very pleased to make your acquaintance, Mr. Jeppson. So you are from Utah?"

"No, I live in California now."

"And you came to Washington to see the sights? Is that how you say it?"

Marc nodded. "Yes, but actually, I'm here on business. Or at least I'm supposed to be." He frowned. "I'm here with three associates, and we're waiting for some meetings to be arranged."

Yaacov tapped his chest with understanding. "I too."

Marc raised an eyebrow, curious but not wanting to pry.

"While I was waiting, I decided to see some of the famous Smithsonian Museum." Yaacov rolled his eyes. "I did not realize the famous museum is a whole city of museums."

Marc laughed. "I know."

"Well." Yaacov looked up one last time at the two aircrafts suspended in midair. "It was delightful to meet you, Mr. Jeppson. Have a good visit to Washington."

"You too, Mr. Shoshani. Good luck to you with your business."

He laughed. "I will need it. *Mazel tof* to you as well."

"Mazel tof and shalom," Marc returned with a wave.

The old man shuffled off, peering up at one of the space capsules.

There was a soft knock on the hotel door. Marc was sprawled out on the bed studying a map of the downtown area, trying to decide where he would go tomorrow if they had another day free. He went to the door, still carrying the map.

It was Jackie, still dressed in the skirt and blouse she was wearing when they had all had breakfast together that morning. "Hi," he said, noticing the weariness around her eyes.

"Hello, Marc. Can you stick your head out a minute while I get Derek? I have a message from Alex."

"Sure." He followed her out into the hallway and watched as she tapped on the next door. When it opened, Derek stepped out, smiling broadly. Then he saw Marc, and the smile faded.

"No luck, yet," she said. "The earliest we can meet with the delegation is tomorrow afternoon."

Marc groaned inwardly. That meant at least another two days here. It just kept mounting up, and every call home was getting to be more and more difficult.

"Alex would like you to be on hand from noon on, just in case, but it will probably be tomorrow evening."

"But nothing tonight?" Derek asked.

"No."

"A classmate of mine from Harvard lives in Alexandria. He wants me to spend the evening with him. If that's okay, I'll call him."

Jackie nodded. "Fine." As Derek went back inside, she turned to Marc. "And what did you spend the day doing?" She pulled a face. "Not sitting in your room drinking, like Derek, I hope."

That surprised him a little.

"You mean you couldn't smell him?" she said in disgust, waving her hand in front of her face.

Marc looked thoughtfully at the door. Derek had had several drinks the night before at dinner, to the point that Alex had finally made a comment. Derek had not liked being called down in front of Marc and Jackie and had bristled. Marc shrugged and turned back to her. "So what about tonight? Do you and Alex want to do dinner again?"

"Alex will be at the State Department until late." There was a fractional hesitation. "Does the offer hold if it's only me?"

Just as he had noticed her hesitation, she noticed his, even though he tried to recover quickly. "Of course," he said. "What time?"

She reached up and rubbed the back of her neck. "Well, I feel like I've been in a gym all day. I'd like to shower and rest for a bit. How about eight-thirty?"

"Eight-thirty is fine. I'll knock for you."

The phone rang in Quinn Gerritt's suite in the Marriott Hotel, and Jessica swept across the room in her satin evening gown to pick it up. "Yes?"

She listened a moment, then called into the bedroom, where

Quinn was putting on a black tie and tails. "Quinn, a Mr. Derek Parkins is downstairs."

He came out, putting on his coat. "Tell him to come up."

She frowned but spoke quickly into the phone. When she hung up, he pulled her into his arms.

"You look lovely, Jessie. As usual." He kissed her lightly, so as not to smear her lipstick, then pulled two tickets from inside his jacket. They were for box seats at the Kennedy Center where *Aida* was playing. He handed her one of them. "Give me five minutes. Then go. I'll catch a cab."

There was a momentary flash of annoyance, then resignation. "Try to hurry, Quinn."

"I didn't think he was coming until we got back." He turned to check his bow tie in the mirror. "But this is important. I'll catch up."

She gave him a quick wave and swept out the door.

Jackie opened the door to her room a few inches, then leaned against it, looking up at Marc. "Thanks for the company. It was a delightful dinner. The thought of eating alone was pretty depressing."

"Thank you. It's easy to be gallant when Alex is picking up the tab."

"Would you like to come in for a few minutes? I think I could find a Seven-up or something equally daring."

He laughed, seeing through her fear of rebuff, then took a deep breath. "Jackie," he started, then stopped and took another breath.

"Don't tell me," she said lightly, trying to keep the hurt out of her eyes. "You want to go to your own room and get smashed on caffeine-free Coke, right? Or," she rushed on, before he could respond, "are you going to be what Alex calls your brutally honest self?"

He put a finger to her lips and shushed her gently. "Just listen, will you?"

Now it was she who took the deep breath, her eyes not meeting his. "I'm listening."

"Jackie, until this year I hadn't gone out but once or twice in the two years since my wife died. I don't think that was caused by any deep and sustained mourning. Within a few months I had come to accept the fact that Lynette was gone. But I was satisfied being alone, just me and the boys."

Finally she looked up, watching him closely as he sought the right words. "Remember that night when you and Alex found Valerie and me in the parking lot? That was my first date with her. I felt like a sixteen-year-old teenager again—awkward, stumbling over my words, feeling like a fool. And then ironically, on that same night I met you for the first time."

Her face softened, and she smiled up at him. "I remember. You and that ridiculous little VW."

"You got out of that Mercedes convertible, and I just stared. You were so striking. So lovely."

Her lips parted softly, and her eyes were suddenly moist as she sensed what was coming.

"And that night on the beach." He shook his head. "I came so close to taking you in my arms and kissing you."

"I wanted you to," she said in a half whisper.

"I know. And I wanted to. But I guess, even then, somehow I knew that as much as I admired you and was attracted to you, we are two different kinds of people. You're a class act all the way. Me, I'm just a farm boy from Willard who strayed into the big city."

"I have no complaints."

He shook his head slowly. "That doesn't change what is."

"And Valerie is part of what is." It wasn't a question.

"Well, I thought she was. I'm having trouble convincing her."

Jackie's chin came up. "Then tell her to get out of the way."

"I can't."

She looked away. He took her chin and brought her gently back to face him. "But it's important to me that you understand this. My turning from you makes you no less charming, no less beautiful, no less a remarkable woman in my eyes, Jacqueline Ashby."

The tears welled up and trickled down her cheeks. He brushed at them with the back of one finger. "I mean that."

She suddenly reached up, brought his head down, and gently kissed him. He could feel her lips quivering, and then she pulled away and buried her face against his chest. "I'm sorry, Marc. I'll go watch "M.A.S.H." reruns and be all right in an hour or so."

Marc nodded, stroking her hair, not knowing what to say.

"Well, well!"

The insolent sneer in the voice spun both Marc and Jackie around with a jerk. Derek Parkin was standing unsteadily in the hallway of the hotel, leering at them. "Isn't this a cozy little scene?"

Jackie touched Marc's cheek quickly and opened the door. "Good-bye, Marc," she whispered and slipped inside.

Marc turned and pushed past Derek without speaking.

"Valerie would love to know how you spend your time while you're on the road."

Marc fished for his room key without turning around. "Derek, why don't you just go to bed?"

"So the fair-haired boy does have some flaws, after all." He shook his head, clucking his tongue. "And all this time, Alex thought his little goody-goody was above reproach."

"Good-night, Derek."

"Well, you're not the only game in town anymore, buddy!" he shouted as Marc stepped inside and shut the door. "You and Alex will find out that I have a contribution to make too."

It was nearly seven-thirty the next morning when Alex stopped by at the breakfast booth. Marc looked up and started to slide over, but he shook his head quickly. "No, I'm on my way to the State Department." He looked at the breakfast menu longingly, then pulled away. "Jackie and I are going to hit it again this morning. But hopefully, by noon, we'll have some word."

"Good. I'm ready."

At that moment, Jackie entered the hotel coffee shop, spied them, and came over. "Good morning, Alex." She looked at Marc quickly, gave him a fleeting, wistful smile. "Good morning, Marc."

"Good morning, Jackie."

"Hi, Jackie," Alex said. "I was just going to ask Marc what's on his agenda today."

Marc lifted his shoulders and let them drop again. "I feel like a knickknack in a bathroom. I may add to the decor, but I'm not terribly useful."

"You just hang on until tonight. Then you'll earn every penny I'm paying you."

"Well, anyway, I thought I'd go down to the kennel and check on the dog again, then—"

"No need to—I presented it to the prince last night."

"You did?"

"Yes." He clapped Marc on the shoulder. "You earned your money right there. Russ Whitaker, the Undersecretary of State, called afterward and just went on and on." His voice dropped to mimic that of Whitaker's: "'A purebred Saluki hound? The famed hunting dog of the Bedouin princes? It was perfect, Alex, just perfect. How did you ever think of that?' I modestly admitted that we had given it quite a bit of thought."

"I'm glad."

Alex looked at his watch. "Well, Jackie, we've got to get out of here. I'll bring the car up and meet you out front."

"Okay." She watched him go, then slipped in across from Marc. "I wanted to apologize for being such a boob last night."

He reached across quickly and took her hand. "Look. You and I have to work together for some time to come. We have two choices. We can go around feeling awkward and averting our faces every time we meet, or we can take it as it is, and be friends and associates—a thing that I would like very much."

She squeezed his hand back. "I would like that too."

"Good."

She rose. "I'll try and call around noon."

"Okay, I'll be in my room."

As she started away, he called after her, "By the way, Derek called and apologized this morning."

"I know. He called me too. I think he felt pretty foolish."

Marc shook his head. "I don't know about him."

Jackie went stern. "Look. You and he have to work together for some time to come. You have two choices. You can go around averting your faces, or I can talk Alex into firing him."

Marc laughed. "Now that's a tough choice."

She sobered again, and this time it wasn't feigned. "Thanks, Marc." She waved and was gone before he could respond.

Marc picked up the menu and began to study it again. A few moments later, he realized someone had come up to him again. He looked up, then smiled in surprise. It was Yaacov Shoshani, the man he had met in the museum.

"No!" Shoshani said, pointing at him. "You are in this hotel?"

"That's right."

"And still waiting?"

Marc laughed. "Yes, still waiting."

"I too."

"Have you had breakfast yet?"

"No, I was just coming down."

"Then join me. I haven't ordered yet."

Shoshani removed his hat, and slid in the opposite side of the booth. "I would be delighted."

Marc leaned over, picked up his watch from where it lay on the lamp table, looked at it, then turned to Yaacov. "I'm expecting a call anytime. Would you mind if we just ordered lunch from room service?"

Yaacov looked at his own watch. "*Oi vavoi!* I have kept you here talking for two-and-a-half hours. You must have other things to do."

"No, no. Really. I just have to be in the room around noon.

I'd like to continue our talk, unless you have something you must do."

Yaacov shook his craggy head quickly. "No. And this has been very enjoyable. You make a persuasive advocate for the Arab cause."

"And you make a very persuasive advocate for the Jewish cause."

"Ah," he said with a slow smile. "But I am Jewish, and you are not Arab."

"I used to teach a class at Claremont on the Arab-Jewish political situation. I would take the first half of one period and present all the arguments for the Arab side. Before I was through, the students would be so angry at the Israelis for all the injustices they have done to the Palestinians and other Arabs. Then I would take the second half of the class and present all the arguments for the Jewish side. By the time I was done, all of the students would be saying, 'No wonder the Israelis do what they do. It is only right. What's the matter with those Arabs, anyway?'"

Yaacov nodded sadly. "That is what makes the whole situation in the Middle East so difficult. Until the hearts of the people—my people as well as the Arab peoples—are changed, there will be no solutions, no lasting peace."

Marc nodded, then got up and found the room service menu. "Well, what would you like for lunch?"

They spent the next half an hour waiting for and then consuming the food. The conversation stayed light—Marc's early life, Yaacov's pilgrimage to Israel in the early thirties, and half a dozen other topics. As they were finishing, Jackie called to report that the meeting with the Saudis had been set for four o'clock that afternoon.

As they finished their meal and turned to two heaping dishes of strawberry shortcake, Yaacov leaned back. "You seem to be a man who thinks deeply about things, so let me pose for you an interesting question. I too teach at a university—the Hebrew University in Jerusalem. I give this problem to my students in philosophy."

"Okay."

"In World War II, the British, through an incredible intelligence feat, cracked the codes of the German High Command."

"Yes, I remember. They called the whole project 'Ultra' or something like that, as I recall."

"Yes. Very good. So you are familiar with that part of the story. Well, one day the British decoded a transmission intended for the Luftwaffe. They learned that a massive bomber raid had been planned against the city of Coventry, England, on a certain night in the near future. Now Churchill and his military staff were faced with an interesting dilemma. They could warn Coventry and save thousands of lives. But if they did, it could easily tip off—is that how you say it? Tip off?"

"Yes. It would tip off the Germans."

"Exactly. If the Germans suspected that the British had cracked their codes, they would change them. The information the Allies were gaining through Ultra was saving thousands of lives."

He leaned forward, bringing his hands together. "What should you do? Warn Coventry and jeopardize thousands of lives? Or not warn Coventry and jeopardize thousands of lives?"

"Well, I remember what they did do."

"Yes. They chose to protect the secret, and many, many innocent people in Coventry were killed. But I ask you. If it had been up to you, what would you have done?"

Marc grinned. "Do I get some time to think about it?"

Yaacov laughed merrily and pulled the shortcake in front of him. "Only as long as it takes for you to consume this delicious monument to the passions of the flesh."

Marc chuckled, pulled over his own plate, and started to eat, lapsing into deep thought.

Finally, he pushed his plate away. "Okay, I think I am ready."

Yaacov scraped up the last wisp of the whipped cream, licked it off the spoon, and then rubbed his hands in delight. "Then proceed. What would you have done?"

"I would have warned Coventry."

"Why?"

"Because it was the greatest known good. The other choice was based on conjecture and hope. They believed that if they protected the secret, they could save a greater numbers of lives. But that was guesswork. What if the Germans, shortly after they bombed Coventry, learned that their codes had been compromised, and changed them anyway? Then the people of Coventry would have died for nothing."

"But they didn't. Ultra saved many other lives."

"Oh, no," Marc protested. "You're using the vantage point of hindsight now. We know what eventually happened, but the people making the choice could only choose on the basis of what they knew or could project. And I say the known value of the human lives in Coventry should have become the overriding factor in their decision. They knew for sure they could save those lives."

The dark brown eyes in the old leathered face were sparkling with enjoyment. "But when you cannot know the future, you must go on probabilities. If there was a good probability that a greater number of lives could be saved by keeping the secret, that is the way you would have to go."

Marc just shook his head. "No, there is another dimension."

"What other dimension? When you are dealing with the future, what other dimension is there but to balance all the known facts and decide as best you can?"

Marc hedged, suddenly a bit embarrassed.

"Yes? What is this other dimension of which you speak?"

Marc took a deep breath. "Faith."

"Explain!" It was a curt command, but not harsh or critical. Yaacov was watching this young professor with increasing interest.

"It's hard to explain." Marc began tentatively, still formulating the thoughts in his own mind. "If one believes there is a supreme being who concerns himself deeply with the affairs of men, and if he also believes that that being gives men laws and principles that they can use to govern their lives, then those principles become

187

the basis for action. They override desire or wants . . . or probabilities."

"Do you know how the leaders of the British military would have responded to such counsel?"

"Yes. They'd laugh me right out of their map room. They would say I was being ridiculous."

"But you don't think you are being ridiculous?"

"Sure, I do. As ridiculous as marching a horde of Israelites into the Red Sea with the Egyptian army at their backs. The British generals would have laughed Moses right out of their map rooms. I mean the probabilities for success there were absolutely zilch."

Yaacov clapped his hands. "Excellent analogy! Zilch. It is a good word. Go on."

"Same principle applies. You use the laws and principles given to make your decisions. You don't trust solely in your own abilities."

The older man was staring down at his hands now, and Marc sensed a sudden sadness in him. He paused, but when Shoshani did not look up, he finished his line of reasoning. "The British sacrificed the lives of the people of Coventry to save Ultra. But what if they had warned the people, yet the Germans still did not suspect what was wrong. The Ultra secret would have been saved anyway."

Finally, Yaacov looked up, nodding very slowly.

"You want to talk about probabilities. Consider that one, that all those people were sacrificed for nothing."

"Exactly," Yaacov said in a voice so low that Marc had to lean forward to hear him. "And so few of my students could ever see that. So very few." There was a long pause. "Including my own son."

Chapter Twenty-One

Alex and Derek were about eighth or ninth back in the line of people coming off the United Airlines flight from Dulles International. Valerie spotted them at the same time Ardith did. "There they are," Ardith said. She waved, and they both started forward, but Valerie suddenly stopped. Two or three paces behind Alex, she saw Jackie, with Marc at her elbow. He was carrying her overnight case along with his own clothing bag and briefcase.

Valerie looked away quickly, the stab of disappointment like a physical blow. So much for the schoolgirl flutter and quickening pulse, she thought bitterly.

Alex kissed Ardith soundly, then looked past her. "Hi, Valerie."

She moved forward slowly. "Hello, Alex."

Derek nodded curtly to her, then shot a quick glance over his shoulder to follow her eyes. Triumph flashed across his face, but almost instantly it was gone, and he was sullen and impassive once again.

Marc saw her then and smiled at her over the tops of the heads.

"Hello, Valerie," Jackie said quietly, as they came up.

Valerie nodded. "Hello, Jackie."

Marc came to stand next to her and gave her a warm smile. "Hi." He looked around. "Where are Mary and the boys?"

"We called, and they said your plane was going to be an hour late. Matt had already fallen asleep by then, and Brett was close behind, so Mom decided to stay home with them."

"We had heavy snow in Denver. They wouldn't let us take off until it cleared a little."

"That's one thing about California," Alex growled. "By late February, we have spring, while the rest of the country is still having winter."

As they moved toward the exit, a small man with dark eyes and olive skin increased his step. He had come off the same plane but had hung back as Alex's group had paused to greet Ardith and Valerie. Now he moved more quickly to keep up. Suddenly he spotted a tall man with flaming red hair. There was no flicker of recognition, but both timed their pace so that one stepped on the down escalator immediately behind the other.

"Any problems?" Yossi Kettleman asked quietly.

Yitzhak ben Tsur shook his head almost imperceptibly. "No. Does Nathan want us to stay with them?"

"No. He and Gondor are waiting for us in Westwood. They want a strategy session as soon as we can get there."

"So how was the trip?" Ardith asked, as they walked through the tunnel area toward the main terminal and the baggage claim area.

"Tremendous!" Alex fairly bubbled. "Better than I'd hoped." He turned to Valerie. "And this young man right here"—he grabbed Marc's elbow—"was no small part of it. You should have seen him charm that delegation. I mean, it was something to watch. Wasn't it, Jackie?"

She nodded, glancing sideways to catch Valerie's expression. "Yes, it was. Marc made a great difference."

Derek grunted, and his lips pressed into a tight line as Alex chattered on about their experience in Washington. When they reached the baggage carousels, he turned to Alex. "Well," he said shortly. "Good night."

"Oh, Derek," Alex said, turning. "We'll meet tomorrow afternoon to start the plans for next week's session."

Marc had just started to say something to Valerie, but that brought him around sharply. "Alex, tomorrow's Saturday."

"I know, I know. But two weeks from today we've got the final meeting in the Hotel LaRoche. We've got a heck of a lot to do before then."

"I promised I would take my boys to the San Diego Zoo tomorrow."

"Fine. Let's make it four o'clock. That should give you plenty of time and give us all a chance to rest up."

"Fine with me," Derek said quickly.

Valerie turned and looked away as an awkward silence fell on the group. She heard Marc take a deep breath, then she turned back to watch the surrender.

"Alex, between South America, the New York trip, and this one to Washington, I've been gone eleven of the last sixteen days. I need to spend some time with my boys."

There was a quick flash of surprise, then slight irritation. "Look, Marc, I know it's been tough, but it all comes together or falls apart in these next two weeks. We can't—"

"I promised them, Alex. All day tomorrow is their day. I can't go back on that."

Valerie's eyes widened, and Jackie looked surprised too.

Ardith laid her hand on Alex's arm. "And you promised me a little time tomorrow too," she said softly. "Can't it wait until Monday?"

That swung Alex around with real anger on his face, but she didn't flinch, just met his gaze steadily. Suddenly he capitulated. "You're right. We'll all do better with a weekend off. But let's hit it early Monday. Say, six-thirty?" There was a bit of a challenge as he looked at Marc.

"Fine. Thanks Alex."

"Good night," Derek said curtly and strode away.

"Well," Marc said, "All I've got is carry-on luggage, so we'll see you all later." He handed the overnight case to Jackie. "I guess you'll want this."

"Yes, thank you, Marc." There was the slightest pause. "For everything." She turned her head slightly and nodded to Valerie. "Good night, Valerie."

The sadness in her eyes was unmistakable, and it took Valerie back slightly. "Good night, Jackie." She hesitated for a moment, then turned. "Good night, Ardith. Alex."

Marc took her by the elbow, and they moved out the front door of the terminal.

As the three of them waited for the luggage to come onto the carousel, Ardith turned to her husband. "Was Marc as good as you say?"

"Absolutely. In more ways than one. I think we've got Quinn Gerritt nearly in the bag. We go to Switzerland next week to wrap everything up with him. That was all Marc's idea. And with the Saudis, Mark was really something."

Jackie nodded. "He was superb. All the rest of us, even some of the Air Force and State Department people, stood around feeling a little bit awkward. But Marc started in with his Arabic, and in ten minutes you would have thought he was a member of the royal family."

Alex gave his wife a searching look. "While we are on the subject of Marc, what's with you challenging me about tomorrow, Ardith? That's not like you."

She shrugged, her eyes thoughtful. "I was trying to help you save face."

"Me?" he blurted. "You bailed Marc out of a hole, not me."

"He wasn't going to back down, Alex. Even if you had pushed harder."

Alex started to respond, then let it die, thinking about what she had said.

"And what about Derek?" Ardith asked.

"What about him?"

"You hurt him deeply tonight when you were so open in your praise of Marc and didn't say a word about him."

"He ought to be grateful I didn't say anything about him," Alex snapped. "Mr. Derek Parkin did not do a lot to endear himself to me on this trip."

The sudden anger in Alex's voice surprised Ardith, but no

less than the expression of contempt that crossed Jackie's face. "What happened?" she asked.

"I think the proper word is boor," Jackie said. "He was an absolute boor."

"Derek?" she said, disbelieving. "Mr. Harvard himself?"

"First of all, he had been drinking," Alex said. "He wasn't drunk, but you could smell the whiskey on his breath. After all that Marc had told us about the Islamic prohibition against liquor."

"He drank for three solid days in his room," Jackie said in disgust. "He and Marc had a lot of free time, and Derek spent it drinking and sulking."

"That really surprises me," Ardith said.

"I think he knows Marc is outpacing him," Jackie said. "And his overinflated ego finds that hard to accept."

"But it was more than the drinking. The Saudis are men of the world; I don't think that would have bothered them." He took a quick breath. Just talking about it was getting Alex angry all over again. "But he nearly ruined things for us at the reception."

"My goodness," Ardith said, looking back and forth between the two of them. "I think I struck a raw nerve in both of you."

"At least!" Alex retorted, with Jackie nodding vigorously. "Everything we are doing depends on how the Saudis feel about us, okay? Marc had told us again and again that there are things you do and don't do in carrying on a conversation with the Arabs."

"It is considered bad manners to discuss religion, politics, or family affairs with strangers," Jackie explained. "It is in especially poor taste to ask about female members of the family. Care to guess how many of those basic rules Derek violated?" Jackie took a deep breath. "Alex finally sent him back to the hotel. He's been pouting ever since."

Alex picked it up from there. "Marc cautioned us that patience is one of their fundamental rules of social etiquette. To break off a conversation abruptly, no matter how good the reason, or to interrupt and try to change the subject is very rude. The Saudis view impatience or undue haste in conversation as either a sign of bad manners, or worse for us, a lack of confidence. Three different times, Derek broke into the conversation and tried to steer it onto the contract. Three different times!"

His eyes were smouldering with the memory. "The last time, I was watching the crown prince. That's when I sent Derek packing."

"For good?" Ardith asked.

The luggage had started to come onto the carousel now, and Alex turned to watch for their bags. She thought he hadn't heard her question, but finally, without turning, he shook his head. "Not yet. He's drawing up the contracts and all of the paper work. He's too far in to change horses now, but I'll tell you, the minute this is over, he's back on his own."

Ardith fell silent as Alex waved to a porter and started pointing out the pieces of luggage. They followed him out the door to the curb. Ardith handed the porter her keys and explained where the car was parked. As he moved away, Ardith spoke again. "And what about Marc?"

"What about him?"

"Do you send *him* packing when the deal is all completed?"

He turned slowly. "Ardith, I've been bringing in men for fifteen years. Why all of a sudden are you interrogating me on how I deal with them?"

"So you are dumping him?"

"Dumping!" he exploded. "Every man who has worked with me has gone on to better things. Even Derek. He'll use this experience to find something better for himself."

"You call it whatever you want, if it makes you feel better, but I want to know if you plan to dump Marc too."

Jackie was watching Alex and Ardith with some concern. These were the two people she felt closest to in her life. She loved them both deeply, but she had never seen Ardith filled with such quiet determination, and it was striking sparks from Alex.

"And what if I do dump him?" Alex said. "Marc's resilient. He'll be fine."

"It's not Marc I'm worried about."

Alex just stared at her.

"You don't even see it, do you?"

"What?"

"The effect that Marc is having on you."

"The effect he's having on me? I've brought that boy out of the doldrums. He's come alive again. He's having a ball."

"Yes, I know."

"Ardith! I can't believe this is you."

"Alex, you run the business and I don't interfere. But I'm telling you, if you throw Marc away, something he has revived in you is going to die once and for all. And that saddens me. More than I can possibly express."

It had been a warm day in Los Angeles, and though the evening overcast had moved in, the night was still pleasant. As Marc and Valerie got in the Chrysler LeBaron, he turned to her. "Do you mind if we put the top down?"

She looked at him sharply, then shook her head. "No. I brought a sweater if it gets too chilly."

"Good." He punched the buttons, got everything secured, and then drove out of the parking terrace. As they drove along Century Boulevard and out of the airport complex, Marc reached for Valerie's hand and pulled her gently toward him. She came an inch or two, not turning her head.

He laughed softly and pulled again. "I traded in my bucket seats, remember? Come on."

Reluctantly, Valerie slid closer, and accepted without response the arm he put around her shoulders. The silence continued, hers strained, his amused, until he turned south on the San Diego Freeway instead of north. Her head came up. "Where are you going?"

"I know a little seafood place in Long Beach that has terrific steak and lobster."

"Marc! It's almost ten o'clock."

He grinned. "They stay open late on Fridays."

"Marc, really. It's too late."

"It's never too late for steak and lobster."

She took a quick breath, not trying to hide her irritation. It only made him smile more.

"I do have a job now, Marc. I'm really tired tonight."

"Tomorrow's Saturday. You can sleep in before we go to the zoo."

"Marc, please. I'd really rather not."

"I used to date a girl in high school," he mused. "Her dad always insisted that I have her home by ten-forty-five. I thought when I passed thirty, all that would change."

She tried to fight it, but a tiny smile pulled at the corners of her mouth.

"You could tell me that your mother told you to be home early, but knowing your mother, she probably told you not to worry about how late it was."

Valerie laughed in spite of herself. "That's almost a direct quote."

"Then, Val, unless you start to scream, you're on your way to Long Beach."

"Marc, I—"

He lifted a finger to her lips and pressed them gently. "Valerie, before you say anything, let me just talk for a few minutes. Okay?"

She looked up at him, searching his face, and he saw the hurt that still lingered in her eyes.

Taking a deep breath, he plunged in. "Look, I know I am incredibly dense, but not so much so that I don't know what's bothering you. I saw your face when you looked up and saw Jackie and me coming off the plane together."

She looked away, not meeting his probing look.

"Jackie is a beautiful, charming, and very capable woman. I told her that at dinner the other night."

Valerie's hands were twisting together in her lap. He reached out and covered them with his. "I also told her that while I was deeply flattered that she should be interested in me, there was a computer programmer from Colorado whom I had found to be a totally lovely woman and whom I couldn't get out of my mind."

That finally brought her head around.

Marc smiled, somewhat sadly. "I also said that I was making that young woman miserable and that I intended to come home to remedy that situation once and for all."

He laughed at her expression. "What I didn't say to Jackie was that I was scared to death one Valerie Robertson wouldn't give me a second chance to show her I could make some changes in my life."

Valerie's eyes were wide, and her lips parted softly. "I'm a sucker for second chances."

"I'm glad." He pulled her closer, and this time she came clear over to sit next to him, squeezing his hand tightly. "My dad has a favorite saying. I heard it so many times when I was a kid, I used to resent it. Now . . ." He shrugged. "I spent a lot of time thinking about it while I was in Washington."

"What is it?"

"He says, 'If your life is out of order, it's because your priorities are out of order.'"

She nodded, looking up in time to see the line along his jaw tighten.

"There are several things in my life out of order right now."

"Such as?"

"Such as making you the pinewood derby mechanic."

She saw the shame in his eyes, and sudden tears welled up in her own as she realized how much this man meant to her and how really good he was deep inside. She laid her head on his shoulder, not trusting herself to speak.

"Such as making other people take my boys to the movies. Such as working nearly every night and every Saturday for the last two months." There was a long pause. "Such as starting to think that the deal is everything."

"So what do you do about it?"

"Put the priorities back in order."

About twenty miles north, six men were sitting around the living room of Moshe Gondor's apartment. Yitzhak and Yossi had just arrived from the airport. Nathan sat in an easy chair across from Gondor. Yehuda Gor sat crosslegged on the floor, drumming his fingers silently on the carpet. Yaacov Shoshani was in a straight-backed chair facing the others, as though he were the witness facing a hostile jury. The air was heavy with cigarette smoke and tension.

Gondor was shaking his head angrily. "Mr. Shoshani, by now I know the whole lecture by heart, okay? What we are facing here is not a theological problem. We have a sale of sixty of the most advanced fighter planes in the world—with a dramatic new advancement in radar technology—to a country that daily reiterates its undying hatred for what we are and what we stand for. And frankly, your talk of spiritual Zionism and returning to the traditional values of Torah and the law of Moses don't make much of a dent in that fact."

When Yaacov spoke, his voice was tinged with deep sadness. "And so you, and so many others like you, press ahead, trying to save the state of Israel while you ignore the very God who made the state of Israel a reality."

"Be that as it may," Gondor said slowly and evenly, "I am in charge of this operation and you are not. To talk to Barclay would do nothing more than reveal our hand in all this. I forbid it."

"Barclay is a man of the world," Yaacov agreed. "Where Gerritt gets his money and how will mean little to him. But Jeppson—he is a man of honor, a man of integrity. If he knew what Gerritt has done, he would persuade Barclay to cancel the deal. I know it."

"Papa," Nathan said patiently, "we know that Barclay has already spent nearly a million dollars setting this up. He will not turn his back on that."

"True. But tell Jeppson about the drug shipments, tell him what they did to Taggart and his family in order to get the radar device, show him the pictures taken by the customs agents on his airplane, and he will either get Barclay to break off the deal with Gerritt or he will quit. I know it!"

Yehuda spoke up. "Jeppson is playing an increasingly important role in the negotiations, but he is not pivotal. If he quits, it is only a setback, not a victory."

"That's right. Jeppson is not pivotal, not by himself. But let me also tell him what we know about Derek Parkin. I'll play him the tape of his conversation with Gerritt in Washington. Barclay will have to fire Parkin."

Gondor started shaking his head, but Yaacov went on doggedly. "That's two of Barclay's key people out. It may not stop him, but it will delay him long enough to buy us the time we need in Washington."

"We cannot let them know that the state of Israel is involved in this affair in any way. We have come this far because we have stayed completely out of sight. There is to be no contact made with either Barclay or Jeppson. Is that clear?"

The men locked eyes for several seconds. When Yaacov made no expression either way, Gondor played his final card. "And appealing this to the Prime Minister is useless. The director has met with him this very day. I have full authorization to determine what action is taken."

"I had no plans to try to go over your head, Mr. Gondor," Yaacov said dryly. He didn't add that such was the case because he had also talked to the Prime Minister earlier and had seen the handwriting on the wall.

"Then it would be most helpful to me if you would let us proceed with our plans without further interruption."

The silence grew heavy, every man in the room feeling awkward and uncomfortable, except for Yaacov Shoshani who was in deep thought on another matter. When there was no response from him, Gondor turned to the others. "All right. Our next task is to get set up for the Hotel LaRoche." He reached for a folder on the table and extracted a piece of paper. He looked around at the operational team, finally settling on Nathan.

"Nathan, here's the list of the rooms Barclay's secretary reserved for the big meeting on the thirteenth. As you can see, they've reserved some pretty high-class suites."

"Barclay is determined to get this deal."

Gondor nodded. "I want someone in every one of those rooms in the next few days. Shana has already made reservations for one night each. The dates are on here too."

He handed the list to Nathan who read it quickly, then looked up. "Okay."

Gondor handed him another sheet. "We've booked the Laguna Suite on the thirtieth floor starting tomorrow night through the meeting. That will be the monitoring center."

"I assume you want every room tapped—Barclay's people as well as the Arabs."

"Barclay, Jeppson, Gerritt. Anybody who comes to that hotel for this meeting."

Yaacov Shoshani stood, shaking his head, and walked out of Gondor's apartment.

Marc pulled the car into the parking lot of the restaurant and shut off the lights and engine. He turned to Valerie. "So that's it, I guess. I'm going to talk to Alex on Monday and tell him where I stand. I hope that's enough to convince Miss Valerie Robertson that I'm serious about getting her back."

She slipped her arm through his and squeezed it happily. "I'm convinced, and I'm so glad. I've never been so miserable in my life before. But what is Alex going to say when you tell him?"

There was a long pause as Marc stared out into the night. "I don't know. The next few weeks are critical. I can't pull back completely, but things are going to change, or else I come back to Claremont."

She watched the disappointment around his mouth and

reached up and touched his face, smoothing the lines along his jaw. "I hope it doesn't come to that."

"No more than I. I've loved these last two months. I feel like I'm alive again." He shrugged. "But . . ." He let it trail off, thinking of what Alex would say.

Valerie gently turned his head, and his eyes softened.

"I love you, Valerie. I want you to know that."

"And I love you, Marc Jeppson." She kissed him then, a long, lingering kiss that held all of the joy she was feeling. "Well," she said a little breathlessly when she pulled away, "I'm famished. Shall we go eat?"

"I thought you were tired."

She dug him in the ribs with her elbow. "Don't get smart."

"Okay, but before we go in, there is one other priority I'd like to get straight first."

"What?"

He reached across the back seat and fumbled until he got his briefcase open. When he straightened back around, he held a small gift-wrapped package. "After your enthusiastic reception of the necklace I brought you from Columbia, I don't know whether I dare do this or not." He handed it to her.

For several moments she just stared at it, then finally looked up at him, her eyes luminescent. "Go on," he encouraged her. "This has very much to do with priorities."

There was no careful opening of the paper, no saving of bows and ribbons. She tore the paper off quickly, then looked up at him again when she saw it was a blue velvet ring box. "Oh, Marc!"

"Come on, I thought you were famished. Open it."

She lifted the lid slowly, then her jaw dropped. The box was empty. Marc laughed at her expression, then gathered her up into his arms. "I actually went to a jeweler," he said, "but then at the last minute I decided I didn't want to pick your engagement ring without you. The man looked at me very strangely when I told him all I wanted was the ring box."

Valerie was rubbing the inside velvet softly, the happiness evident in her eyes.

"If you'll accept an empty ring box for now, we could get back early from San Diego and go shopping together. I think—"

She clamped her hand over his mouth. "Will you be quiet and kiss me, please?"

Chapter Twenty-Two

Jackie opened the door to Alex's office and stuck her head in. "Alex, I'm going home now. Is there anything you need before I leave?"

Alex did not look up at her, just kept staring at Marc. "I'd like you to hear this, Jackie. Come in."

Jackie came in tentatively, sensing the tension crackling in the air, and sat down next to Marc. Marc took a deep breath. He had been afraid it wasn't going to go down easy.

"Go on, Marc, tell Jackie."

Marc glanced at her, then turned back to Alex. He took another quick breath and began, talking slowly and quietly. "You were in the meeting this morning, Jackie. Between now and next week, when we go to the LaRoche, Alex has set up three more trips. He wants you and me to leave with Derek in the morning and go to Switzerland to meet with Gerritt. Then there'll be another trip or maybe two to Washington. And if all goes well at the LaRoche, then it's off to Saudi Arabia for two or three weeks. In the meantime, we'll be over our heads trying to get everything put into place."

Jackie nodded, waiting.

"Brett's teacher called Mary, my housekeeper, while I was in Washington. In the last few weeks, Brett's performance in school has nose-dived. For the first time, he is a behavioral problem. Matt has started to wake up every night now and has to sleep with an adult."

"So," Alex cut in, "Marc informs me that he cannot give his full devotion to Barclay Enterprises anymore."

"Alex, that's not what I said."

"All right, what did you say?"

"I said that my family is going to start taking a higher priority than it has. I've got to spend some time with my boys."

Alex swore. "You know, Marc, when you first came on board with me, you said you couldn't work on Sundays. I've honored that, even though there have been times when the rest of us have had to. Now, this. This is not an eight-to-five job, Marc. You don't get eighty-five thousand a year for eight-to-five jobs."

Marc bit back an angry retort, fighting to keep his voice even. "I have never asked for an eight-to-five schedule, and you know it. But I am asking that I have some time with my family. We work every Saturday. Night after night I'm gone, or when I am home, I'm working on something. And now you tell me the real pressure is just beginning."

"You'd better believe it. You think these deals just put themselves together? If you can't stand that kind of heat, then you'd better get out of the kitchen, kid."

Marc flushed as Alex turned to Jackie. "Can you believe this? And Friday night Ardith is trying to tell me how valuable he is to me. I was even thinking of bringing him into partnership with you and me." He gave a derisive hoot of disgust. "And now this!"

Jackie looked at Marc, who had looked up again in surprise. "That's right. He mentioned it to me this morning. Marc, I know it's been rough. On all of us. But you can't quit now."

"I'm not talking about quitting. I'm just saying that my family is no longer going to come second. I'll still give a hundred percent."

"Sure! But he gets to say when and where the hundred percent goes." He was still talking to Jackie as though Marc were not in the room. "I can't believe it! I take him from some jerkwater college, double his salary, bring him up to a full executive level, and what do I get? I mean a cruise to Mexico, trips to South

America, bonuses, a company car—and what do I get? He comes in and starts crying about being overworked."

"Alex," Jackie said, trying to soothe him.

"Alex nothing!" He jerked back around to Marc. "You owe me, Marc! And I'm calling in the markers." He sat back, breathing heavily, glaring at him.

Marc stood slowly, looked first at Jackie, who looked away, then at Alex. "I'm not one of your markers, Alex, and I'm not much for playing poker with people. You'll have my resignation in the morning."

Alex's mouth dropped open as Marc moved to the door. He stopped and turned back, fishing for his keys from his pocket. He pulled two of them off the ring and tossed them on the desk. "There's your company car, Alex. I'll find my own way home, like I should have that first night at UCLA."

And he walked out.

For several seconds Alex and Jackie both sat there, half stunned by the suddenness of Marc's departure. Then Alex swore again. "I can't believe it! I can't believe it!"

"And I can't believe you," Jackie said softly.

He whirled on her, raging. "Don't you start on me! If I hadn't given into Ardith the other night, he wouldn't be in here demanding his rights."

"Alex Barclay," she went on, as if he hadn't spoken, "the master of leverage. The man who gives lectures on how to bind people to him. And you just violated every principle, I mean every principle, you ever taught on the subject."

His mouth opened, but Jackie bored in on him. "I don't think Marc is right on this, but do you think you bought him with company cars and Mexican cruises? Derek, yes. Even me, maybe. But not Marc Jeppson."

He sat back, his eyes still smouldering, but getting control again. "All right, I'm listening."

"I guess the first question is, do you want him back or not?"

"You know I do."

"Simply to keep the deal together?"

He paused, then sighed wearily. "You know it's more than that too."

"You have leverage with Marc, Alex, but not through any of the things you tried to use right now. You called in the wrong markers."

"Come on, Jackie! We're in the biggest deal of our lives right now. I can't have him just waltzing all over me with his personal demands."

"I guess you're right. And you surely straightened him around on that account."

He winced. "Okay, okay. Between you and Ardith, I'm starting to feel like a dog on a freeway. So what are the right markers?"

"Friendship. Loyalty. Integrity." She took a deep breath, then proceeded to explain, talking earnestly for five minutes.

When she finally sat back, Alex stared at the ceiling for almost a full thirty seconds. When he turned back to look at her, it was with a rueful expression. "Do I pay *you* enough?" he asked.

She smiled. "We'll talk about that later."

Suddenly he straightened. "If he's on foot, he can't get too far. See if you can find him."

Jackie stood. "Maybe we both ought to try to find him."

But ten minutes later, when Alex drove back into the parking lot in front of the warehouse, Jackie was waiting next to her car, shaking her head.

"Matt," Marc said firmly, "we are not going on our walk until you get all those towels folded."

Brett scowled at his younger brother. "Hurry, Matt! Valerie and I are all ready." He walked over and knelt beside him. "Look, let's pretend we're making a mountain. You fold the towel, and then put it on top of the mountain. You've only got three or four left."

"I'm not making a mountain," he said matter of factly, starting to fold more rapidly.

"What are you making?"

"I'm making the Entire State Building."

"The *Empire* State Building," Brett corrected, as Marc and Valerie both laughed.

At that moment, the phone rang. Brett darted to it and picked it up. "Jeppson residence." He listened for a moment, then held the phone out toward his father. "Dad, it's Mr. Barclay."

Valerie turned slowly, unconsciously starting to twist the diamond ring on her left hand. Marc gave her a questioning glance, then took the phone. "Hello."

He listened for several seconds, his face expressionless, then finally nodded. "Yes. I'll be here."

When he hung up, he turned slowly, looking at Valerie. "He and Jackie are over on Indian Hill Boulevard. They want to talk."

"Good."

He shook his head. "I don't know if it is or not."

"Yes it is. You don't want to leave it like this." She put her arm around his waist. "I'll take the boys for the walk so you can be alone."

He kissed her lightly. "Okay."

He turned to Brett, dropping into a squat, and pulled him around to him. "Son," he began, fumbling for words. "As you know, Mr. Barclay and I are having some problems right now. I know I promised you a long walk, and I'll join you as soon as I can. Okay?"

Brett nodded, very adult. "I understand, Dad. It's all right."

Marc swung one arm and pulled him in tight. "Thanks, Brett. It shouldn't take long."

He straightened, looking glumly at Valerie. "There's not a lot to say."

"You're not wrong, Marc," she said earnestly. "He'll try and talk you out of your decision. But you're not wrong."

"I know. My mind is made up. It just isn't going to be very pleasant."

Valerie nodded then turned. "Matt, get your jacket. Brett,

207

will you take the Entire State Building and put it in the linen closet?"

Alex sat on the couch in Marc's living room, as close to true nervousness as Marc had ever seen him. Jackie sat next to him. Marc was in a chair where he could face them both.

"Marc, I . . ." He took a deep breath. "I'm sorry. That was stupid of me to get angry."

Marc nodded. "I understand. I shouldn't haven't gotten in a huff and walked out."

Jackie stirred. "How did you get home? We came looking for you."

Marc smiled fleetingly. "I found a cab. The driver was delighted to make the run to Claremont. And I talked to my banker. He thinks he can get me a second mortgage to cover the fare."

Alex laughed. "I'll cover the fare." He held up his hands quickly at Marc's expression. "No conditions. It's my fault. I'll cover it."

Marc shrugged and sat back. There was silence for several seconds. Alex glanced once at Jackie, who nodded in encouragement, then turned to Marc again. "Marc, let me tell you some things about myself that not a lot of people know."

Marc nodded. "As you've seen, Ardith and I live rather well. Home on the Palos Verdes Peninsula, yacht, private plane, fancy sports car."

Again Marc just nodded, not sure where this was leading.

"I'm good at what I do," Alex continued, without any false modesty, "and it pays off. But that doesn't mean I don't have financial challenges. I buy on credit just like you do. The only difference between you and me is my payments. If you count the house, the boat—all the rest—my payments run about fifty or sixty thousand dollars a month."

Marc gave a low, soundless whistle.

"That," Alex added dryly, "keeps my cash flow needs at a moderately high level."

"Slightly," Marc said, still a bit shocked at the figure.

"If we pull this sale off with the Saudis, all of that will change. But for now, I'm hurting. I've let other deals go to pursue this one. And we're talking significant out-of-pocket expenses for the deal even at this point. I've already had to put up more than half a million on that bauxite ore deal. Then you count the quarter of a million Gerritt is demanding up front for his part of the agent's fees. Add travel, what we've already paid to the five percenters in Saudi Arabia, your salary, Derek's." He shrugged. "I'm not trying to give you a sob story, just laying out the realities of life. And we're just beginning. I figure I'm in close to a million five already, and that could double or triple before we start seeing the first returns."

Marc remained silent, seeing where Alex was leading, and knowing that in spite of himself, the figures were staggering and rocking his determination.

"We're borrowing to the hilt to bring it off." He spread his hands. "I guess what I'm saying is, if this deal goes down, I go down with it."

Jackie leaned forward. "There's something else, Marc. And Alex doesn't know I'm going to say this. In fact, he doesn't even know I know it."

Alex turned to her with a quizzical look on his face, but she ignored him. "Alex has a heart problem. A serious heart problem."

From the instant surprise on Alex's face, Marc knew this had not been part of the script. Jackie had caught Alex completely off guard. Ardith's reaction at the restaurant in Ensenada when Alex had lit a cigarette flashed into his mind. Marc had not seen him smoke since. And Alex had started an exercise-and-weight-loss program that he joked about from time to time.

Jackie was watching Marc intently. "Two weeks ago, the doctor told him that he was on the verge of having a major heart attack or a stroke. He has high blood pressure. He's had pains in his chest. He's on medication."

"Jackie, that's enough," Alex said quietly.

She whirled on him. "No, it's not enough!" she cried. "Ardith is terrified." Suddenly there were tears in her eyes, and she brushed at them quickly. "And so am I." She turned back to Marc. "The doctor says he's got to get out from under the stress. It's killing him."

Marc looked at her, then at Alex, who was looking at the floor. Finally his head came up to meet Marc's gaze, and Marc saw something in Alex's eyes he had never seen before. Alex was pleading. "Marc, I . . . I understand about your family. But I need you. I can't give it to Derek. You know that. And Jackie and I can't do it alone."

Now it was Marc that looked at the floor.

"You can set your own hours. Take what time you need. I know you won't neglect the work." He paused. "But I won't try to deceive you. These next three to four weeks are going to be unbelievably hard."

Marc's head finally came up. "I know."

Jackie's lips parted, and the tears welled up again in her eyes. "Does that mean yes?" she asked softly.

Marc nodded, his eyes sorrowful.

Alex was up and to him in an instant. "Do you really mean that?" he said, his voice husky.

Marc stood slowly to face him. "Yes," he finally murmured. He looked down, realizing that Alex was pumping his hand.

As they came out on the porch ten minutes later, Alex reached in his pocket and pulled out a set of keys. "Would it offend you if I gave you back your company car?"

There was a brief laugh, tinged with some sadness. "No."

"We parked it around the corner." He pointed. "We didn't know if you'd open fire on us if you saw it out front."

"There's no way we can postpone the Switzerland trip?"

Alex shook his head. "No. We've got to tie Gerritt up once and for all. I'd go, but the Jakarta people will be here tomorrow, and—"

"I know," Marc sighed, then turned to Jackie. "I'll see you at the airport at nine."

Alex stuck out his hand. "Marc, I—" As Marc gripped it, Alex's voice faltered. Suddenly he pulled Marc to him and embraced him. "I won't forget this."

He pulled free and turned to Jackie. "Well," he said gruffly, "let's you and me be going."

Jackie nodded. "Go ahead. I'll be right there."

They watched him go down the walk and get in the Lamborghini. Then Jackie turned to Marc, her dark eyes moist. "Thank you."

"You knew I didn't stand a chance, didn't you?" It was said sadly, almost wistfully.

"I did," she whispered, "because I know what kind of man you are." She went up on tiptoes, reached up and pulled his head down, and kissed him hard on the lips. Then she averted her head, turned, and ran down the sidewalk to the car.

Valerie had just rounded the corner with the boys when she saw Alex come down the walk and get in his car. She stopped. "They're just going," she said to Brett, pulling him and Matt back so the shrubbery hid them from view. Puzzled that Alex was alone, she moved forward enough to see the front of Marc's house.

A moment later she stumbled back, grabbed Brett by the shoulders, and turned him around. "We'll go around the block the other way."

Brett looked up at her sharply. "What's the matter, Valerie?"

She shook her head, groping blindly for Matt's hand. "We're going to walk around the block the other way, that's all."

"Brett, you and Matt go watch TV for a few minutes. I need to talk to Valerie. Then we'll have root beer floats."

"I want root beer floats now," Matt cried plaintively.

Brett looked up at Valerie, who was staring out the living room window, not seeing. He grabbed Matt's hand. "Come on. We'll watch that video again."

Marc moved behind Valerie and put his arms around her. She jerked away from him, still keeping her back to him. "I knew you would."

Her voice was caustic and sharp and rocked him back. "You knew I would what?"

"You're going back, aren't you?"

"Val, will you listen?"

"I'm listening."

He talked quietly for several minutes, trying as much to convince himself as to convince her. Throughout, she stood at the window, not turning.

"So you leave for Switzerland in the morning?"

"Yes," he answered, barely audible.

"I'll tell Mother." She started away from him, toward the door.

"Val!" he cried, shaken by the implacability in her. She stopped, and he put his hands on her shoulders and turned her gently. "Val, I can't just walk away from him now."

"I know. That's exactly the point."

"You won't even try to understand?"

She wouldn't meet his gaze, just continued to stare at his chest.

"Valerie, can't we talk about it?"

"I thought we had talked about it Friday night."

"You know I meant what I said, but there are new factors now I didn't know about before."

"I see." She slipped the engagement ring off and held it out to him. "There are new factors for me too."

He gaped at it blankly. "You're not serious?"

"You don't want a wife. You want a babysitter. And as much as I love your boys, I need more than that, Marc." She set the ring on the lamp table and walked out the door.

Chapter Twenty-Three

The LaRoche Hotel on Wilshire Boulevard in Santa Monica downtown Los Angeles, is a stunning architectural achievement. Circular towers cluster together, thirty-five stories of mirrored glass reflecting the soaring skyscrapers surrounding it. Inside, the five-story central nave captures and recaptures the circular motif. Curves, ellipses, parabolas, spirals, arches, cambers, bends—all are dazzling to the eye but yet curiously restful. The Gallery—a miniature mall—along with restaurants and cocktail lounges fill the first five levels of the hotel complex. The main lobby itself is like a gigantic atrium, with fountains, lakes, trees, and shrubbery.

As Marc walked swiftly through the main lobby with General Amani and Sheik Ahmed al Hazzan, vice-Minister of Defense, they drew curious looks from the people. Amani was in uniform, which looked much like American Air Force dress. Hazzan wore a business suit but also had the red-and-white checked headdress. But Marc hardly noticed the attention they drew. His eyes lifted to the spectacular architecture towering above them, and he thought of Valerie with a sharp pang. This would be perfect for a honeymoon.

He shook the thought away in self-derision. Before that happened, they would have to move beyond the point of nodding politely to each other at church. She had not been to the house since that night two weeks before when she had given back the ring.

General Amani noted the frown as they stopped at the elevators and punched a button. "Worried?"

Marc pulled out of his thoughts. "About tonight?"

Amani nodded, and Marc saw the sudden interest in Hazzan's eyes. "No. You have prepared well. We have prepared well. All will go as planned." He paused for a fraction of a second. "*Insh'allah.*"

Amani laughed in delight. "Do you even think like an Arab?"

Marc just grinned without answering.

Each bank of elevators in the LaRoche ascends up through the central enclosure and emerges at about the sixth floor to glide the rest of the way on the outside of the main towers. All but the back wall of the elevator is glass, providing a dizzying view of the city lights spread out below as far as the eye can see. Both Amani and Hazzan commented quietly on that view as they rose to the thirty-first floor. But Marc was back with his thoughts of Valerie.

Insh'allah. God willing. Many Westerners accused the Arabs of fatalism, for this was their standard injunction for any event, and the customary response to whatever befell them—be it blessing or curse. But it was more than simply fatalism; it was a form of a prayer, an invocation on any undertaking. I am going to get through to Valerie, he thought, *insh'allah.*

Even her mother, Mary, couldn't penetrate the stone wall of silence and hurt she kept between them. At first, Mary had been distinctly cool at the news that Marc had gone back on his decision with Barclay. But she had thawed when she saw the efforts he was making, in spite of a staggering schedule, to spend time with his sons.

He frowned again. If Mary had said anything to Valerie to that effect, it had made little difference.

The doors opened, and the three of them moved to the La Jolla Suite. Marc took a deep breath. Amani and Hazzan were the last ones in from the airport. They were about to launch into the final negotiating session, and there would be no trial runs.

The La Jolla Suite occupied the entire top floor of one of the outer glass towers, providing a sweeping two hundred seventy degree view of the city of Santa Monica and beyond that, Los Angeles. The suite was like a large house, with nearly twenty-six hundred feet of floor space. It had a large parlor, a dining room, a library, five bedrooms with walk-in closets and full baths, a wet bar, and serving pantries. It was the finest accommodation in the hotel and ran just over thirteen hundred dollars a night. Marc knew because he had helped Jackie make the arrangements. He had felt extravagent, staying on the eighteenth floor in one of the San Simeon Suites for a hundred and eighty-five dollars a night, until he saw what they were paying for the Saudi suite.

Alex broke away from the small group clustered around a table when he saw the three enter, and he came over, smiling broadly. "General, good to see you again." They shook hands warmly. "I hope your six o'clock has been clear."

It was jet jockey slang, and Amani warmed to it noticeably. To have an enemy in the six o'clock position puts him looking right down your tail pipe, the most vulnerable position a fighter pilot can face. The general nodded and smiled. "And yours as well."

Marc half turned. "Alex, may I present Sheik Ahmed al Hazzan, the honorable vice-Minister of Defense. Sheik, this is Alexander Barclay, president of Barclay Enterprises."

Again there were the formal bows, a quick shaking of hands, then Alex took the two men in tow and moved them over to where General Taylor Canning, Russell Whitaker of the State Department, and the crown prince were standing. Marc stepped back, moving to the window, out of the way and yet where Alex could beckon to him.

There were nearly thirty people in the dining room and the parlor, almost half of them Saudis. Some, including the prince, were in flowing robes and headdresses, some in business suits. A good share of the Saudis were part of the royal body guard, and as Marc studied them, he decided he would rather not find out how efficient they were at their jobs.

Quinn Gerritt was off in one corner conversing with a major and a colonel in Saudi air force uniforms. State Department per-

215

sonnel in suits mingled with the Arabs, and Marc recognized a face or two from the reception in Washington. There were no women present. This was to be a business session, and not even Jackie would be allowed to participate. Nor was Derek here. Alex had booked him a suite alongside Marc's and Jackie's, but he would be called only if absolutely necessary.

A waiter brought a tray of hors d'oeuvres and soft drinks, and Marc helped himself, knowing the social hour would continue for some time before the prince gave the signal to move to the next phase. Then the work would begin. It would be bone-crunching, head-to-head, nerve-banging work—all done, of course, with the finest of manners and courtesy. When it came to the fine art of negotiating, the Saudis were some of the best in the world.

He turned to the window, took a sip of his Seven-Up, and fell back to thinking about Valerie.

The Israelis were in the Laguna Suite on the thirtieth floor, directly below the La Jolla Suite. Nathan and his team had spent many nights in the hotel in the past two weeks. The result of all that was a large bank of tape recorders and listening devices along one wall. Every room booked by Alex Barclay had tiny, almost invisible microphones. The man whom Gondor had given Nathan was one of the best, and the Israelis were confident their surveillance devices could survive even a professional security sweep. In addition, every phone was tapped through the main circuitry downstairs.

The hotel staff thought of the group in the Laguna Suite as a group of well-heeled European businessmen. They were quiet, well-mannered, and ate all of their meals in the finest of the hotel's restaurants.

Yehuda Gor was at the console with a pair of headphones on. The reels on three banks of tape recorders were turning slowly off to one side. Nathan and Yossi were at a table playing a desultory game of gin rummy. Gondor was asleep in the nearest bedroom, and Yitzhak and two other men in the one next to that. They had maintained the surveillance around the clock and took turns sleeping. Yaacov was on the couch, reading a book.

"Nathan," Yehuda called softly. "I think they are preparing to start work."

Nathan nodded, slipped into the bedroom, and a moment later reappeared with Gondor.

"Yes," Yehuda confirmed. "The prince has suggested they move the chairs into a circle. I think the social time is over."

Gondor grunted, sat down, and picked up another set of headphones as the others came around to listen.

Nearly two hours later, Valerie got out of her car and handed the parking attendant her keys. As he drove away, she turned and saw the signs pointing to the main lobby.

Ardith was waiting for her near the reception desk and came quickly over. "Thank you for coming."

Valerie nodded, still not sure what to make of the telephone call and the insistence that she come. "I've got a table reserved for us in the Paris Cafe if that's all right."

"That's fine."

As they walked, Ardith watched Valerie's eyes lift to stare at the mass of curved lines rising in every direction above them. "Isn't this an incredible place?" she said.

Valerie nodded and let her eyes drop to take note of the women passing by them or seated around the lobby area. There was no question that she was mingling with the moneyed class. The dresses were expensive, the hair flawless, the jewelry abundant. Valerie was at least grateful she had followed her impulse to wear her camel-colored wool suit and cream-colored silk blouse. And yet as she looked around, she felt the gnawing sense of plainness dogging her heels again. A quick stab of pain hit her as she thought of Marc here in this setting with Jackie.

Ardith reached out and took her hand as they sat at their table. "You look lovely tonight, Valerie."

Valerie gave her a sharp look, wondering if Ardith had

known her thoughts, but the waiter came at that moment to take their order.

When he walked away, Ardith looked up. "I really do appreciate you coming."

Valerie waited, not sure how to respond to that.

"I took the liberty of booking a room for you."

That completely knocked her off guard. "You what?"

"It's late and a long drive back home."

"I . . . I can't do that."

"Barclay Enterprises is picking up the tab," Ardith said evenly. "When I told Alex what I wanted to do, he agreed instantly."

Valerie was nonplussed. "But my mother is expecting me back."

Ardith shook her head. "I've already talked to your mother. She thought it was a wonderful idea."

Valerie sat back, dazed. "You talked to my mother?"

"Yes." She took a deep breath. "Look, Valerie, at the risk of seeming like a meddling old lady, let me come right to the point. Alex and I owe a debt that needs to be paid."

"To Marc?" Valerie asked.

"Yes."

"Does he know I'm here?"

She laughed quickly. "No. And if he finds out we've had this little talk, he'll probably kill me."

Valerie watched with deepening bafflement as the smile quickly faded and Ardith grew very serious. "Valerie, your mother told me why you gave Marc the ring back."

"My mother talks too much," Valerie said softly.

"Your mother loves you very much." She paused, studying her hands. "As does Marc Jeppson."

Valerie gave a little shake of her head, suddenly fighting tears.

Ardith leaned forward. "Do you know how happy Jackie is that you've given Marc back your ring?"

"What Jackie feels is not my affair."

"You saw Jackie kiss Marc that night on the porch, didn't you?"

Valerie's head jerked up. She hadn't even told her mother that.

Ardith smiled kindly. "Jackie told me. I just put two and two together. Let me tell you exactly what happened that night, and why Marc went back on his promise to you. And why Jackie kissed him. Then maybe you'll understand why I insisted you come here tonight."

It was nearly midnight when Marc got off the elevator on the eighteenth floor. He was exhausted but exuberant. The session had been a success. The Saudis were still holding out on one or two minor items, but the agreement was made. Alex Barclay had just sewn up his deal.

As he came around the curved hallway toward his room, he stopped dead. Valerie was leaning against the wall next to his door.

"Hello," she said softly.

"Valerie?" he asked, not believing his eyes.

"I understand there's a little restaurant downstairs that serves a pretty good hamburger until one o'clock on Friday nights."

He was still speechless, just staring at her.

"Unless you start to scream, I was thinking of taking you down there and buying one for you."

Quinn Gerritt got off the elevators and moved purposefully to his suite. He glanced around quickly. At this hour, the corridors were empty. Extracting a card from his shirt pocket, he inserted it into the computerized door lock. The lock clicked softly, and he stepped inside.

Derek Parkin stood almost instantly, leaving his drink sitting on the coffee table. Quinn nodded as he took off his jacket and hung it in the closet. "Did anyone see you come up?"

"No. I've been here almost an hour."

"Good." He walked to the phone, punched some numbers quickly. "We're ready."

Ignoring the curious look on Parkin's face, Quinn poured himself a drink and sat down in the chair.

"Well?" Derek asked, his hands nervously pulling at some unseen lint on his shirt.

"It's done," Gerritt answered with satisfaction. "There are a few more tricky things to be ironed out, but it's done."

"Great!"

Gerritt just nodded, not revealing how great it was. Gerritt Industries had just been pulled back from the edge of disaster. He thought of that morning in Lauterbrunnen when his two top executives had cried wolf. Wait until you hear the crack of the hammer before you say we're belly up, he had told Shurtliff. Well, the hammer had been set aside. Now, they were about to move from the edge of disaster to something very much more attractive.

With a soft click the lock shot open again, and the door opened. Derek whirled in surprise as a small dark man, carrying a thin and very expensive-looking briefcase entered. Gerritt stood quickly and went over and shook hands with Andrew Hadlow.

"Would you like a drink?"

Hadlow shook his head, and Gerritt turned to Parkin. "This is Derek Parkin."

There was a curt nod, and Derek noted return introductions were not forthcoming. Gerritt motioned to the chairs, and they all sat down. Gerritt sipped his drink, watching Parkin thoughtfully for several moments. Then he smiled.

"Derek, I've been very happy with our little arrangement."

Parkin picked up his own drink and gulped the remaining third of it down quickly, aware of the sudden prickling sensation down his back. He had come expecting the fifteen thousand dollar payoff Gerritt had promised him. Now he sensed that something else was in the wind.

Hadlow opened the briefcase and pulled out an envelope. He handed it to Gerritt, who tossed it to Derek. Parkin nearly dropped his glass as he caught it. He checked it furtively, counting the fifteen bills quickly. When he looked up, he saw the quick look of distaste on the small man's face.

"The information you have given us has been most helpful," Gerritt went on expansively.

"Thank you."

"This, along with the bonus Barclay will pay you, should fix you up for some time to come."

Parkin's eyes narrowed. "What bonus?"

Gerritt looked surprised. "Alex has promised Marc Jeppson a bonus of one hundred thousand dollars when the deal is finalized. You mean . . . ?" He looked a little embarrassed at having revealed something he should not have.

Derek slammed his glass down on the table and swore bitterly.

"Jackie, too, from what I understand," Gerritt lied smoothly.

Derek swore again, his face dark with anger. "That doesn't surprise me. Barclay has been squeezing me out ever since his darling Marc Jeppson came on board."

Gerritt nodded sympathetically, watching this sullen man brood, wondering how Barclay had ever come to hire such a liability. He stood, got the bottle of whiskey, and poured Derek another drink. As Parkin drank deeply, Gerritt glanced at Hadlow, who gave a quick inclination of his head.

"How would you like to make that bonus and a great deal more?"

Parkin's head snapped up like Gerritt had yanked on it with a baling hook. The sudden hunger in his eyes was unmistakable.

Gerritt held out his hands, a bland expression on his face. "As you know, I am now a limited partner with Alex in this thing. I'll get five percent of the total commissions."

"Yes, I know."

"It seems to me that Alex is treating me as shabbily as he is you. I mean, if it weren't for my radar system, there would be no deal with the Saudis."

"That's right. Alex has said that again and again."

221

"And yet Alex takes ninety-five percent. I get five. Marc gets a hundred thousand bonus, and you get nothing. Somehow, that doesn't seem right to me."

"It's rotten, that's what it is!"

Gerritt leaned forward suddenly. "How would you like to change all of that?"

Derek, suddenly very sober, set his drink down carefully. "How?"

"You know about Alex's heart condition?"

Derek nodded, a sudden chill hitting him at the base of the neck.

"If he were to have a heart attack about now, that would take him out of the action for a time. Perhaps long enough that a different deal would have to be negotiated."

Derek was absolutely motionless now, his eyes following every nuance on Gerritt's face.

"Who would be a more logical choice for a replacement than me? I've got the contacts with the aircraft company. I have the radar system. The Saudis already know me, and I've been in on the negotiation phase from the beginning." He paused as Derek licked his lips. "And who would I need by my side but the man who has already drawn up all the contracts and knows the ins and outs of all the paper work?"

Hadlow opened his briefcase again and extracted something, but when he shut it, whatever he had gotten was in the palm of his hand, and Derek couldn't see what it was.

"The commissions are going to run around sixty million, Derek," Gerritt continued. "I'd be willing to give you a ten percent partnership. I'm not talking about hundred thousand dollar bonuses. I'm talking six million dollars!"

Hadlow leaned over and handed Gerritt a small brown prescription bottle and a plastic card. Gerritt looked at them curiously, his gray eyes hooded and veiled. Finally he looked up.

"Alex is on medication for his heart. He takes one pill every night before going to bed."

Derek's face was suddenly gray.

"He is not back in his room yet. He's down in the main bar celebrating his victory with General Canning and Whitaker from the State Department."

"What are you saying?" Derek whispered.

"This medication, which looks identical to his, will trigger the heart attack we were just discussing. Here is a card that will get you in his room."

"Are you mad? What if it kills him?"

Hadlow spoke for the first time, mildly and quietly, but it frightened Derek even more than Gerritt's calloused blandness. "It won't. This has been prepared very carefully. We don't want Barclay dead. Only out of commission for a while."

"I can't!" Parkin said hoarsely. "If something went wrong, you're talking murder!"

"Nothing is going to go wrong!" Gerritt snapped. "All we're going to do is make the inevitable happen at a more convenient time."

Derek was shaking his head in horror.

Hadlow leaned forward. "Do you know Jonathan Taggart, Mr. Parkin?"

For a moment, Derek was blank, then recall came. "The designer of the radar system?" he asked Gerritt.

Both men nodded.

"Let me tell you a little story about Jonathan Taggart," Hadlow said quietly.

Chapter Twenty-Four

Valerie twirled around slowly in front of Marc.

"You look terrific!" He turned to the salesgirl. "She'll take it."

"Marc!"

He ignored her. "Can she wear it?" he asked.

The woman smiled, liking this handsome young man's assertiveness. "Certainly. I'll put her other dress in a box."

"Good. I'll clip the tags on this one." He stepped to Valerie and took out his fingernail clippers. Valerie turned her head. "Marc! I can't take this!" she whispered.

"Why not? You said you liked it."

"I love it, but—"

"You only have the dress you wore. You need something for the celebration luncheon today."

"I know, but it's a hundred and seventy dollars!"

He spun her around and kissed her firmly. "Right now, I'd pay five hundred dollars just to have you here."

"You're crazy," she laughed, thoroughly delighted.

"I know, and I also know who made me that way." He finished clipping the tags. "Come on, let's go pay for this and go to some other stores. The morning is still young. You'd better take advantage while I'm in this affluent mood."

Half an hour later, they were just coming out of a hotel gift shop, laden with packages for the boys, when an urgent cry spun them around. Jackie came from the direction of the elevators, half running.

"Marc, wait!" she called.

They turned on their heels and walked swiftly toward her. She stopped, trying to catch her breath. "Marc. I've been looking all over for you."

"What's the matter?"

"Alex has had a heart attack. They've just rushed him to the hospital."

When Ardith came out into the waiting room, everyone stood. Her face was drawn, her eyes swollen and red. Russ Whitaker, Undersecretary of State, stepped up to meet her. "How is he?"

She took a deep breath, then sighed heavily. "They've taken him into surgery. They're going to have to do a bypass. But the doctor is very optimistic."

Derek sagged back and sat down heavily, relief coursing through him like a cold mountain stream.

Gerritt shot him a warning glance, then stepped forward. "Ardith, if there's anything we can do, let us know."

"Thank you, Quinn. For now, there's nothing really." She turned to the others. "Really, I so much appreciate you coming, but you may as well return to the hotel. It will be several hours before anything further develops." She looked to Marc. "I would like Marc, Jackie, and Derek to stay for a few minutes."

The others offered quick condolences and took their leave. Valerie murmured something to Marc and started to turn, but Ardith moved quickly to her side. "I'd like you to stay too, Valerie."

Once the others were gone, Ardith motioned to the chairs. "Sit down, please." She waited until they were seated in a semicircle facing her, then pulled a chair around.

"Alex wouldn't let them put him under until he made me promise to do this." A fleeting expression of desperation crossed her face. "There he was, so sick he could barely talk, and—" Tears welled up, and she fumbled for a Kleenex in her purse. "And he wouldn't let them take him until he made sure I knew what to do."

Jackie nodded, her own eyes red and swollen.

Ardith turned to Marc. "Alex was worried sick something like this would happen. Once you agreed to stay with him, he had all the papers drawn up and executed. You are now the acting president of Barclay Enterprises, Marc."

Marc rocked back, stunned. Jackie took a quick intake of breath. Derek stared, his mouth working but making no sound. Valerie, wide-eyed, was watching Marc's reaction.

"You have full power and authority to act." She stopped, fighting again for control. Finally, sniffing back the tears, she was able to continue. "He begged me to tell you not to wait around here, Marc. He said you've got to act immediately, or everything will start to fall apart."

Marc nodded slowly, still dazed as Valerie reached out and squeezed his hand. Derek jumped up, his mouth a thin hard line. "Well," he hissed. "I guess that makes it clear where I stand with Alex." He shot Marc a withering glance, then whirled and stalked out.

Jackie reached over and touched Marc's arm. He was staring after him in shock and bewilderment. "Don't worry about him, Marc. He'll be all right. He's just extremely jealous."

"I . . ." He shook his head, then turned back to Ardith. "I don't know what to say."

Ardith smiled despite her tears. "Don't say anything. Alex has tremendous confidence in you." She turned to Jackie. "He would have made you the president if the Saudis didn't have this thing about dealing with women."

Jackie was up instantly and put her arms around her. "Ardith, you don't have to explain anything to me. All I care about is Alex getting better."

"I know," Ardith said, the tears starting again. She looked at Marc. "So go, Marc. You've got to keep things together." Her voice caught. "If he loses this, it will kill him."

Valerie and Marc were at the entrance to the hotel parking garage. She reached up and kissed him quickly. "You don't need to be worrying about me right now. I'll go and stay with the boys and Mother."

He shook his head, still a little dazed. "I . . ." He finally nodded. "I guess you're right. Thank you for understanding."

She threw her arms around him. "I love you Marc Jeppson. I'm sorry I've been so difficult."

He held her tightly. "Just knowing you're back is enough. If it weren't for that . . ." He kissed her hard, not wanting her to leave, but knowing she was right.

She pulled back, her eyes shining. "Did you take the ring back to the jeweler?"

He smiled, touching her cheek. "It's in the top drawer of my dresser."

"Will you get me for breaking and entering if I go get it?"

"Won't matter," he said gruffly. "A man can't testify against his wife anyway."

By four o'clock that afternoon, the scramble for repositioning was starting to settle. The parlor of the La Jolla Suite had become the equivalent of the *majlis*, the council room, where so much of Saudi business and social interaction takes place. The men were seated in a rough circle, drinking the bitter coffee ground fresh from the beans they'd brought with them from Saudi Arabia. Except for the luxurious surroundings and the business suits scattered here and there, it could have been a gathering of sheiks in the black, goat-skinned tents of the Bedouins.

Quinn Gerritt had been the first to come, oozing reassurances that the deal was in no way jeopardized. Then with subtlety, but clarity, he made them a new offer.

Marc Jeppson came an hour or so later with the announcement of his new authority and calm assurances that all would be well.

Now they sat in council, sipping the bitter coffee. General Amani spoke first, shaking his head firmly. "Do not trust this Mr. Gerritt. If he so quickly turns on Barclay in a time of tragedy, he will as quickly turn on us, given half a chance."

Several others nodded their agreement, but Sheik Hazzan was adamant. "Gerritt has the radar system. And he has offered to work with us for ten percent less commission. That is a substantial difference."

Prince Khalid, full brother to the crown prince and the king, and Commander-in-Chief of the Saudi Armed Forces, spoke softly. "Do the Saudis change camels in the middle of the race? Last night we agreed that Mr. Barclay would represent us."

Hazzan nodded in deference but was still firm. "Alex Barclay is lying in a hospital. That changes everything."

"He has designated Mr. Jeppson as his legal representative," General Amani pointed out. "And while nothing has been signed, Khalid is right. Our honor states that we must wait to see if Barclay Enterprises can carry through what they have promised."

"Mr. Jeppson is a young, inexperienced agent. He has no expertise."

The crown prince stirred, and the others turned to watch. His eyes were bright and alert, his face handsomely etched. For several moments, he looked above their heads, considering all that had been said. Finally he spoke. "Ahmed is right in one thing. Our first concern is to make the best arrangements we can make for our government."

The vice-Minister of Defense tipped his head, acknowledging the support.

"However, my brother also makes a telling point. I would not have it be said that when a stranger trips on the tent peg, the Saudis use his body for a carpet."

They all nodded, thinking of Alex Barclay lying in a hospital bed. The crown prince turned to the general. "You know this Jeppson best. What is your assessment?"

Amani spoke slowly, choosing his words with care. "He is young. In that Feisal is correct. He is also inexperienced in the area of being a representative."

Hazzan was nodding vigorously.

Amani hesitated, then spoke quietly. "Ibn Saud was twenty-six when he recaptured Riyadh from the hated Ibn Rasheed." It was a telling point, for he was referring to the apex of modern Saudi history. In 1902, Abdul Aziz, the leading son of the famed house of Saud, had crossed the incredibly fierce environment of the Empty Quarter with a small force of loyal followers to fall on Riyadh and reclaim it for the house of Saud. It was the beginning of the modern kingdom and the center of song and legend.

Amani let the point sink in, then continued. "Jeppson is a man of honor, and Barclay evidently has great confidence in his abilities. And," he paused, to give emphasis to what he felt was an important factor, "he knows our people and respects and admires what we have achieved. He will not use us and throw us aside when he is done."

The crown prince was impassive, letting that rest on the others' as well as on his own mind. He looked around, but when no one else wanted to speak, he nodded. "Then we will see what the young Mr. Jeppson can do." He turned to Amani. "Convey to Mr. Gerritt our interest in his proposal, but that for now we regretfully feel we must honor our commitment with Barclay Enterprises."

One floor below, the Israelis were also holding council. Gondor was at the head, the rest were scattered around the suite watching him attentively. Eli Weissman, the deputy director was a new addition, having just arrived from Washington, D.C., about twenty minutes earlier. There was a small chalkboard, and on it Gondor had listed the current status of the various participants in the drama unfolding in the Hotel LaRoche.

"That's where it stands now," he said to Weissman. "At first, it looked like the pieces of the tapestry would start to unravel, and Barclay's tragedy would prove to be a blessing for us. But Barclay's foresight and Jeppson's quickness seem to have pulled things back together. The Saudis are committed to follow through if he can deliver.

"And he withstood Gerritt?" Weissman asked.

He turned to Yehuda. "Udi, you were monitoring that line. Tell us again what happened."

Yehuda shrugged. "Parkin came straight from the hospital to Gerritt with the news that Jeppson had full authority. So Gerritt acted swiftly. He went to the Saudis and tried to undercut Barclay and to squeeze him out. When that failed, he called Jeppson to his room. He threatened to pull out of the deal unless Marc cut him in for half of the total commission. Jeppson seemed at first stunned, but he held his ground. Gerritt has already signed all the agreements with Barclay. Jeppson told him flatly that if he tried to pull out, he would have a massive law suit on his hands."

Weissman nodded. "Go on, Moshe."

"We cannot wait any longer," Gondor continued. "Our options are narrowing fast. The sabotage teams will hit Gerritt's laboratory and plant tomorrow night. The bauxite shipments will be the next targets."

Yaacov, who had sat quietly in the background for most of the last four hours, sat up. "Would you add shame to the shame we have already brought upon ourselves?"

Gondor spun around, fire in his eyes. "I told you that we were not monitoring Gerritt's room! We had listening devices in eleven rooms. You cannot listen to eleven conversations at once. We did not learn about the switch of the medicine until we heard the tapes several hours later."

"Does negligence lessen the shame?"

"It was not negligence, Papa!" Nathan exploded. "We've told you that. If we had known what Gerritt was doing, we would have warned Barclay, but all of us were focusing on the Saudis."

"And now you take the law in your own hands."

Gondor threw up his hands in disgust and turned to Weissman, his expression clearly asking for deliverance. Weissman was thoughtful for a moment, then turned to face the white-haired patriarch on the couch. "Mr. Shoshani, I know the prime minister has great confidence in you. I also know that you know the gravity of our present situation. Though we disagree in philosophy, we both want to stop the sale of these planes to our enemies. What do you suggest?"

"Let me talk to Marc Jeppson."

Gondor snorted in derision behind him. "And tip our hand. You know that from the very first we've had to be very careful that the Americans don't find out we're in this."

Yaacov didn't turn, just watched Weissman steadily. "I have a good friend who is an FBI agent. They already know some of what we're doing, and they want Gerritt and Hadlow badly. They're willing to work with us."

Gondor started to say something, but Weissman motioned him to stay quiet. He had read all the reports. He knew what Yaacov had proposed and why it was rejected. But that was before Barclay had turned over the reins to Jeppson. He also knew of some things starting to transpire in Washington, if only they could buy some time. Finally he nodded.

"You've got until noon tomorrow. If Jeppson turns you down, then we move."

Chapter Twenty-Five

Brett stood before his father, ramrod stiff, submitting to the quick inspection.

"Do you have your toothbrush?" Marc asked.

"Yes."

"Pillow?"

"Don't need one. Jed's mom says they've got plenty."

"Okay." Marc looked him up and down. "Now look, kid, this is your first sleepover. You know how Jeppsons are supposed to act?"

"Yes, sir."

"Polite."

"Yes, sir."

"Always say 'Thank you.'"

"Yes, sir."

Valerie had come to the kitchen door and was watching the interaction fondly.

"Help with the dishes," Marc continued.

Slight hesitation, a little less enthusiasm. "Yes, sir."

"Have a great time."

Brett's eyes widened. "Yes, sir!"

"Get out of here!"

"*Yes, sir!*" Brett whooped and was out the door like a shot.

Marc sighed, shook his head at Valerie. "One down and one to go." He walked to the hall just in time to see his youngest son dart across the hall and into the bathroom.

"Matt! Come on!"

"Just a minute, Daddy. I'm putting gasoline on my lips."

"You're what?"

Valerie poked her head around from the kitchen. "I think the word is Vaseline."

"Oh," Marc laughed. Sure enough, a moment later Matt emerged, his lips glistening. "All right, you," Marc ordered gruffly, "into bed. You've had your drink, you've said your prayers, you've been to the bathroom, and you've got gasoline on your lips. Now get in there, and I don't want to hear another peep."

Matt disappeared through the doorway, then peered back around at his dad. "Peep!"

Marc stomped a foot. There was a squeal and the sound of a running dive onto the bed.

When he came back into the kitchen a few moments later, Valerie was smiling.

"What are you smirking at?"

She turned back to the counter where she was putting the final touches on a chocolate cake. "Peep, peep!" she said in a tiny little voice.

He laughed and came up to her, putting his arms around her. "What do I have, rebellion on every hand?"

Before she could answer, the doorbell rang. They both looked up in surprise. "I'll get it," Marc said.

As he opened the door and stepped back, his mouth dropped. The man standing in his doorway was Yaacov Shoshani.

"Hello, Marc," Yaacov said, smiling faintly.

"Yaacov. How did you . . . ?" He caught himself, still a little dazed, looked at the second man, who smiled politely. "Come in," Marc said, opening the door wider.

Yaacov took off his hat and stepped inside. The other followed, and Marc noted he was carrying a briefcase. He was a heavy-set man but trim and very fit. He was dressed in suit and tie, like Yaacov.

"Marc, this is Lynn Braithwaite. Lynn, Marc Jeppson."

They exchanged greetings as they shook hands, and Marc noted the strong grip of the other. Valerie stepped into the entryway from the kitchen, taking off her apron.

Marc beckoned to her to join him. "This is my fiancée, Valerie Robertson. Val, this is Yaacov Shoshani. I met him in Washington, D.C. He's from Israel."

Valerie tossed the apron into the kitchen and came to stand by Marc. "I'm pleased to meet you."

"And this is Lynn Braithwaite." He motioned to the chairs. "Sit down, please." When they had done so, he and Valerie sat together on the couch and Marc turned to Shoshani. "What a surprise this is. How did you ever find me?"

Yaacov took a deep breath. "Marc . . ." He stopped, took another quick intake of air, and let it out in a weary sigh. "Before we begin, you ought to know that I am here on behalf of the Mossad, Israel's intelligence service, and Mr. Braithwaite is a special agent for the Federal Bureau of Investigation."

If Marc had gaped at the first sight of Shoshani, now he was dumbfounded. He glanced at Valerie, who was as stunned as he.

"We have something you need to hear, Marc."

Valerie started, then looked at Marc. "I'll go in with Matt." She moved to get up.

Yaacov shot Braithwaite a quick look and got an imperceptible nod. He turned to Valerie. "Miss Robertson, we think it might be well if you heard what we have to say. It could have implications for you as well as Marc."

She sat back, and Marc reached out and took her hand.

With Yaacov leading out and Braithwaite filling in, they laid it all out for them, starting with the account of the financial state of Gerritt Industries and a visit in October from Andrew Hadlow. The agent took the lead then, sketching in brief but sobering detail the interest the federal government had in Andrew Hadlow and his sponsor, Lyman Perotti.

To that point, Marc was shocked but puzzled. So Gerritt had Mafia connections. He wasn't sure why they were telling him all this. But then they began describing a trip to Bogotá. They handed him more than two dozen black-and-white photographs. He looked at them slowly, the puzzlement growing at first, then turning to a cold fury as Yaacov talked quietly. It was all there. Alex's plane parked at the airport, two men jimmying the door, the same two carrying sacks inside, the close-ups—much more clear and sharp now—of sacks of cocaine stuffed into the paneling of the cabin. The last had been taken by federal narcotics agents as Marc and Jackie had sat inside the terminal for three hours waiting to clear customs. When he finally looked up, his mouth was drawn into a hard, tight line.

"Understand, Marc," Braithwaite said, noting the expression. "There is not the slightest suspicion that either you or Miss Ashby had knowledge of the fact that you were being used as couriers. It would be helpful if you could tell us how you came to make that trip for Mr. Gerritt."

Marc did so, his voice low and filled with loathing. Braithwaite took out a small notebook and scribbled quickly as Marc talked. When Marc finished, the agent leaned forward. "The ones we're really after are Hadlow and Perotti, but I think for the first time we have a shot at getting them if we can get Gerritt."

Valerie was seething. "You and Jackie could have been arrested. Thrown into prison."

Yaacov cleared his throat. "I do not wish to deceive you, Marc. The FBI's interest in all this is clear. But you are probably wondering why Israeli intelligence is involved in an American crime case."

Marc nodded, his eyes never wavering from those of Yaacov's. "Yes. That's exactly what I was wondering. What *is* your interest, Yaacov?"

The old man sighed again, a sound filled with pain and sorrow. "My country knows about the sale of the F-22s to Saudi Arabia. Our interest is to see that the sale does not take place."

"And the chance meeting in Washington—"

"It was not by chance. I took it upon myself to meet you and get to know what you were like."

The pieces were beginning to fit together for Marc. "And you're telling me all this now so I will no longer deal with Quinn Gerritt, thus stopping the sale."

Yaacov hesitated, then decided that this young man deserved to be told the truth. "That is our hope."

"The Israelis have provided us with some very helpful information," Braithwaite spoke up. "Unfortunately, we cannot use anything they have obtained as evidence. We need your help to nail Quinn Gerritt and his associates and send them away for a very long time."

"What about the drug shipments?" Valerie asked. "Isn't that enough evidence?"

"Not much of that will stand up in court. Gerritt is cunning and has covered his tracks well. And Perotti and Hadlow are pros, Marc. You don't just pick them off the streets."

"Gerritt is evil, Marc," Yaacov said. "And the men he runs with are evil. They live by marketing filth and destruction."

Marc leaned forward. "I know that. But what can I do? I hope you nail Gerritt to the wall, but I can't just throw away a deal Alex has worked toward for three or four months."

"There is more, Marc," Yaacov said sadly. "Much more."

Braithwaite stood abruptly and went to the door. He opened it and beckoned. A moment or two later, Jonathan Taggart, chief engineer and designer of the VSM-430 radar system, walked in.

When Taggart finally left fifteen minutes later, Marc had his head down in his hands. Valerie was staring at the door in horror and revulsion. "That poor man," she whispered.

"It is not a pretty picture is it, Marc?" Yaacov said quietly. "But now you see the kind of man with whom you are partners. Gerritt has managed to get in on this deal only through criminal action—extortion, coercion, drug smuggling, using innocent people, including yourself. Are you really willing to work with a man like that?"

Marc finally looked up. "You don't understand—this is not my choice. If it were, Gerritt would be out this instant, but I am only Alex's representative."

"Barclay has given you full power and authority to act."

"To act in *his* name! Not go off on my own and overturn everything he has worked for."

"So you just turn your head aside? Ignore what Gerritt is and what he has done?"

"You can't!" Valerie cried. "You can't work with that man!"

"Don't you understand? It will ruin Alex!" He turned to Valerie. "And right now, that could cost him his life."

"Could?" Yaacov challenged him softly. "Aren't you talking probabilities, Marc?"

Marc's head came around.

"I remember a young man telling me that there are higher considerations than probabilities. Things like faith and integrity and trust in a supreme being."

Marc just stared, unblinking, almost dazed.

"To save a friend, or destroy an enemy? You have your own Coventry dilemma, Marc Jeppson. I do not envy you."

For several seconds Marc's breathing was the only sound in the room. As Valerie watched her fiance struggle with the decision, she suddenly loved him more intensely than she had cared for anything or anyone in her entire life. She took his hand, gripping it tightly, not knowing what to say or how to help him, only knowing that the one thing she wanted at this instant was to stand by him and strengthen him in whatever he decided to do.

Yaacov watched the inward struggle, knowing with terrifying clarity what he had laid on this man's shoulders. When he finally spoke again, his voice was low and grave. "Marc, there is one more thing you must know." He took a cassette from his pocket, and Braithwaite opened his briefcase and brought out a small tape recorder. Yaacov put the cassette in the machine and pushed the play button. "This was recorded last night in Quinn Gerritt's suite at the LaRoche approximately eight hours before Alex Barclay's heart attack. I think you'll recognize the voices of Gerritt and Derek Parkin. The third man is Andrew Hadlow."

•   •   •   •   •

Long after the two men had left, Marc was still standing at the living room window, staring out into the darkness. Valerie came back from covering Matt, stopped and watched him for a moment, then walked quietly to stand by his side. His arm came up and around her shoulders.

"Val, what do I do?"

"What would Alex want you to do?"

There was not an instant's hesitation. "Stick with Gerritt and see the deal through."

"Even if he knew what Gerritt tried to do to him?"

Marc nodded, the sureness of his conviction not helping his emotions. "Yes. I know Alex. 'We'll worry about that later,' he would say. 'Right now, you just worry about putting that contract to bed once and for all.'"

Valerie knew he was right. "Surely those tapes are enough to convict Gerritt. Then it's out of your hands."

Marc shook his head quickly. "You heard Braithwaite. The tapes were illegally obtained. They are not admissable as evidence."

He fell silent, struggling with the emotions raging within him. Finally Valerie broke the quiet, "Are there any other options?"

"Like what?"

"I don't know. But so far all you've considered is whether to stay with Gerritt and compromise with evil or dump him and destroy Alex. Couldn't there be a way to dump Gerritt and still see the other through?"

He turned slowly, looking at her in wonder.

She smiled up at him. "After hearing how you crashed the door at Mervyn's last fall, I have great faith in your ingenuity."

His face softened, as he chuckled with the memory. "Can you believe I did that?"

She shook her head firmly. "No. Not my level-headed, basically serious Marc Jeppson."

"I could have won, you know. The store security guy was trying his darndest not to laugh when I told him how I got through that door. But suddenly I said to myself, 'What are you doing? You're a college professor, not some juvenile delinquent trying to con a woman out of a sack of marbles.' "

She slipped her arm around his waist. "So put some of that ingenuity to work now."

Turning, he pulled her into his arms and kissed her. "Where did you come from?"

She laughed, her eyes sparkling with a mixture of tears and joy. "I jogged in from Colorado, remember?"

He didn't smile, just suddenly pulled her in tight against him. "Do you know, can you even begin to fathom, what you mean to me?" He sighed, coming back to the realities facing them. "I need to think this through. Do you want to go for a walk?"

She looked up again, searching his face, then finally shook her head. "You go. I'll be here when you come back, and then we can talk."

It was almost one-thirty when Marc opened the front door and came into the living room. Valerie was sitting in the dark, the light from the entryway putting her face in soft shadow. Marc came slowly to her, sat down, and took both her hands in his.

She waited as he sorted out his thoughts, wanting to touch his face and make the deep lines go away.

"You know what this is all about?" he began.

"What?"

"What Alex calls leverage points. Everything in this whole situation comes down to one person or group of people trying to leverage others. Alex and Jackie leveraged me into staying by telling me about Alex's condition. Quinn Gerritt leveraged Derek into betrayal with money and by nursing his hurt ego. Jonathan Taggart was leveraged by playing on the terror of his wife and daughter. The Saudis leverage just about everyone with their incredible wealth. It goes on and on."

Valerie leaned her head against his shoulder. "But Alex is a born infighter, and Hadlow and Gerritt knew they could neither scare him out nor buy him out, so they leveraged him out with a heart attack."

"Exactly, which then gives Yaacov Shoshani the perfect opening to leverage me, because he knows I can't just look away from that."

"And you can't, can you?"

"How could I? No matter what Alex would do, how can I just turn and look the other way?"

"And what about Alex?"

He stood and walked to the window, pulled the curtains back, and stared out into the night. "You know the answer to that, too. For all his faults, for all his bluster and blow, Alex Barclay is a decent man. He has been very good to me and for me. I won't ruin him."

"So?" she asked again.

"So, maybe it's time I start using what the master taught me. I'm not the only one in this game who can be leveraged."

She went to him, and he held out his arms. "So you found another way!"

"Yes, I think so. I think I can get Gerritt out and and still save the deal."

"Marc, that's wonderful!"

He was shaking his head slowly. "No, it's not. When Gerritt finds out . . ." He let it hang, not wanting to finish.

Valerie went cold, remembering the look on Jonathan Taggart's face as he described what had happened to his wife and daughter. Marc was watching her closely, and when she looked up, he nodded.

"That's right. If you want to talk about my ultimate leverage point, it is you and the boys." He pulled her to him, holding her with a fierceness that frightened her. "Valerie, if I just let everything ride, there would be no threat to you."

She looked up at him for several seconds, feeling the fear tightening her stomach. But she shook her head. "You can't deal with Gerritt." She buried her head against his chest. "You just can't."

"Okay," he said with sudden determination. "Call your mother. Tell her to pack some things for both you and her."

Valerie's head came up swiftly.

"I don't think they will bother Mary, but we can't be sure. So all of you have to go."

"But where?"

"I'm taking you to Utah."

"Right now?"

"As soon as we can get some things packed for the boys. If you'll do that, I'll go get Brett from his sleepover."

It was two-thirteen A.M. when Marc carried two suitcases out and put them into the trunk. Mary locked the front door of her home, then walked hurriedly with Valerie to the Chrysler Le-Baron, where she got in the back seat next to two very sleepy little boys. As Marc came around and got in the front seat with Valerie, Yitzhak ben Tsur, in a car half a block away, lowered the binoculars and picked up the microphone.

"This is Claremont One. We have definite confirmation. The fiancée's mother has been picked up with her luggage. The bird is in flight."

Chapter Twenty-Six

They left Claremont, California, Sunday morning at two-fifteen A.M. and drove straight through, stopping only for gas, food, and one time when Marc made a half-hour call to Washington, D.C. They arrived in Willard, Utah, shortly after five that evening. By five forty-five they were back on the road south again, this time not in Marc's car, which had been left locked in his father's garage, but in his father's minivan. There was a quick, tearful farewell at the Salt Lake International Airport, with urgent warnings from all that Marc be extremely careful. Even Brett sensed the somber mood of the adults and was subdued. Matt, exuberant at the thoughts of two weeks at a small mountain resort with his grandma and grandpa, was the only one whose spirits weren't dampened.

Marc disembarked from the Salt Lake to Los Angeles flight at ten thirty-two that night, California time, made one quick phone call, then rented a car and drove directly to a fashionable neighborhood in Cypress, about twenty-five or thirty miles southeast of Los Angeles.

Jonathan Taggart always watched the news at eleven, then late night reruns before going to bed. When the doorbell rang at ten minutes to twelve, he looked up in surprise, fighting down the instant fear that had become a part of his life since he had pushed open the door to find a headless cat lying on his porch. Hurrying, before the bell rang again and woke his wife, he padded into the living room, leaving the lights out, and peeked quickly out a window. His eyes widened when he saw the two men. He stepped back quickly, turned off the porch light, and opened the door.

"Mr. Taggart," Marc said, "we apologize for the hour, but it is very important that we talk to you."

Taggart's eyes were frightened. "Why did you come here?" he demanded. He peered up and down the street, then opened the door wider. "Please come in. Quickly!"

It was one-nineteen A.M., Monday, March 16, when the phone rang in Yaacov Shoshani's apartment. He was awake instantly and picked it up.

"Yaacov, this is Marc Jeppson. I have Lynn Braithwaite with me. How soon could you get your people together? We would like to talk with them."

Marc could feel the burning behind his eyelids and knew that if he looked in a mirror, he would find them terribly bloodshot. The physical weariness was also starting to seep into his mind and dull his thought processes. He had slept for three or four hours while Valerie and Mary took turns driving, and caught another half an hour on the plane back to L.A. Other than that, he had been up for about forty-two hours. He stood up, shaking it off, willing himself back into alertness.

The others were also a little bleary-eyed from being yanked out of bed in the middle of the night, but in addition to having slept more recently, Yaacov had also served coffee to all the others, and it was starting to have it's effect. Except on Lynn Braithwaite. He was in the large overstuffed chair, his coffee on its arm, untouched. His head had tipped down onto his chest, and he was dozing. Nathan Shoshani sat near his father on the couch, talking quietly. Moshe Gondor was at the table, staring into his cup, lost in his own thoughts.

The doorbell rang, and they all started. Yaacov hurried to answer it and came into the room a moment later with Eli Weissman, the Deputy Director of Operations for the Mossad. The others all came to the table. Gondor introduced Weissman quickly to Marc, they shook hands, then they all sat down.

"Sorry to be so long in getting here," Weissman apologized, without explanation. Then he turned to Marc. "Mr. Jeppson, you called us together. Let's hear what you have to say."

Marc nodded. He had rehearsed this often enough in the last twenty-four hours, but now that the moment had arrived, he found a sudden tightness in his throat. He took a deep breath and plunged in.

"Mr. Braithwaite and I have come to ask for your help." Gondor stirred, but Marc went on quickly. "Before telling you exactly what it is we need, let me say a couple of things as prelude to our request."

He paused, but every eye was on him and no one spoke, so he continued. "As you know, Yaacov's coming to my house put me into a moral dilemma, as I'm sure you meant it to. I have now resolved that dilemma, at least partially."

Again he paused, choosing his words carefully. "I have made two decisions. Number one, as acting president of Barclay Enterprises we are breaking off all relationships with Gerritt Industries." All four of the Israelis stirred, but he went on smoothly. "That decision goes into effect immediately, though we will not tell Gerritt until Mr. Braithwaite and his people decide when the timing is most advantageous for their purposes."

"Decision number two. I have agreed to work with the FBI in helping them obtain sufficient evidence to convict Mr. Quinn Gerritt and those who work with him."

"Bravo!" Yaacov said softly. "I knew you could not do otherwise."

"Excellent!" Gondor beamed. "Excellent."

Yaacov suddenly sobered. "And what of Mr. Barclay?"

"That is something else I want to lay out clearly before I say more." He was more hesitant now, knowing this next part was crucial. "My decision to see Gerritt brought to justice in no way lessens my determination to act in Mr. Barclay's best interest, speaking both of his physical health and as his official representative."

"What's that supposed to mean?" Nathan said warily.

Marc straightened, looked around at the others. "Alex Barclay will be in intensive care until Wednesday or Thursday. I will use that time to make every effort to put together another deal that the Saudis will find acceptable, in spite of the fact that Gerritt Industries is out."

Gondor came half out of his chair. "What!"

Yaacov was stunned. "But—" He caught himself and clamped his mouth shut.

"I fully expect that you and your people will continue to make every effort to prevent that from happening. Fine. But know that I plan to explore every possibility to hold the deal together. If, on Thursday, I can tell Alex that the deal is still alive, even with Gerritt out, that will significantly lower the stress on him, and I will have solved my dilemma."

Weissman was thoughtful. "In three days? No way, Mr. Jeppson."

Marc smiled now for the first time. "The oddsmakers would certainly bet with you, Mr. Weissman."

Yaacov's mind was racing. They needed time. That was the purpose of his visit to Marc in the beginning, and they had gotten that. Weissman was correct. Marc was bright, and it would be dangerous to underestimate him. But not in three days. And yet . . . There was a confidence in Marc that was unnerving.

"And that brings us to the basic question," Marc said to Weissman. "We need your help."

Gondor had just taken a sip of his coffee and nearly choked. "You tell us you plan to go ahead and sell planes to our enemies, and you want us to help you?"

"We need your help in bringing Quinn Gerritt to justice. I expect nothing more."

"You're a fool!" Gondor snapped, his face incredulous. "Break off the sale, then you'll have our help."

Marc ignored Gondor, just watched Weissman steadily. The round face was impassive, unmoved. There was no way to fathom what was going on behind those mild, brown eyes.

"You people used my sense of honor and integrity, Mr. Weissman. You used it in a calculated and cunningly devised manner to achieve your ends. Now all I ask of you is the same. You too claim to be men of honor, men of principle. You know what Gerritt is as well or better than I. We want you to help us bring an end to his freedom. Or is all this talk of principle and integrity mere rhetoric, an expediency used only when it suits your convenience?"

"No!" Yaacov cried hoarsely.

Marc whirled around. "I'm not asking you, Yaacov!" Then his voice softened. "I know how *you* feel." He turned back, his words coming out sharp and clipped. "What I do not know is how Eli Weissman and Moshe Gondor and Nathan Shoshani feel."

The silence in the room was heavy as Marc leaned forward, breathing hard. Gondor glared back at him, but finally looked away under the glittering challenge of Marc's gaze. Nathan was staring into his cup, his dark eyes unreadable.

"He asked the question of all of us," Weissman finally said mildly. "Moshe, how do you answer?"

"Of course we do not condone what Gerritt is or what he has done. But we are official representatives of the state of Israel. We cannot interfere in the domestic affairs of the U.S., unless that interference would be of direct benefit to our government."

"Courageously spoken!" Marc said with mocking praise.

Weissman grabbed Gondor's arm as he shot out of his chair. He pulled him back down, not looking at him but turning instead to the younger Shoshani. "Nathan?"

Nathan finally looked up. He glanced quickly at his father, then turned back to Weissman. "I say we help." Yaacov sat back, the tenseness that had stiffened his body, suddenly gone. He smiled at his son.

Weissman nodded slowly. "I agree." He turned back to Marc. "What did you have in mind, Mr. Jeppson?"

Marc felt a lurch of relief but kept his face expressionless. "You know what happened to Jonathan Taggart. You also know he has a deep and abiding hatred for Quinn Gerritt but is too terrified to come forward and testify against him."

They nodded. Marc went on swiftly. "He has agreed to come forth if we can absolutely guarantee his safety and that of his family."

Weissman turned to Braithwaite. "Protective custody is not an unusual request. Why come to us?"

Braithwaite spoke for the first time since entering the apartment. "Hadlow and Perotti have both openly bragged that they have sources of information in every police department." He dropped his eyes momentarily. "Even the FBI. We think that is bluff, but if we're wrong, it would mean death for Taggart."

"We want Taggart and his family taken to Israel," Marc said quietly.

For the first time, Marc broke through Weissman's aplomb. His eyes widened, and he swallowed in surprise.

"They must disappear without a trace and remain totally incognito until the time is right."

As quickly as he had lost it, Weissman recovered and was back in control. "What else?"

"I was followed to Utah yesterday. I assume that was your people."

Now it was Nathan and Gondor who rocked back. Marc grinned. "A blue Ford sedan. Then a red-and-white pick-up. Those two vehicles I'm sure of. Others I could guess."

When neither man answered, the grin faded. "Come on," Marc said, "if they were not your people, then I have cause to worry."

"They were ours," Weissman said.

Marc breathed a sigh of relief. "Good. So you know where my fiancée and my boys are?"

"Yes."

"You know that when Gerritt finds out I'm going after him, he'll try to get to them, use them against me."

"I think the probability is high."

"I would appreciate it if you could see that nothing happens to them. Again, we can't rely on the FBI or other law enforcement agencies for the same reason as before."

Weissman shook his head.

"Why not?"

The deputy director chose his words carefully. "While we can appreciate your concern, providing protection for your family frees you up to pursue the deal with the Saudis. That works directly counter to our interests and is not in the same moral realm as the help with Taggart."

Marc had anticipated that and was ready. "It will not directly aid in the arms sales. I will pursue that with or without your help. But I do have a *quid pro quo* to offer."

Weissman's eyes narrowed. "What?"

"I was in contact with the State Department yesterday," Marc said blandly. "As yet, Gerritt Industries has refused to let your technical advisors get a close look at this new radar system."

Weissman gave an almost imperceptible nod.

"Sooner or later, I suppose you'll get those plans." Marc shrugged. "I am proposing it be sooner."

"Go on."

"All things considered—the sale of the F-22 to Saudi Arabia, the pressure being brought to bear by your government, the help you are providing in the Gerritt situation—considering all of that, the State Department, with direct permission of the president, has authorized me to make you an offer."

The room was almost totally silent as the Israelis waited for his next sentence. Marc smiled faintly. "They have agreed that they would look the other way if Jonathan Taggart were to take a set of plans for the VSM-430 radar system with him to Israel."

Chapter Twenty-Seven

The alarm went off at eight-thirty Monday morning, and Marc groaned and rolled over, groping for it blindly until he found the button and hammered it down. Up on one elbow was as far as he made it. For the life of him, he couldn't remember what it was that had been so urgent that he had set his alarm for just three hours after he had arrived home. With a long sigh of surrender, he collapsed back onto the pillow, vowing to reset the alarm for sometime around Thursday morning.

The insistent ringing of the phone brought him up again with a start. He peered at the clock radio as he grabbed the phone. It was ten-sixteen A.M.

"Hullo." His voice was a clear confession of what he had been doing.

"Marc?"

"Yeah." He shook his head, trying to bounce a brain cell or two off the walls of his mind to get them functioning again.

"This is Jackie."

He swung his feet off the bed and let them drop to the floor with a thud. "Oh, hi, Jackie," he said, barely stifling another moan.

"Marc, were you asleep?"

"Well, not really. It's just an act to throw you off."

She laughed. "At ten-fifteen in the morning, Marc Jeppson is still in bed? I can't believe it." She paused but when he didn't respond, went on. "Where in the world have you been? I tried to get you all day yesterday."

Finally, the Jell-o in which his synapses were immersed began to melt, and he felt some modicum of alertness returning. "Oh, yeah. I took the boys on a little trip. I got back kind of late."

"I tried Valerie's house too."

"No answer?"

"No. Not even late last night."

"Hmmmm." He managed to sound really puzzled. "Generally one or the other of them is home. How's Alex this morning?"

"Still in intensive care, but he's improving all the time."

"I called the hospital yesterday and got to talk to Ardith. She seemed much more optimistic than she did on Saturday."

"Yes, he's doing very well, which is such a relief."

"Are they still projecting he'll be out of intensive care on Wednesday or Thursday?"

"The doctor told Ardith this morning that it will be Thursday, just to be safe."

"Good." For more reasons than one. This was going to be a busy three days. "Still no visitors till then?"

"Only Ardith."

"Well, I've got to go down to the LaRoche this afternoon anyway, see the Saudis one more time before they take off for home. I'll stop by the hospital while I'm down there, see how Ardith's doing."

"She'd like that." There was a moment's pause. "Well," she said, getting down to business. "The phone has been ringing like crazy here. Are you coming in this morning?"

"Uh . . . Well, probably not. A couple of critical things have come up that I need to follow through on. Who's called?"

"Gerritt. He's the most insistent. Even called me yesterday at home. Said he's been trying to reach you. Says he wants to talk about the offer he made you Saturday."

Marc frowned. Knowing Gerritt, he had hit on some new angle for intimidating the acting president of Barclay Enterprises. "Can you stall him? Tell him you finally reached me, but I was flying out the door to get to the LaRoche. Which is nearly true. I'm starting to taxi out onto the jetway now."

She laughed. "I can tell."

"Have him call me there after three." By which time he would be gone again. "Who else?"

"The sales rep from Northrup. The executive vice-president of Hughes. Seems like word is out that we're representing Gerritt Industries on the radar system. There's been a lot of courtesy calls about Alex. Also, Jakarta called, but I think Derek can handle that one all right."

Marc's mouth tightened subconsciously, and he began to tap the table top with his index finger. "Is Derek there?"

"Not yet, but he called and is on his way."

"Okay. Listen, Jackie, some of this I'm in on could have important implications for us. Can you and Derek meet with me about five-thirty?" He considered that. "No, make that six."

"Well, yes, I'm sure that would be all right." He could hear the question in her voice and hated himself for putting her off.

"Great! Thanks for the wakeup call. I might have slept right through 'Days of Our Lives.'"

"Good-bye, Marc," she laughed merrily. "See if you can't get your wheels off the ground so I won't have to lie to Gerritt."

"That's a big roger, Control Tower, ten-four, over and out."

But as he hung up, the humor in him died, and the smile on his face slowly faded away. He found his pants, dug out his wallet, and got the slip of paper he had put in there on Saturday, then picked up the phone again.

"Hotel LaRoche." It was a pleasant female voice, and he pictured her as being the attractive blond who had checked him and Valerie out Saturday.

"Yes. Could I speak with the La Jolla Suite."

"I'm sorry, sir, calls to that room are restricted."

"Yes, I know that. This is Marc Jeppson. I'd like to speak with General Sayeed Amani. I'll hold."

The line went dead for several seconds, then Amani's voice came on. "Good morning, Marc."

"Good morning, General. How is everything with you this morning?"

"Very good. And how is Alex this morning?"

"Doing much better thank you."

The small courtesies continued for almost a minute. Halfway through them it suddenly hit Marc that the Israelis had a tap on the line. If they had bugged Gerritt's suite, they had certainly tapped into the Huntington Suite as well, and that would include the phones.

When an appropriate opening occurred, Marc broke in smoothly. "I was hoping to get a chance to say good-bye to you and the crown prince before you leave."

"He would be pleased."

"I'll be in Los Angeles this afternoon."

"Good. Hold a minute." The phone was covered, and Marc could hear muffled Arabic rapidly spoken. Then, "The prince would be honored if you could join us for lunch in our suite."

The thoughts of talking into Israeli microphones did nothing for him, especially with what he planned to say to the Saudis. He cursed his stupidity for not thinking of it sooner. "I would be much more honored if you would allow me to take you and the prince and Sheik Hazzan to lunch at a favorite restaurant of mine." He would have to do some quick thinking to decide what favorite restaurant he was talking about.

Again there was the muffled consultation. "Marc, the prince insists. We shall have lunch up here. Shall we say one-thirty?"

Marc's face fell. "General, that is most kind and generous of the prince, but he has done so much already. Tell him it would be the greatest of honors if he would but allow me to host the lunch this last time we are together."

He clenched his fist. Come on, General. Think! You know I wouldn't offend the prince by refusing his hospitality unless there was a very important reason. "The restaurant is not far from the hotel. It would be a delightful opportunity for all of you to see another part of Los Angeles before you leave."

This time the pause was long. Marc strained to hear, but if they were talking now, it was inaudible. A moment later, Amani spoke again. "The crown prince is most grateful for your generosity. If you insist, he will accept your invitation."

Marc's shoulders sagged in relief. "I insist. I'll come by your room at one-thirty. Shall we make the reservation for your whole party?"

Again the brief pause. "No. The prince suggests there will just be the three of us."

"Very good," Marc said, and hung up.

A little later Marc stopped at a phone booth a few blocks from the Barclay warehouses in El Segundo. He punched in the phone number he had memorized early that morning, then hit the numbers for his credit card. It rang twice, then Marc recognized the deep voice of Eli Weissman, Deputy Director of Operations for the Mossad.

"This is Marc. How did it go with Taggart?"

"Very nicely."

"So they are gone?"

"Yes. The plane left New York forty minutes ago. They're in the air."

"Thanks. We'll put the backfield in motion."

"I beg your pardon."

"It's an American expression. It means we start the ball rolling."

"That one I understand. Good luck."

Jackie suggested that they meet in Alex's office, but Marc decided that looked a little too presumptuous, so they gathered in his. It was small but well decorated and comfortable. He waited until Jackie and Derek were both seated, then took a deep breath.

"I appreciate you staying late, both of you. I was hoping that things would work out so we didn't have to have this meeting, but . . ." His face became very grave, and he finally just shook his head in disbelief.

"What, Marc?" Jackie asked with concern.

"I'm dumping Quinn Gerritt."

Jackie rocked back. Derek's jaw dropped, and he gaped at Marc. Jackie recovered first, her eyes incredulous. "What!"

"Gerritt's out of the deal as of this afternoon."

"Are you crazy?" Derek blurted hoarsely.

Marc sat back, letting the worry and fear he had felt for the last two days show clearly on his face. "I have no choice."

"Gerritt is central to everything!" Jackie said in alarm. She couldn't believe he had said what he did.

"I have no choice!" Marc repeated firmly.

"But why?" Derek demanded, his voice thin and reedy with the shock.

Marc let out a long sigh of pain and weariness. "I had visitors Saturday night."

"Who?"

"Israeli intelligence."

If the news of Gerritt had dumbfounded them, that declaration left them completely speechless.

"They know about the sale of the planes to the Saudis. They're trying to stop it."

"Alex expected as much," Jackie finally said, "but why did they come to you?"

"They've been investigating all of the principals in this— Alex, you, me, and Quinn Gerritt." He picked up the folder with the photographs. "Jackie, remember when we went to Bogotá for Gerritt?"

"Yes."

"And we were surprised how easily we were able to solve what was supposed to have been a major crisis?" She nodded again, and he handed her the photographs and watched as she thumbed through them with growing bafflement. Derek moved his chair closer and leaned over to see.

"What are these?"

"Recognize the plane?"

"Sure, it's the company plane, but who are those men?" She held up another photo. "And what are these sacks?"

"Cocaine."

The photos lowered slowly into her lap as she stared at Marc. "That's right. The copper crisis was merely a guise to get us down there. You and I became the couriers for somewhere around ten million dollars worth of cocaine."

"The Israelis gave you these?" Derek said contemptuously. "Yes."

"How do you know this isn't just a set-up and you're playing right into their hands?" Derek's mouth was an open sneer. "They want you to break off the deal!"

"There's more." Marc told them about the other drug shipments, then sketched out the story of the intimidation and extortion of Jonathan Taggart.

Jackie was reeling, but Derek was furious. "And you just sat there and let them tell you all that garbage and never even questioned their motive?"

"Of course, I questioned their motive!" Marc snapped. "I know what their motive is! But their motive has nothing to do with this. The point is, Quinn Gerritt is a man with no scruples, a man who has flagrantly violated the law, and used us as dupes in doing so."

"According to the Israelis!" Derek shouted. "Talk about being duped!"

When Marc spoke, his voice was quiet, but the edge in it was unmistakable. "I talked with Taggart personally," he said. "And I will not deal with Quinn Gerritt for one more minute."

Derek threw up his hands. "So you blow a sixty million dollar deal because your conscience is tweaked? Come on, Marc. This isn't your decision."

Jackie took a breath. "Derek's right, Marc. We can't just drop everything."

"And it doesn't matter to you that you—Jacqueline Ashby—were used to bring in ten million dollars worth of cocaine?"

"Of course, it bothers me!" she flared. "It makes me physically sick, but—"

"There are no buts!" Marc cut in sharply. "We will not deal with him!"

Derek's lips had pulled back into an angry snarl. "You're a generous man with Alex's money."

"Marc," Jackie pleaded, "this will kill him. If the deal falls apart, it will kill Alex."

Marc lifted his hands in a gesture of helplessness. "I'm not going to let the deal fall apart. I'm going to see what we can do to save it."

"Wonderful!" Derek seethed. "He's going to see what he can do to save it. And what about the contracts we have already signed with Gerritt?"

"We won't say anything yet. This is strictly hush-hush. Everything is to continue as though its status quo until we have something else set up."

"And when do you tell Alex all of this?" Jackie asked quietly, deeply shaken.

"Not until he's much stronger," Marc said, not looking at her. "I hope by next week I'll know more. If I can show him the deal is still in place without Gerritt, then I won't worry as much about what it will do to him." He gave her a stern look. "Jackie, you're not to tell Alex anything yet. Not until he's considerably better than he is right now."

She met his stare sullenly, not giving in.

"I mean it, Jackie. You tell him too soon and it could kill him."

"If you lose this deal, you'll kill him anyway. You can't do this on your own, Marc. Wait until Thursday, then let Alex decide."

"He won't be strong enough yet. And I can't wait that long. I've got to act now if we hope to salvage anything."

"Salvage!" Derek cried. "The only thing that needs to be salvaged is what you're destroying right now!"

"You have no right!" Jackie said bitterly. "I know you have the authority, but you have no right."

Marc put his hands to his head and rubbed his temples with his fingertips, starting to question all over again the path he had chosen for himself. Finally he looked up at Jackie, stricken. "I have no choice."

When Andrew Hadlow opened the door of his palatial home in Pacific Palisades, his eyes were smouldering with anger. He nodded to the guard who had escorted Quinn Gerritt and Derek Parkin up from the main gate, and the man turned on his heel and left them.

"What are you doing here?" Hadlow demanded of Gerritt even before the man had gone. "I told you never to come to my home."

"This is urgent!" Gerritt snapped back, in no mood for cloak-and-dagger mentality.

Ten minutes later, when Derek had finished his account of the meeting at Barclay Enterprises, Hadlow was in a cold fury. "We've got fourteen million dollars invested in you," he said to Gerritt. "You lose that radar system, and my people will not look kindly on that."

" 'My people!' 'My people!' " Gerritt shouted. "What about me? It's my corporation. It's my life that's being ruined. You're the ones who terrified Taggart. If he talks—"

"Taggart won't talk!" Hadlow said flatly. "The question is Marc Jeppson. What happens if we take him out as well?"

Derek swallowed hard, his fingers fluttering nervously at his tie.

Gerritt hesitated too, but obviously it wasn't because Hadlow's words had shocked him. "No," he said finally. "With Alex down, everything is hanging in the balance anyway. It could break off everything. No, all we need to do is bring him into line."

"Money?" Hadlow said. "What if we offer him a hundred thousand cash now, another when the deal is completed?"

"No." Gerritt was firm. "The money wouldn't phase him."

"Blackmail? Is he into anything kinky? Or what about Barclay's secretary? Didn't you tell me she was kind of sweet on him? What would she be willing to do for ten or fifteen thousand?"

Both Derek and Gerritt were shaking their heads.

"Come on!" Hadlow hissed. "Everybody's got a handle. What's Jeppson's?"

Both men looked to Derek. He could feel the sweat trickling down his back. He licked his lips nervously, looking cornered.

"What, Parkin? What is there?"

"He's got two little boys. And a fiancée."

Hadlow spun around and walked to the phone. He punched the buttons with sharp, deliberate jabs, then turned his back.

"Mr. Perotti," Derek heard him murmur. "We've got some complications here. I need a couple of men."

Gerritt grabbed Derek's arm. "Let's go." They exited as Hadlow continued to speak softly into the phone.

Derek Parkin fished for the key to his apartment, feeling a sudden surge of fear. Two men had gotten out of the car that had pulled up behind his. Now they were coming up the walk toward him. He finally got the key out and jammed it in the lock.

"Derek Parkin?" one of the men called.

Derek turned around slowly, feeling his knees turn into cotton. "Yes?"

The lead man flashed a badge. "FBI. You'll have to come with us, please."

Lynn Braithwaite turned off the tape recorder and sat back. Marc, sitting across the desk from him, didn't look at him. His mouth was set in a hard line, and his eyes had narrowed to dangerous slits. They had just listened to the recording made of the conversation that had taken place at the Hadlow home and Hadlow's phone call to Perotti.

"Well," Braithwaite finally said. "We knew they would play rough."

"Weissman had better keep a tight watch on Valerie and my boys."

"I called Weissman and played this for him as well. He knows the stakes are getting higher and higher."

"So what happens when Hadlow's men can't find Taggart or Valerie?"

Braithwaite shook his head slowly. He was a plain man with thinning hair, horn-rimmed glasses, and a heavy beard. He hadn't shaved since morning, and it gave him a slightly sinister look.

"They come after me, right?"

Braithwaite pursed his lips, considering the options. "You heard Hadlow. He wants a handle, and if there's no handle, he'll break the jug."

Marc nodded glumly, trying to ignore the ball of brass that had suddenly settled in his stomach.

"Marc, are you sure you want to go through with this? You can bet Perotti will have nothing but professionals."

"Thanks," Marc said dryly. "Have you ever thought of going into counseling? You have a way of comforting the troubled soul."

Braithwaite gave a short, mirthless laugh, then sobered instantly. He leaned forward and tapped the cassette tape in the recorder. "The only consolation is this—for the first time we've linked Perotti in directly."

"And you're sure these will be admissable in court?"

"Absolutely. Your testimony and Taggart's gave us sufficient probable cause. Getting the court order was a snap. Everything now is strictly legal."

"It's too bad the tape of Derek and Gerritt planning Alex's heart attack is not."

"True," Braithwaite mused. "But it's still been of great value. Derek tried to stonewall it until we played that to him. Then he broke, and he's been talking nonstop ever since."

Marc's mouth pulled down. "And he gets immunity from prosecution?"

The FBI agent shrugged philosophically. "I know it galls you, but Parkin is a little fish—one that stinks, that's true—but if we can use him to reel in the big ones, I can live with throwing him back in the pond."

Marc stood abruptly. "Well, I'm going to try to get a good night's sleep."

"In a motel?" Braithwaite asked innocently.

Marc jerked around.

"Look," he went on. "I think you're fine until they discover Taggart and your family are not available. But these guys play rough. We've got men covering you, but a motel lessens the risk."

Marc nodded soberly. "All right." He turned and started for the door.

"So," Braithwaite persisted, "I'm asking you again. Are you sure you want to go through with this?"

Marc frowned deeply. "If we stop now, how much will Gerritt and Hadlow get?"

"So far, all we've got them for is conspiracy and extortion. We might be able to make the drug thing in Colombia stick, but I'm not sure. I'd guess five to ten years, with eligibility for parole in three or four."

"And for attempted murder?"

"I think we could double that." He paused. "But if they can't find Taggart or Valerie, there'll be no actual attempted murder. Just conspiracy to commit murder."

"I wasn't thinking of Taggart or Valerie," Marc said grimly.

Chapter Twenty-Eight

It was a private room on the third floor, and the buildings of Los Angeles were visible through the hospital curtains. The heart monitor was mounted to the wall above the bed, and two chairs were pulled up alongside where Alex lay. Marc let the door shut softly behind him, and the sound caught the attention of all three in the room.

The look on any one of their faces would have been sufficient to tell Marc what he had already suspected. Jackie had told Alex everything. Jackie's head lifted in defiance as Marc looked at her. Ardith's face held a mixture of anger and imploring beseechment. Alex, drawn and pale from the operation, looked like one of the Furies from hell itself.

Marc took a deep breath and came into the room. He had considered bringing flowers or a gift, then under the circumstances, settled only for the tape recorder and cassette.

"Before you say anything, Alex," he said quietly. "There's something I want all of you to hear."

"What?" Alex demanded with heavy sarcasm. "More evidence from the Israelis?"

Marc ignored that, just plugged the tape recorder in and set it on the stand in front of Alex. "You'll recognize Gerritt's voice and also Derek's. The third man is Andrew Hadlow. This tape was made last Friday night, approximately eight hours before you had your heart attack."

Five minutes later, when Marc reached up and pushed the

stop button, Ardith had gone white. Jackie was staring at him in horror. Marc turned to Alex and saw that he was deeply shaken too.

"Did you know this Monday when you talked to Derek and me?" Jackie's voice was hollow and filled with loathing.

He nodded.

"Have you told the police?" Ardith whispered. Her fingernails were digging into the palms of her hands.

"The FBI. But the tape was gotten illegally by the Israelis. It cannot be used in court."

Alex raised up weakly on one elbow. "Maybe the Israelis made the tape. They'd do anything to stop this sale from—"

"Right, Alex." It was a gentle reproof. "And it was nice of you to have your heart attack to coincide with it."

He fell back on the pillow. "All right, all right. But it still doesn't change anything."

That brought both Ardith and Jackie up sharply.

"We'll deal with Gerritt when the time is right. But you are not to break off the deal, Marc. Do you understand me?" He clutched at Marc's jacket. "You are not to break off the deal under any circumstances."

"Alex!" Ardith was staring at him in wide-mouthed disbelief. "Quinn Gerritt tried to kill you."

"No," he said, breathing heavily. "No, he just tried to squeeze me out. And I won't squeeze." He turned back to Marc. "Don't you see, Marc. This is exactly what the Israelis want."

Marc took Alex's hand and laid it back across his chest gently. "Alex, listen. I've talked to the Saudis. They won't automatically cut us off if we break with Gerritt. They're willing to listen. I can put another deal together without Gerritt."

"No! You'll lose everything if you start tampering with things at this point."

"That's right, Alex," Marc said with soft bitterness. "The deal is everything, isn't it. Hang the principles. Stuff the ideals. Just keep the deal together."

"Yes!" He had tried to shout it, but it had come out weakly, pathetically impotent.

Ardith stepped to his side quickly, shooting Marc a warning glance. Marc touched her arm. "Ardith, I didn't want to go through this until he was stronger, but now that he knows, it's got to be resolved." He turned back to Alex. "You know I'll try everything I can to make it work. But I will not work with Quinn Gerritt."

"You fanatic!" Alex cried hoarsely. "Don't try to jam your lofty ideals down my throat! Just do what I say!"

Jackie's sharp intake of breath behind him registered only peripherally in Marc's mind, as did Ardith, who was trying in alarm to calm her husband. The only thing that was vivid in Marc's perception was Alex, lying on the pillow, breathing in quick, shallow breaths, eyes burning into Marc's flesh like pokers drawn from a fire.

"You really mean that?"

"This is my deal. Don't you mess with it!"

When Marc spoke it was with a deep calm and soft sadness. "Alex, you once told me that my commitment to values was what you admired most about me. Now that commitment has become inconvenient for you, and you want me to change. Well, fanatic or not, I am what I am. If you don't like it, then take me out. Because if you leave me in, you take me as I am."

The door burst open, and a nurse rushed in. "What's going on in here?" She darted to Alex's side where Ardith was stroking his face, trying to soothe him.

Marc glanced at Jackie. Tears were streaming down her face. "I'm sorry," she said in an agonized whisper, "I shouldn't have told him."

"He had to know sooner or later," he said simply. He laid his hand briefly on Ardith's shoulder. "I'm sorry, Ardith." And he turned and walked to the door.

"Marc?"

It was a hoarse whisper, but it jerked Marc around like a rifle shot. Alex had turned his head, one hand raised in supplication, and Marc stepped back quickly and gripped it.

"I'm sorry, Alex. I didn't want to make you go through this now."

There was an attempt to shake his head, but it failed. He took a breath, then another, then his eyes raised to meet Marc's. "I want you in," he whispered. "As you are."

"Please!" the nurse exclaimed. "He must be left alone now." She put one hand on Marc's arm and started to turn him away, very firmly, but Alex held Marc's with a sudden fierce determination.

"Will you stay?" Alex whispered.

Marc grasped the trembling hand with both of his, looked deep into the haggard eyes, then finally nodded. "Yes, Alex. I'll stay."

Willard, Utah, is a small farming community in northern Utah, known for its fruit orchards and nearby Willard Bay on the Great Salt Lake. Since Interstate Fifteen was completed several years ago, the old highway that ran through the town had lost ninety percent of its traffic.

It was on the same morning Marc was visiting Alex that two men left the bank in Willard and drove along the old highway to the nearest phone booth. Both were in their early thirties, dressed in suits and ties and neatly groomed. That, coupled with their badges and I.D. cards, made it easy for the people of Willard to accept them for what they claimed to be, two special investigative detectives from the Los Angeles Police Department.

The shorter of the two dialed a number and waited for several seconds while the private phone in Andrew Hadlow's office rang. Hadlow himself answered.

"Mr. Hadlow?"

"Yes." There was no need for further identification. Hadlow recognized the voice instantly.

"We've come up short here."

"Nothing?"

"No. There's no question that Jeppson brought them here. His car is in the garage. A couple of the neighbors saw him drive up with the women and the boys. They left a few minutes later in his parents' van. From there they just disappear. They left a note for one son to take care of the dog and the yard, but he has no idea where they are."

For one moment Hadlow nearly pushed them on that. Maybe the son or some of the neighbors were lying, but then he shook his head. These men were the best, and they would have known.

"We even checked the bank for cancelled checks or some kind of clue, but there's nothing. Maybe in time . . ." He left it hanging, making it clear how much chance he thought there was of that.

"No." Hadlow's mind was racing. They had underestimated Jeppson's ingenuity. The Taggarts had also disappeared without a trace, and time was running out. "How soon can you get back?"

"We can be back to the airport in an hour. We'll take the first flight."

"Okay, but not to L.A. Go to the house in San Diego. Wait there."

"Yes, sir. We should be there by late afternoon or tonight."

"Good. We'll have need of you by then."

He hung up the phone and stared out the window onto the towering buildings of downtown Los Angeles. His fingers drummed silently on his desk; the dark eyes were sulfurous. Then he made up his mind, grabbed his briefcase, and walked out to his secretary.

"Call Mr. Gerritt, please. Tell him I'm on my way over to see him."

"But they've got to be somewhere!" Gerritt blurted. "They can't have just disappeared."

"Of course they're somewhere!" Hadlow snapped, deeply irritated by Gerritt's growing intransigence. "If we had another week or two, my men would find out where. But we don't. Jeppson leaves tomorrow for Saudi Arabia. If he makes that trip, you're out." His voice dropped to a soft menace, like the soft snick of a pistol's breech being pulled into place. "And if you're out, Mr. Gerritt, you have real trouble."

Gerritt paled. "Then what do we do?"

Hadlow came to the desk, took a pad, and wrote quickly. "Here's an address in San Diego. I want you to bring Jeppson there tonight."

"San Diego? How do I get him there?"

Hadlow just watched him steadily. Gerritt swallowed hard and nodded. "Okay, then what?"

"You just get him there."

Marc hung up the phone and turned to look at Jackie and Lynn Braithwaite, sitting in front of him in his office at Barclay Enterprises. "Surprise. Gerritt wants me to meet him in San Diego."

Jackie's eyes widened. One of Braithwaite's men had already called to appraise them of the conversation between Hadlow and Gerritt taped moments before in Gerritt's office.

"You played it just right," Braithwaite praised him. "If you had given in too easily, they might have suspected something."

"Marc," Jackie said, "I don't think you ought to do this. What if something goes wrong?"

He gave her a wan smile. "That's it. Fire me with enthusiasm before I hit the beach."

"I mean it!" she cried. "They plan to kill you!"

"Which means all that money I spent on that assertive leadership course was for nothing."

Braithwaite sighed. "She's right, Marc. Even I'm starting to have second thoughts."

"Come on, Lynn!" Marc exclaimed. "Don't you start! I'm already scared spitless. I'm counting on you and your people to make sure this whole thing comes off."

Braithwaite merely nodded, thinking of how many things could go wrong in an operation like this. When he spoke, it was with more confidence than he felt. "We're just going to have to make sure we leave nothing to chance."

266

Chapter Twenty-Nine

Marc paused for a moment before the hotel door, keenly aware of the dryness in his throat, took a deep breath, then rapped on the door. Gerritt answered almost immediately.

"Ah, Marc. Thank you for coming. Let me get my jacket." He stepped back into the room, then reappeared, putting on a suit coat. He shut the door and steered Marc down the hall.

"Did you drive down?"

"No, I came down on the company plane. I'm anxious to get back as soon as possible. I leave first thing in the morning."

"I have my car." He put his hand on Marc's arm. "I know this is a terrible time to ask you to break away, what with your trip overseas tomorrow, but I think you'll find it worth the time. If it proves to be as good as it sounds, you should know that before you see the Saudis."

"And who are these men again?"

"General Dynamics, aircraft division. They're biggies."

"So they know about the VSM-430?"

He punched the elevator button, then shrugged. "Word's out all over the place. But if they can combine their system with ours, we could really have something."

Marc nodded, trying to ignore the pounding of his heart. "Well, let's hope they can. Where is it we're going?"

"They have a house out by Mission Bay. It's not far."

·   ·   ·   ·   ·

It had rained earlier in the evening, and the walks were still damp. A heavy gray mist had moved in from the ocean and left little rainbow halos around the street lamps. As they got out of the car and walked to the door of the home in the Mission Bay area, Marc had to fight the temptation to peer out into the night for some sign of Lynn Braithwaite and his men.

This must be what weightlessness feels like, he thought. A curious lightheadedness, perpetual queasiness in the pit of the stomach, surrealistic detachment from reality. He was vaguely aware that Gerritt had made some comment to him, and forced himself to smile and nod, hoping it was an appropriate response.

A pleasant-looking man in a business suit opened the door and smiled briefly. "Mr. Gerritt?"

"Yes."

"Good. Mr. Hadlow said you would have some form of identification from him."

"Yes." Gerritt already had it out and handed it to the man.

He looked at it carefully, grunted in satisfaction, then stepped back. "Come in."

Marc felt a sudden prickling sensation as they walked into the entryway. "This is Marc Jeppson, president of Barclay Enterprises."

Marc smiled grimly to himself. Gerritt's last official act had been to promote him from acting president to the full title.

The man grunted and ushered them into the living room where a second man of approximately the same age stood near the couch. His suit jacket was off, and he wore a shoulder holster. A thirty-eight Smith and Wesson hung heavily beneath his armpit.

Marc stopped short at the sight of it, but the man behind him was instantly at his back, and there was a jab of steel against the base of his neck, so sharp it made him gasp.

"Come in, Mr. Jeppson."

"What!" Marc blurted. "What is this? Who are you?"

The other man grabbed his coat from the couch and put it on. He took out the pistol, then got a short stubby cylindrical object from his pocket. He began to screw the silencer onto the barrel, all the time his eyes never leaving Marc's face.

"All right," the first man said. "We're going out the back. I suggest that resistance would be very foolish, Mr. Jeppson. Gerritt, you lead the way."

Gerritt blanched. "Me! I'm not going."

The second man nodded. "Hadlow said you're to see it all the way through so you're up to your neck in this as much as he is."

"I've got to get back," he stammered, "I can't—"

The man behind Marc fixed Gerritt with a hard stare. Gerritt swallowed hard, then nodded. "All right."

Marc swung his head around. There was no need to fake the fright. The hard pressure of the steel was an effective prompter. "Gerritt?" he whispered hoarsely.

"Move!" the man behind him said, giving him a shove. Gerritt didn't look at Marc, just stumbled out ahead of him in his own daze of confusion.

There was a dark maroon Ford LTD in the garage in the alley. Gerritt and the man with the silencer got in the front. Marc was shoved in the back, the pressure against his neck never lightening for a moment. As they drove out and onto the street, Marc risked a glance out the side window. Come on, Braithwaite, he urged fervently. Don't lose me now.

They stayed to the back streets, and the traffic was light until they turned onto the main street leading to Interstate Five.

The driver looked up at the rearview mirror for the fifth or sixth time in a minute. "We're being followed."

Marc's heart plummeted as both Gerritt and the man at his side whirled to peer out the back window.

"It's a blue Chevy sedan, about eight cars back, and he's been with us since the house."

The man next to him swore softly. "You're sure?"

The driver nodded.

"It could be Israelis," Gerritt said. "They've been following him trying to stop this deal we're working on."

"I don't care who it is," Marc's companion answered bluntly. "Get rid of them."

Again the driver just nodded, concentrating on his driving.

When they stopped at a red light just west of the freeway, Marc considered jumping out for one wild moment but fought it down. *The one thing you've got to fight is panic,* Braithwaite had said in his final instructions. *You're going to be in a tense, risky situation. Just keep your head.*

They turned south on I-5 and drove steadily for almost ten minutes. They passed downtown San Diego, then entered National City. Signs were indicating they were headed for Tijuana, and there was a sudden clutch in Marc's chest. Could the FBI cross the border and follow them into Mexico?

But they didn't go that far. The driver kept the Ford at an even speed until they reached Chula Vista, then took the E Street exit and turned east. Once again they went off the main thoroughfare and into quiet residential streets.

"All right, hang on." The driver hunched lower in the seat, and the others tensed. He came to an intersection, signaled for a right turn, and took it slowly. Marc caught a quick glimpse of some headlights about two blocks behind. But the instant they were around the corner and out of sight, the driver jammed the accelerator to the floor. The car shot forward, engine howling. They covered that block and half of the next in a matter of seconds, then were slammed forward as he hit the brakes. The tires screamed in protest as he laid the car into a hard slide, then shot into a narrow alleyway that ran through the center of the block.

The headlights went off instantly, and the speed dropped to a sedate twenty miles an hour. But it was enough. Marc jerked around along with his guard and peered back down the alley the way they came. There were no street lights here, and with the heavy overcast and mist, the darkness was total. A moment later, a pair of headlights flashed by, and they could hear the howl of an engine under hard acceleration. It was at that moment Marc Jeppson's last flicker of hope was blown out.

"All right," the man next to him growled to the driver. "Let's head for the reservoir."

"Out!" his captor commanded, giving him a hard shove with the muzzle of the pistol.

Marc stumbled out of the car, the man hard on his heels. In the nearly total darkness, Marc saw the faint gleam of water and heard the soft sounds of waves lapping at the shore. Crickets and night birds could be heard in the distance.

"Just stand there by the car, Mr. Gerritt," Marc heard the driver say as the other two car doors opened and shut.

The driver walked around to face him, the pistol and silencer in his hand. He raised it until it was pointing at Marc's chest. At that point the pistol held against the back of his neck was removed. The man behind him jerked his arms behind his back, and there was the sudden burn of rope against his wrists. Then he was led roughly to the edge of a sharp incline. He could hear the soft lapping of water below.

At that moment, Marc passed beyond fear and felt a sudden icy calm. There was an intense burst of sorrow, not for his own life, but because he wouldn't have one last chance to gather Matt and Brett in his arms and tell them how much he cared for them. And Valerie. That brought a pain so sharp and intense that he had to bite his lip quickly and felt a burning in his eyes.

The man who had ridden next to him made a last check of Marc's bonds, then backed away. The driver stepped forward, pistol steady.

"Gerritt," the first man called sarcastically. "You want to do this?"

The president and chairman of the board of Gerritt Industries dropped his head, feeling suddenly sick.

The other man laughed contemptuously. "What's the matter? Haven't got the stomach for it?"

When Gerritt still didn't answer the first chimed in again. "We can stop right now if you want. We've all but scared this poor dude to death anyway." He laughed raucously, and Marc felt a tiny surge of hope.

Gerritt's head came up, and he was staring at the two men. "Whaddya say, Gerritt?" the first needled. "Shall we call it a night?"

"No!" It was a hoarse, desperate cry. "Just do it!"

"Gerritt," Marc called softly.

Gerritt's head jerked up, and he stared at the dark shape standing apart from the other two.

"You think you've won, Gerritt." Marc's voice floated to him out of the darkness. "But you haven't. I—"

There was a sharp but muffled crack. A massive hammer blow hit Marc full in the chest. He stumbled back. Crack! The second shot caught him in the stomach, knocking him over the incline. There was a brief sensation of falling, a dim awareness of his body hitting water with a tremendous splash, a sudden rush of coldness, then darkness—a suffocating, all-encompassing darkness.

Gerritt stared at the two dark shapes standing in the night. One moved to the edge of the incline and peered at the water. Gerritt heard a soft grunt of satisfaction, then the two men moved toward the car. Only gradually did Gerritt become aware of the sound of lapping water and crickets off somewhere in the night.

"Get the car turned around," Gerritt heard the one say. "Let's get out of here."

The sharp buzzing of the phone brought Hadlow up from his book, and he checked the clock on the mantle. It was past eleven. He set the book down and reached for the phone.

"Yes."

It was the guard at the front gate. "Mr. Hadlow, a Mr. Gerritt and two other men are here, sir."

"What?"

"They say you wanted to see them."

Hadlow's face twisted with anger. "Put Gerritt on."

"This is Gerritt."

"What are you doing here?" Hadlow hissed. "Are you crazy? I told you to go home."

"What am I doing here? It's your men that insisted we come and report."

"They what?" Hadlow bellowed, the fury boiling over.

"They said you wanted a first-hand report. So let's get it over with. I want to get out of here."

Hadlow swore. "Those fools! I told them to stay in San Diego." He slammed a fist against the table. "All right, get up here!"

When Hadlow opened the door two minutes later, Gerritt was standing on the step, the two men close behind. The angry rebuke forming on his lips froze as he gaped at the men with Gerritt. "What!" he shouted. "These aren't my men!"

As Gerritt whirled, the nearest man jerked open his suit jacket, and the .38 Smith and Wesson was instantly in his hand. The other man, the gunman who had shot Marc Jeppson, reached inside his coat and brought out a thin leather wallet. He flipped it open to an ID card. "FBI, Mr. Hadlow. You're under arrest."

Chapter Thirty

There was a soft knock at the door.

"I'll get it," Ardith said and walked quickly to open it.

Marc and Valerie were seated next to Alex's hospital bed and looked up curiously as Ardith stepped back and a man entered the room.

"Lynn!" Marc jumped up and gripped Braithwaite's hand, pumping it hard. They were both grinning like old combat buddies who had just found each other after the war.

"Come in, come in," Marc said. "Let me introduce you. This is Ardith Barclay, Alex's wife."

Braithwaite nodded. "Mrs. Barclay."

Marc turned to where Valerie sat next to Alex. "You can probably guess which of these two is Alex."

Braithwaite laughed and stepped forward to shake Alex's hand. "I think I can. You're looking very well, Mr. Barclay."

That was true. The week that Marc had spent in Saudi Arabia had brought a notable improvement in Alex's condition. The color was back in his face, he was much stronger, and more of the old Alex was evident when he talked.

Marc motioned toward Valerie. "You already know my fiancée."

Yes. Hello, Valerie."

"Hello again."

"Come in and sit down," Alex said, smiling. "We were just talking about you."

"Then I'd better sit down. I can imagine what this guy has been telling you."

"I've been telling them I have some questions for you," Marc said. "What kind of a guy are you anyway? First, you have me shot. Then you pull me out of the reservoir, shake my hand, and disappear into the night."

Braithwaite shrugged. "I wanted to be sure you were okay, then I had to join the strike teams. We had a busy night that night, as you'll remember. Sixty-four warrants, forty-two arrests, including Gerritt, Perotti, and Hadlow."

There was no attempt to lessen his feeling of pride. It had been a great night, the culmination of several years work for Lynn Braithwaite. "And then you left for Saudi Arabia first thing the next morning. When did you get back?"

"I just got back last night."

"How did it go?"

"Oh, no you don't. I want some answers. How did you engineer that whole thing?"

"It was simple enough. We had Hadlow's phone bugged and recorded the full conversation with his two hit men. That made it easy to pick them up and substitute our own. Gerritt had never seen them, so that ploy was safe. Actually, you deserve the credit. We had tape recorders in the car and on both men. I've listened to those tapes again and again, and you played your part to perfection. Even your voice was trembling there at the last."

Marc pulled a face at him. "It was your men who were convincing. I wasn't playing a part. *I was scared.* Why didn't you tell me?"

"If you had known those were our men, what would you have done?"

"Been much more relaxed!"

"Exactly the point. We had to be absolutely sure Gerritt thought this was for real, to see if he would follow it through all the way. He did, and now we've got him."

Valerie shuddered, even now hearing the horror that tinged Marc's voice as he described those last final moments.

"Besides," Braithwaite went on, "you had on that bullet-proof flak jacket. Didn't you remember that?"

Marc shook his head. "Not till after! Remember, I had worn that thing for several days by then. I wasn't even conscious of it anymore. And when I entered the house and saw that both men had guns, all I could think of was, 'When is Braithwaite and the cavalry going to ride in and put an end to this?' Then we lost you . . ." The memory welled up, and he had to stop for a moment.

"Yes, losing your tail. That was a nice touch, don't you think?" Braithwaite grinned.

Alex laughed right out loud at Marc's expression.

"But why did you have to use real bullets?" Valerie demanded. "What if your men had missed the jacket, or if it didn't stop them?"

"You've got to remember that we had to have Gerritt accompany our two men back to Hadlow. If Marc's 'death' had been the least bit suspicious, we would have had trouble. But actually, we didn't use 'real' bullets in the full sense of the word. We used what we call a wad cutter. We use them in target practice. It takes less powder, uses a flat slug, and has only about half the regular muzzle velocity."

"Don't tell me they weren't real!" Valerie retorted. "You should see the bruises on his chest."

Braithwaite nodded. "I know. That's why I have complete confidence in those flak jackets. I took a direct hit in the stomach once from a three fifty-seven magnum at point-blank range. It never even pierced the skin, but I couldn't move for a week. So we knew we'd be all right with the wad cutters."

He turned to Marc. "The trigger man moved in close to be sure he hit you where you wouldn't be hurt. He also happens to be our best marksman."

Ardith shook her head, then looked at Alex. "Well, it was one thing for Gerritt to change your medicine and cause a heart attack since he didn't think he was going to kill you. But to par-